The Underdogs
Pictures and Scenes from the Present Revolution

The Underdogs
Pictures and Scenes from the Present Revolution

A Translation of Mariano Azuela's
Los de abajo
with Related Texts

Translated and Edited by
Gustavo Pellón

Hackett Publishing Company, Inc.
Indianapolis/Cambridge

15 14 13 12   2 3 4 5 6

The selections from Anita Brenner's "Blood and Struggle of Mexico Incarnate in *Under Dogs*" (*New York Evening Post,* August 31, 1929) and *Idols behind Altars* (1929) appearing on pp. 117–119 and 159–173 are reprinted by generous permission of the Brenner Estate.

"The Mexican Invasion" by Waldo Frank, pp. 120–123, was originally published in the October 23, 1929 issue of The New Republic.

For further information, please address:

Hackett Publishing Company, Inc.
P.O. Box 44937
Indianapolis, IN 46244-0937
www.hackettpublishing.com

Cover design by Abigail Coyle
Text design by Carrie Wagner
Composition by Agnew's, Inc.

Library of Congress Cataloging-in-Publication Data

Azuela, Mariano, 1873–1952.
    [Los de abajo. English]
    The underdogs : pictures and scenes from the present revolution : a
translation of Mariano Azuela's Los de abajo with related texts / translated
by Gustavo Pellon.
        p. cm.
    ISBN-13: 978-0-87220-834-6 (pbk.)
    ISBN-10: 0-87220-834-6 (pbk.)
    ISBN-13: 978-0-87220-835-3 (cloth)
    ISBN-10: 0-87220-835-4 (cloth)
    1. Azuela, Mariano, 1873–1952. Los de abajo.   I. Pellon, Gustavo.
    II. Title.
    PQ7297.A9L613 2006
    863'.62—dc22

…o clear explanation for constant fight.

Contents

nas mythical element to it

Translator's Note

This is not the first translation of Mariano Azuela's *Los de abajo*. There have been four previous translations. Enrique Munguía's *The Under Dogs* (1929) appeared only five years after the novel became widely known in Mexico. It was followed by Frances Kellam Hendricks and Beatrice Berler's *Two Novels of the Mexican Revolution: "The Trials of a Respectable Family" and "The Underdogs" by Mariano Azuela* (1963), and then by Frederick Fornoff's translation in 1992. Stanley L. Robe's *Azuela and the Mexican Underdogs* (1979) is a translation of the serialized 1915 version of the novel as it appeared in *El Paso del Norte* and differs in some respects from the book version revised by Azuela that modern readers know.

Why a new translation, then? In the note on his translation of *Los de abajo*, Fornoff explains why the previous three translations of the novel are unsatisfactory:

> Robe's translation is mildly verbose, especially in the dialogue, and seems intended more as an aid to the reading of *Los de abajo* than as a literary equivalent. The two earlier translations are now dated. . . . Both the Berler and Munguía translations conventionalize Azuela's epigrammatic presentation of narrative image and dialogue through standard novelistic paragraphing, which closes off access to the austere simplicity and intensity of the original. . . . The Munguía translation and to a lesser extent Berler's tend to inflate descriptive passages, a practice that works against the tonal sobriety and "epic texture" of the work. (xvii–xviii)[1]

I agree with Fornoff's evaluation of the previous translations. I would add that in Munguía's translation there are many inaccuracies and one truly confusing moment. It occurs when Demetrio Macías, the leader of the insurgents, tells his men to fire down at the climbing Federales: [—A los de abajo. . . . A los de abajo—siguió gritando encolerizado.] "Get those

---

[1] Mariano Azuela, *The Underdogs*, trans. Frederick H. Fornoff (Pittsburgh: University of Pittsburgh Press, 1992).

coming up from under! *Los de Abajo!* Get the underdogs!" he screamed." Since the title of the novel is *Los de abajo* (literally "the ones below," or those who are on the lowest rung of the socioeconomic scale) and they are represented in the novel by Demetrio and his men, to associate the federal troops who represent the interests of *"los de arriba"* (those high on the socioeconomic scale) with the title of the novel is to seriously confuse the reader.

Although Fornoff's translation does correct many of the infelicities of the previous translations, he also introduces new ones. In particular he adds profanities where there are none in the original Spanish. Here are a few examples:

1. "¡Mueran los ladrones nixtamaleros!"
(Cátedra edition, 84)

FORNOFF: "Fucking *tortilla*-eaters!"

MY TRANSLATION: "Die you corn-grinding thieves!"

2. "¡Hombre, Anastasio, no seas malo! . . .
Empréstame tu carabina. . . . ¡Ándale, un tiro no
más! . . ." (85).

FORNOFF: "Anastasio, man, don't be a shit! . . . Lend
me your rifle. . . . Come on, just one shot!"

MY TRANSLATION: "Anastasio, don't be mean! . . .
Give me your carbine. . . . *Ándale,* just one shot! . . ."

3. "¡Ya me quemaron!—gritó Demetrio, y rechinó los
dientes—. ¡Hijos de . . . !" (86).

FORNOFF: "Shit, they got me!" screamed
Demetrio, and gritting his teeth he snarled:
"Sons of bitches!"

MUNGUÍA: "Goddamn their souls, they've branded me!"
Demetrio cried, his teeth flashing."

MY TRANSLATION: "They got me!" Demetrio cried,
and ground his teeth, "Sons of . . . !"

At times the Fornoff translation overlooks nuances that are important:

"Hombres malvados, me han matado mi perro!" (77)

"You bastards! You killed my dog!" (Fornoff, 6).

I feel my translation, "Wicked men, you killed my dog! . . ." captures the woman's reproach and sadness. It also captures the biblical overtones of the Spanish phrase.

In other cases, in addition to the insertion of profanity, Fornoff's translation is also inaccurate. The passage, "¡Ah, es mocho! [. . .] ¿Y por qué no le metiste el plomo mejor en la mera chapa?" (92) is rendered by Fornoff as "So, he's a fucking conservative! [. . .] So why didn't you put that piece of lead in his eye instead?" (16) *Chapa* (badge) in this case means "heart" as explained by Marta Portal in the Cátedra edition of the novel. There is no expletive in the original Spanish.

Mexican insurgents commonly referred to the federal soldiers as *pelones* because of their regulation army haircuts. I feel that Fornoff's use of "skinhead" for *pelón* introduces anachronistic images of German neo-Nazis. I prefer to leave the word in Spanish and include it in the glossary.

Many of Demetrio's men have nicknames rather than names: la Codorniz [the Quail], el Manteca [Lard], and so on, and Fornoff uses "Quail" but leaves *Manteca* untranslated. To avoid confusion, I follow a uniform policy throughout the translation, leaving their names in Spanish and explaining their meaning in the glossary. Overall, despite some improvements over previous efforts, Fornoff's translation leaves much to be desired in terms of accuracy and sensitivity to the nuances of Azuela's text.

The text I translate is the Cátedra edition of *Los de abajo* (1988), edited by Marta Portal, which itself is based on the definitive edition revised by Azuela and published by the Fondo de Cultura Económica (1958). In preparing my translation I consulted many works that were of great help. In addition to the existing translations of *Los de abajo* and Robe's translation of the serialized 1915 version of the novel, Jorge Ruffinelli's critical edition of *Los de abajo* with its excellent glossary was of great use. Most valuable of all, however, was the classroom edition of *Los de abajo* prepared by John E. Englekirk and Lawrence B. Kiddle (Prentice Hall, 1971; Waveland Press, 1992) because the editors were able to consult Mariano Azuela in their preparation of the glossary and footnotes. Their command of Mexican expressions helped me avoid some pitfalls of previous translators.

John Reed's journalistic account of his experiences during the Revolution, *Insurgent Mexico* (1914), a work published a year before Azuela's novel, was of great help to me in finding contemporary English equivalents and in helping me to establish an appropriate tone. Likewise Cormac McCarthy's *Border Trilogy* novels provided an excellent model of prose that effortlessly blends English and Spanish.[2]

---

[2] *All the Pretty Horses, The Crossing,* and *Cities of the Plain.*

One thing I learned from reading McCarthy's novels is that even readers in the United States who don't know Spanish know a lot more Spanish than they think. In this regard, as a translator I have an advantage over Munguía who in 1929 had to translate many words that are now familiar to readers in the United States. I therefore use Spanish phrases that capture the Mexican flavor of the original like *ándale, vamos muchachos,* and *bandido* which by now are well-known to most U.S. readers. Although I am not as radical in my approach, in McCarthy's *Border Trilogy* novels whole phrases of Spanish are untranslated but understood through context. Other lesser known words like *cacique* (political boss), *pelón,* and *mocho* (a pejorative term for conservatives) are translated in the glossary.

My goal has been to try to preserve accuracy as far as what Azuela actually wrote without introducing extraneous material. Insofar as possible I also wanted to preserve the contrast between the telegraphic style of most of Azuela's narration and the rare poetic passages that are sprinkled throughout the text. Accustomed to novels that presented a more sanitized and idealized vision of the world, early readers of Azuela's *The Underdogs* were jolted by its modernity, by the brutal realism of his prose, and by its "virility," as one Mexican critic put it. I have tried to retain as much of that excitement as possible.

I want to thank my colleagues of the University of Virginia's Department of Spanish, Italian and Portuguese, for their support when I presented this project at the Tibor Wlassics Faculty Talk. I am most grateful to my daughter Sofía for serving as a bilingual sounding board when I found myself in dire translation dilemmas. In particular I want to thank her for suggesting "the Seven Sisters" as a translation for *las cabritas.* I could no more imagine Anastasio referring to the Pleiades than a cowboy speaking of Ursa Major instead of the Big Dipper. I am grateful for the support of my wife Karen who read a draft of the translation and made valuable suggestions.

Chronology of Mariano Azuela's Life

January 1, 1873:   Born in Lagos de Moreno, Jalisco. His father owns a grocery store and a ranch.

1892–1899:   Studies medicine at the University of Guadalajara.

1899:   Returns to Lagos de Moreno to practice medicine.

1900:   Marries Carmen Rivera. They eventually have ten children, five girls and five boys.

1907:   Publishes novel *María Luisa*.

1908:   Publishes novel *Los fracasados*.

1909:   Publishes novel *Mala yerba*.

1911:   Publishes novel *Andrés Pérez, maderista*.

1911:   After Madero's election to the presidency, Azuela is named *jefe político* of Lagos. Resigns two months later when he realizes the governor will undermine Madero's work.

1912:   Publishes novel *Sin amor*.

October 1914:   Joins the band of Julián Medina, one of Pancho Villa's generals, as his medical officer. Begins writing the work that will become *The Underdogs*.

December 1914–January 19, 1915:   Azuela is named director of public education of the State of Jalisco. Medina and his followers are driven from Guadalajara in January by Carranza's troops.

April 16, 1915–October 1915:   Villa is defeated by Obregón and Medina withdraws to Lagos de Moreno, where Dr. Azuela remains to tend the wounded. Driven by Carranza's forces, Azuela and eighty men flee to Tepatlitán and then Cuquío, and are attacked in the canyons of Juchipila. They withdraw to Aguascalientes. From there Azuela travels by train with the wounded to Chihuahua. The advance of Carranza's troops forces Azuela to take refuge in Ciudad Juárez and then to cross the border to El Paso, Texas.

October 27, 1915–November 21, 1915:   *The Underdogs* is published in the newspaper *El Paso del Norte*.

December 5, 1915:   *The Underdogs* is published in paperback format by the Paso del Norte press.

1916:   Dr. Azuela returns to Guadalajara. Moves with his family to Mexico City. Resumes his medical practice and withdraws from politics.

1917:   Publishes novel *Los caciques*.

1918:   Publishes novels *Las moscas* and *Las tribulaciones de una familia decente*.

1923:   Publishes novel *La malhora*.

1925:   Publishes novel *El desquite*.

1932:   Publishes novel *La luciérnaga*.

1937:   Publishes novel *El camarada Pantoja*.

1938:   Publishes novel *San Gabriel de Valdivias, comunidad indígena*.

1939:   Publishes novel *Regina Landa*.

1940:   Publishes novel *Avanzada*.

1941:   Publishes novel *Nueva burguesía*. Receives the literary award of the Ateneo Nacional de Ciencias y Artes.

1942:   Admitted to the Seminario de Cultura Mexicana. Is also invited to join the Academia Mexicana de la Lengua, but declines.

1943:   Mexican government names Azuela one of the twenty founding members of the Colegio Nacional.

1944:   Publishes novel *La Marchanta*.

1946:   Publishes novel *La mujer domada*.

1949:   Publishes novel *Sendas perdidas*. Receives Premio Nacional de Artes y Ciencias.

March 1, 1952:   Dr. Mariano Azuela dies of heart failure.

1955:   Posthumous publication of Azuela's novel *La maldición.*

1956:   Posthumous publication of Azuela's novel *Esa sangre.*

1958:   Posthumous publication of Azuela's novel *Madero: Biografía novelada.*

Chronology of the Mexican Revolution

October–November 1910:   Revolutionary movement against Porfirio Díaz initiated by Francisco Madero, uprisings throughout Mexico.

May 25, 1911:   Díaz goes into exile.

November 6, 1911:   Madero is elected president.

February 1913:   Part of the army in Mexico City rebels against Madero.

February 18, 1913:   Victoriano Huerta, commanding general of government troops, joins the rebels, forces Madero to resign, and assumes the presidency.

February 22, 1913:   Madero is shot, presumably on Huerta's orders.

February 1913:   Civil war breaks out. Venustiano Carranza, Pancho Villa, Álvaro Obregón, and Emiliano Zapata lead uprisings against Huerta.

April 1914:   American Navy seizes Veracruz to keep Huerta from receiving German arms.

July 1914:   After series of defeats, Huerta goes into exile.

November 1914:   Aguascalientes convention fails to settle differences of Constitutionalist factions.

December 1914:   Civil war breaks out with Carranza and Obregón on one side and Villa and Zapata on the other.

December 1915:   Carranza controls most of Mexico.

1915–1920:   Carranza serves as president.

April 10, 1919:   Zapata is assassinated.

April 23, 1920:   Obregón revolts against Carranza.

May 21, 1920:   Carranza is assassinated.

1920–1924:   Obregón serves as president.

all involved in → *many fronts fighting each other*

July 28, 1920:   Villa comes to terms with Obregón and retires from politics.

July 20, 1923:   Villa is assassinated.

July 17, 1928:   Obregón is assassinated.

1929: Plutarco Elías Calles founds the National Revolutionary Party, the ancestor of today's PRI (Institutional Revolutionary Party). The party holds power in Mexico until 2000.

→ *fought against esp. by zapata.*

(social inequality)

btwn landowners v. no land is immense *even larger ↑ than the gap today.*

socialist approach.

ex. nationalize oil industry.

when things begin to normalize again.

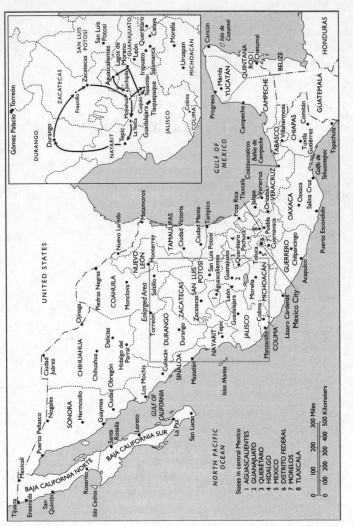

MAP OF MEXICO with inset of the region showing the itinerary of Macías' band.

The Underdogs

Part One

I

"It's not an animal. . . . Just hear Palomo bark. . . . It's got to be a person."

The woman's eyes searched the darkness of the sierra.

"Maybe *Federales*," answered the man who squatted, eating in a corner, a clay pot in his right hand and three rolled *tortillas* in the other.

The woman did not answer; her senses were concentrated outside the hut.

They heard the sound of hooves in the nearby gravel, and Palomo barked more furiously.

"You should hide just in case, Demetrio."

Calmly, the man finished eating, grabbed a *cántaro,* and lifting it with both hands, drank water in gulps. Then he stood.

"Your rifle is under the mat," she whispered.

The small room was lit by a tallow candle. A yoke, a plow, a goad and other farming tools rested in a corner. From the roof hung ropes holding up an old adobe mold that served as a bed, and on blankets and faded rags a child slept.

Demetrio buckled on the cartridge belt and picked up the rifle. Tall, strong, red-faced, beardless, he wore a white cotton shirt and trousers, a wide-brimmed straw *sombrero* and *huaraches.*

He walked out slowly, fading into the impenetrable darkness of the night.

Palomo, furious, jumped the corral fence. Suddenly a shot was heard, the dog let out a dull cry and barked no more.

Some men on horseback arrived shouting and cursing. Two got down and another remained to mind the animals.

"Women . . . something to eat! . . . Eggs, milk, beans, whatever you've got, we're starving.

"Damned sierra! Only the devil could find his way!"

1

"He'd get lost, sergeant, if he were as drunk as you. . . ."

One of them had braid on his shoulders, the other red stripes on his sleeves.

"Where the hell are we, woman? . . . Anybody home?"

"Then why the light? . . . What about the kid? Woman, we want to eat, now! Are you coming out or do we make you come out?"

"Wicked men, you killed my dog! . . . What did my poor Palomo ever do to you?"

The woman went into the house dragging the dog, white, fat, only the whites of his eyes showed now and his body was limp.

"Sergeant, look at her rosy cheeks! . . . Sweetheart, don't get mad, I'll make your house into a love nest, but for God's sake . . .

> *Don't look on me with angry eyes . . .*
> *Don't let us fight . . .*
> *Look on me with love,*
> *Light of my eyes,"*

the officer sang in his *aguardiente*-soaked voice.

"*Señora*, what do they call this place?" the sergeant asked.

"Limón," the woman replied sharply, as she blew on the embers and placed more wood on the fire.

"So this is Limón . . . home of the famous Demetrio Macías! . . . Hear that, lieutenant? We're in Limón."

"Limón? . . . I couldn't give a hoot! You know, sergeant, if I'm going to hell, better now . . . and riding a good horse. Just look at her little cheeks! Apples ready to bite! . . ."

"You must know that bandido, *señora*. . . . I was in the Escobedo Penitentiary with him."

"Sergeant, bring me a bottle of tequila. I've decided to spend the night in the charming company of this little brunette. . . . The colonel? . . . Why bring up the colonel now? . . . He can go to . . . ! And if he gets mad, I don't care! . . . Sergeant, go tell the corporal to unsaddle and feed the horses. I'm staying here. . . . Listen, honey, let the sergeant fry the eggs and warm up the *tortillas*, you come over here with me. Look, this wallet stuffed full of bills is just for you. Because I feel like it. Just think! I'm a little drunk and that's why I'm a bit hoarse. . . . I left half my throat in Guadalajara and on the road I've been spitting out the other half. Who cares? That's what I want. Sergeant, my bottle, my bottle of tequila. Honey, you're too far, come over have a drink. What do you mean, no? . . . Afraid of your . . . husband . . . or whatever he is? . . . If he's in some hole tell him to come out. . . . I don't care! . . . Rats don't bother me."

A white silhouette immediately filled the dark mouth of the door.

"Demetrio Macías!" cried the sergeant fearfully stepping back.

The lieutenant stood, suddenly silent, cold and motionless like a statue.

"Kill them!" shouted the woman, her throat dry.

"Forgive me, *amigo!* . . . I didn't know. . . . But I respect really brave men."

Demetrio stood there looking at them, an insolent smile of disdain wrinkling his features.

"I not only respect them, I also like them. . . . Here's my hand in friendship. . . . All right, Demetrio Macías, you reject me. . . . Because you don't know me, you see me doing this damned dirty job. . . . What do you expect, *amigo!* . . . I'm poor and I've got a large family to support! Sergeant, let's go. I always respect the house of a brave man, a real man."

After they disappeared, the woman hugged Demetrio tightly.

"Holy Virgin of Jalpa! What a scare! I thought it was you they'd shot!"

"Go straight to my father's," Demetrio said.

She tried to stop him, begged, cried, but pushing her away sweetly, he answered somberly:

"I've got a feeling they'll all be back."

"Why didn't you kill them?"

"I guess their time hadn't come!"

They went out together, she holding the child in her arms. At the door they went in opposite directions.

The moon peopled the mountain with vague shadows.

At every ridge and every bush, Demetrio still saw the sad silhouette of a woman with a child in her arms.

After many hours of climbing when he turned to look, at the bottom of the canyon near the river, huge flames rose. His house was burning. . . .

II

All was still shadows when Demetrio Macías started his descent to the bottom of the ravine. The narrow escarpment sliced a trail between the fissure-streaked rock face and the hundreds of meters of slope.

During his swift and agile descent he thought:

"Now the Federales are sure to pick up our scent and track us like dogs. Lucky they don't know the trails, entrances or exits. Except if someone from Moyahua guides them. The people from Limón, Santa Rosa and other mountain villages are loyal. They'd never betray us. . . . The *cacique* who's had me chased from hill to hill is from Moyahua. He'd love to see me swinging from a telegraph pole with my tongue hanging out about a foot. . . ."

And he got to the bottom of the ravine just as it was becoming daylight. He threw himself on the stones and fell asleep.

The river dragged along singing in tiny cascades; the birds chirped hidden in the *pitahayo* cactus, and the monotone cicadas filled the mountain solitude with mystery.

Demetrio woke up startled, forded the river and made for the opposite slope of the canyon. Tenacious like an ant, he climbed up the crest, his hands clasped the rocks and branches, the soles of his feet clasped the stones of the trail.

//When he reached the summit, the sun was bathing the plateau in a lake of gold. Toward the ravine you could see enormous sliced rocks, promontories that rose like fantastical African heads, *pitahayo* cactus like the fossilized fingers of giants, trees leaning toward the bottom of the abyss. And amid the arid boulders and dry branches, the fresh San Juan roses shone like a white offering to the star whose gold threads were already gliding from rock to rock. //

Demetrio stopped at the summit, reached back with his left hand and grabbed the horn slung on his back. He raised it to his thick lips and, filling his cheeks, blew three times. Three whistles beyond the facing slope answered his signal.

In the distance, from a conical cluster of reeds and rotten straw, one by one emerged many men with bare chests and legs; they were dark and polished like old bronze.

They rushed to meet Demetrio.

"They burned my house!" was his answer to their questioning looks.

There were curses, threats and boasts.

Demetrio let them get it off their chests; then he drew a bottle from his shirt, took a swig, wiped it with the back of his hand and passed it to the man next to him. The bottle made its way from mouth to mouth and was emptied. The men licked their lips.

"God willing," Demetrio said, "tomorrow or even tonight we'll look the Federales in the eyes. We'll show them around, what do you say, *muchachos?*"

The half-naked men jumped, shouting with joy. Then their insults, curses and threats multiplied.

"We don't know how many they are." Demetrio observed, searching their faces. "In Hostotipaquillo, Julián Medina and half a dozen field hands with knives sharpened on their *metates* stood up to all the cops and Federales in the town and kicked them out. . . ."

"What do Medina's men have that we don't?" said a strong, compact man with thick, black eyebrows and beard and a sweet look in his eyes.

"All I know is," he added, "my name ain't Anastasio Montañés if tomorrow I ain't got a Mauser rifle, a cartridge belt, trousers, and shoes. I mean it! . . . Don't you believe me, Codorniz? I got half a dozen bits of lead in my body. . . . Ask my *compadre,* Demetrio, if you don't believe me. . . . Bullets scare me as much as a little ball of candy. Wait and see."

"*Viva* Anastasio Montañés!" shouted Manteca.

"No," Anastasio replied, "*viva* Demetrio Macías, our leader, and God in Heaven and his Holy Mother."

"*Viva* Demetrio Macías!" they all shouted.

They lit a fire with dry grass and wood, and over the glowing embers they stretched pieces of fresh meat. They gathered around the flames, sitting on their haunches, sniffing hungrily as the meat twisted and crackled in the fire.

Near them, in a pile, was the golden hide of a cow on the blood-soaked ground. From a rope strung between *huizache* trees the smoked meat hung, curing in the sun and air.

"Well," said Demetrio, "besides my thirty-thirty, we've only got twenty rifles. If there are few Federales, we won't leave a single one alive, if there are many at least we'll give them a good scare."

He loosened the sash at his waist, untied a knot, and offered the contents to his comrades. "Salt!" they cried out with joy, each taking some grains with the tips of his fingers.

They ate avidly, and when they were sated, they lay belly-up in the sunshine and sang sad, monotonous songs, punctuated by piercing screams after each verse.

III

Amid the brush of the sierra, Demetrio Macías' twenty-five men slept until the signal horn woke them. Pancracio sounded the alarm from the top of a ridge.

"This is it, *muchachos,* look alive!" said Anastasio Montañés, checking the action on his rifle.

But an hour went by and they heard nothing but the song of the cicadas in the grass and the croaking of the frogs in the puddles.

When the white of the moon glow faded into the slightly pink stripe of dawn, the outline of the first soldier stood out against the highest edge of the trail. After him others appeared, then ten more, then a hundred more, but they all disappeared quickly into the shadows. The first rays of the sun revealed that the precipice was covered with people: tiny men on miniature horses.

"Ain't they pretty!" Pancracio exclaimed. "Come on *muchachos,* let's play with the toy soldiers!

The little moving figures would disappear into the dense chaparral and then show up black against the ochre boulders.

The voices of the officers and the soldiers could be heard distinctly.

Demetrio made a signal, and the bolts of the rifles clicked.

"Now!" he ordered in a whisper.

Twenty-one men fired as one, and twenty-one Federales fell from their horses. The rest, surprised, were motionless, like bas-reliefs carved into the boulders.

A new volley, and another twenty-one men rolled from rock to rock, their heads split open.

"Come out, *bandidos!* . . . Peasant scum!" . . .

"Die, you corn-grinding thieves!" . . .

"Die, you cattle-rustlers!" . . .

The Federales shouted at their enemies, who from their hiding places calmly and quietly continued to display the marksmanship for which they were already famous.

"Look, Pancracio," said Meco, who was all dark except for the whites of his eyes and teeth, "this is for the one just passing the *pitahayo* bush! . . . Son of a . . . ! Take that! . . . Right smack on his pumpkin! You see? Now for the one on the dapple-gray horse. . . . Down you go, *pelón!*"

"I'm gonna give the one riding on the edge of the trail a bath . . . I'll dunk you in the river, damn *mocho!* . . . How's that? You see?"

"Anastasio, don't be mean! . . . Gimme your carbine. . . . *Ándale,* just one little shot! . . ."

Manteca, Codorniz and the others who had no weapons pleaded, they begged as a great favor to take just one shot.

"Come out if you're men!"

"Poke your heads out . . . You patched up louse-heads!"

From one mountain to the other the shouts were heard as clearly as if across a street.

Suddenly, Codorniz showed himself, buck naked, holding his trousers like a bullfighter's cape, taunting the Federales. Then a rain of bullets fell on Demetrio's men.

"Ay! Ay! A swarm of bees is coming at my head," said Anastasio Montañés, already flat against the rocks, not daring to look up.

"Codorniz, you son of a . . . ! Now go where I told you!" Demetrio roared.

And, crawling, they took new positions.

The Federales stopped firing and were loudly celebrating their triumph, when a new hail of bullets confused them.

"Now there's more of them!" the soldiers shouted.

In a panic, many turned their horses around ready to flee, others dismounted and scrambled over the rocks looking for refuge. The officers had to fire on the fleeing soldiers to restore order.

"Shoot the ones below, the ones below!" Demetrio shouted, pointing his thirty-thirty toward the crystal thread of the river.

A Federal trooper fell right into the water, and they continued to fall unerringly one by one with each new shot. But only Demetrio was shooting toward the river, and for each one he killed, ten or twenty made it up the other incline.

"Shoot the ones below, the ones below!" he kept shouting in a rage.

The comrades now shared weapons, picking targets and making hefty bets.

"My leather belt if I don't hit the one on the dark horse on the head. Lend me your rifle, Meco. . . ."

"Twenty Mauser rounds and half a *chorizo* if you let me knock down the one on the black horse with a white star on its forehead. Good. . . . Now! . . . See him jump! Like a deer! . . ."

"Don't run *mochos!* . . . Come meet your father, Demetrio Macías."

Now it was their turn to insult the Federales. Pancracio shouted, raising his hairless face, immutable, rock-like, and when Manteca shouted all his neck muscles showed, his face contorted around his frowning murderer's eyes.

Demetrio continued firing, and warning the others about the impending danger, but they did not heed his desperate voice until they felt the whizzing of the bullets on their flank.

"They got me!" Demetrio cried, and ground his teeth, "Sons of . . . !"

And he quickly let himself slide toward a gully.

IV

Two were missing: Serapio the candy man and Antonio, who played the cymbals in the Juchipila Band.

"Maybe they'll catch up to us later," Demetrio said.

They came back gloomy. Only Anastasio Montañés still had the sweet expression on his sleepy eyes and bearded face, and Pancracio, the repulsively immutable, hard profile, with his projecting jaw.

The Federales had left, and Demetrio was recovering all their horses, hidden in the sierra.

Suddenly, Codorniz, who was marching ahead, screamed: he had just seen their missing comrades, hanging from the arms of a mesquite.

It was Serapio and Antonio. They recognized them, and Anastasio Montañés prayed between his teeth:

"Our Father, who art in heaven . . ."

"Amen," the rest murmured with their heads bowed and their hats over their breasts.

And they quickly headed north on the Juchipila canyon, not resting until well into the night.

Codorniz did not leave Anastasio for a moment.

The silhouettes of the hanged men, with their flaccid necks, their arms dangling, their legs stiff, swaying softly in the wind, would not leave his memory.

The next day, Demetrio complained a lot about his wound. He couldn't ride his horse anymore. From then on they had to bear him on a stretcher they had improvised with some oak branches and bundles of grass.

"You're still bleeding a lot, *compadre* Demetrio," said Anastasio Montañés. And with a tug tore off a sleeve of his shirt and tied it tightly around the thigh, above the bullet wound.

"Well," said Venancio, "That will stop the blood and take the pain away."

Venancio was a barber; in his town he pulled teeth and applied caustics and leeches. He enjoyed a certain prestige because he had read *The Wandering Jew* and *El sol de mayo*. They called him "the doctor," and he was very proud of his knowledge, and was a man of few words.

Taking turns by fours, they carried the stretcher across flat, stony mesas and up very steep slopes.

At noon, when the dust made it difficult to breathe or see, together with the incessant song of the cicadas you could hear the rhythmic and monotone moans of the wounded man.

In every *jacalito* hidden between abrupt rocks, they stopped and rested.

"Thank God, you can always find a compassionate soul and a *tortilla gorda* stuffed with chilies and beans!" said Anastasio Montañés belching.

And the mountain folk, the *serranos,* after giving their calloused hands strong handshakes, exclaimed:

"God bless you! God help you and keep you on the right path! . . . You go now; tomorrow we too will run from the draft, chased by these damn government soldiers who have declared war to the death on all poor people; who steal our pigs, our chickens and even the little corn we have to eat; who burn our houses and carry off our women, and when they finally run into you, they finish you off like a mad dog."

When the sun began to set in a blaze that tinted the sky the brightest colors, a few houses stood out dark in a clearing, between blue mountains. Demetrio had them carry him there.

They were a few poor *jacales* made of grass, scattered along the riverbank, between plantings of corn and beans that had just sprouted.

They lay the stretcher on the ground, and Demetrio, with a weak voice, asked for a drink of water.

The dark mouths of the huts were crowded with colorless *chomites,* bony breasts, disheveled heads, and right behind them, bright eyes and fresh cheeks.

A chubby boy, with shiny, dark skin, came over to see the man on the stretcher; then an old woman, and after that everyone else came, making a circle around him.

A kind young woman brought a gourd full of blue water. Demetrio took the vessel in his trembling hands and drank avidly.

"Don'tcha want more?"

He raised his eyes; the girl had a very common face but there was much sweetness in her voice.

With the back of his hand he wiped the sweat that was beading on his forehead, and turning on his side, he said in a tired voice, "God bless you!"

And he began to shiver with such force, that he shook the grass and the legs of the stretcher. The fever made him sleep.

"You can feel the *sereno,* the night air, and that is bad for an ague," said Señá Remigia, a barefoot old woman, who wore a *chomite* and a scrap of calico on her chest by way of a shirt.

And she invited them to bring Demetrio into her *jacal.*

Pancracio, Anastasio Montañés and Codorniz sat at the feet of the stretcher like faithful dogs, waiting on their master's wishes.

The rest dispersed in search of food.

Señá Remigia offered what she had: chilies and *tortillas.*

"Imagine . . . I had eggs, chickens and even a goat that had just had kids, but those damned Federales cleaned me out."

Then, cupping her hands around Anastasio's ear, she whispered: "Imagine! . . . They even carted off Señá Nieves' girl! . . ."

V

Startled, Codorniz opened his eyes and sat up.

"Montañés, you hear? . . . A shot! Montañés . . . wake up. . . ."

He gave him a couple of strong shoves, until he got him to move and stop snoring.

"Son of a . . . ! You're at it again! . . . I tell you the dead don't come back," Anastasio muttered, half-awake.

"A shot, Montañés! . . ."

"Go to sleep, Codorniz, or I'm going to sock you one. . . ."

"No, Anastasio, it's not a nightmare. . . . I already forgot the hanged men. It really was a shot, I heard it loud and clear. . . ."

"A shot, you say? . . . Let's see, gimme my Mauser. . . ."

Anastasio Montañés rubbed his eyes, stretched his arms and legs lazily, and stood.

They left the *jacal*. The sky was studded with stars and the moon was rising like a thin sickle. Out of the hovels came the confused murmuring of frightened women, and the noise of the weapons of the men who had been sleeping outside and were waking up now.

"You idiot! . . . You wrecked my foot!"

The voice was heard clearly and distinctly nearby.

"Who goes there? . . ."

The shout echoed from boulder to boulder, through the crests of the hills and the hollows, until it was lost in the distance and in the silence of the night.

"Who goes there?" Anastasio repeated in a stronger voice, sliding the bolt of his Mauser.

"Demetrio Macías!" they answered nearby.

"It's Pancracio!" said Codorniz, overjoyed. And then reassured, he rested the butt of his rifle on the ground.

Pancracio was leading a young man covered with dust, from his American felt hat to his coarse big shoes. There was a stain of fresh blood on his trouser, near one foot.

"Who's this *curro?*" Anastasio asked.

"I was on guard duty, I heard a noise in the grass and I yelled: 'Who goes there?' 'Carranzo,' this guy answered. . . . 'Carranzo . . . ? Don't know the guy. . . . Here's a Carranzo for you!' and I put some lead in his paw. . . ."

Smiling, Pancracio turned his hairless face expecting applause.

Then the stranger spoke.

"Who's the boss here?"

Anastasio raised his head haughtily, standing up to him.

The young man's tone came down a notch.

"Well, I'm a revolutionary, too. The Federales drafted me and I was enlisted, but during combat the day before yesterday, I managed to desert, and I have come, on foot, looking for you."

"Ah, he's a Federal!" many interrupted, looking at him thunderstruck.

"Ah, he's a *mocho!*" said Anastasio Montañés, "So why didn't you shoot him in the ticker?"

"Who knows what he's up to! Says he wants to talk to Demetrio, has to tell him something or other! . . . But nothing doing, there's time enough for all that," Pancracio answered, preparing his rifle.

"But what kind of imbeciles are you?" the stranger said.

And that's all he got to say, because Anastasio knocked him down with one swipe and his face was bathed in blood.

"Shoot that *mocho!* . . ."

"Hang him! . . ."

"Plug him . . . he's a Federal! . . ."

Agitated, they shouted, howled, got their rifles ready.

"Hush . . . hush, shut up! . . . Looks like Demetrio's trying to say something," Anastasio said, calming them down.

Indeed, Demetrio wanted to know what was going on and he had them bring the prisoner to him.

"This is an infamy, chief, just look . . . just look!" said Luis Cervantes, showing the blood stains on his trousers and his swollen mouth and nose.

"So, who the hell are you?" Demetrio asked.

"My name is Luis Cervantes, I'm a medical student and a journalist. Because I said something in favor of the revolutionaries, they came after me, grabbed me, and took me to a barracks. . . ."

The account of his adventure, that he continued to give in detail and in a declamatory tone, caused great hilarity in Pancracio and Manteca.

"I have endeavored to make myself understood, to convince you that I am a true coreligionist. . . ."

"A core . . . what?" Demetrio asked cocking an ear toward him.

"A coreligionist, *jefe* . . . that is to say, that I pursue the same ideals and defend the same cause all of you defend."

Demetrio smiled:

"And what cause do we defend? . . ."

Disconcerted, Luis Cervantes found no reply.

"Look what a face he makes! . . . Why all this fuss? . . . Do we shoot him now, Demetrio?" Pancracio asked eagerly.

Demetrio's hand reached for the lock of hair that covered his ear, scratched for a long time, pensively; then, not finding a solution, said:

"Get out . . . it's starting to hurt again. . . . Anastasio, put out the wick. Lock this one up in the corral. Pancracio and Manteca, keep an eye on him. Tomorrow we'll see."

VI

Luis Cervantes was still not used to discerning the precise shape of objects by the dim light of starlit nights, and looking for the best place to rest, lay his tired bones on a pile of moist manure, at the foot of the vague bulk of a *huizache* bush. Exhausted rather than resigned, he stretched out fully and closed his eyes resolutely, determined to sleep until his fierce guards woke him or until the morning sun burned his ears. Something like a vague warmth beside him, and then a rough, labored breathing, made him tremble. He spread out his arms, and his fearful hand touched the rigid bristles of a pig that grunted, definitely bothered by his proximity.

Then all his efforts to sleep were in vain, not because of the pain in his wounded limb, nor that of his battered flesh, but because of the sudden and precise picture of his failure.

Yes, he had failed to appreciate in a timely manner the difference between wielding the scalpel, blasting the "thieving insurgent rabble" from the columns of a provincial newspaper, and chasing them, rifle in hand, to their very lairs. He suspected he had made a mistake after the first leg of the expedition, when he was relieved of his rank as second lieutenant in the cavalry. The brutal fourteen-league ride left him with stiff hips and knees, as if all his bones had been soldered into one. He finally understood he had made a mistake eight days later, at the first encounter with the rebels. He could swear, with his hand on the sacred image of Christ, that when the soldiers aimed their Mausers, someone with a booming voice behind them had yelled: "Every man for himself!" This was clearly so, since his own spirited and noble steed, a combat veteran, had turned tail, bolted and refused to stop until even the rumor of bullets could not be heard. And this was just as the sun was setting, when the mountain began to fill with vague and disquieting shadows, when darkness was climbing at full speed from the hollows. What could be more logical, he thought, than to seek shelter among the rocks, rest his body and spirit, and attempt to sleep? But a soldier's logic is the logic of the absurd. Thus, for example, the next morning his colonel wakes him by giving him a few sound kicks and pulls him out of his hideout with a swollen, battered face. Furthermore, this elicits the hilarity of the officers to such a point that, laughing with tears in their eyes, they unanimously implore that the fugitive be pardoned. And the colonel, instead of having him shot, gives him a good kick in the hindquarters and sends him to the rear to help in the kitchen.

This grave insult bears poisoned fruit in the long run. Luis Cervantes becomes a turncoat, of course, although for the moment only mentally. The sorrows and miseries of the dispossessed now move him to compassion; their cause is the sublime cause of oppressed people who demand justice, only justice. He gets close to the humble soldiers, and lo, the sight of a pack mule that died of exhaustion on a stormy expedition moves him to tears.

Luis Cervantes, therefore, won the confidence of the troops. Some soldiers boldly confided in him. A very serious soldier, noted for his temperance and shyness, told him: "I'm a carpenter. I had a mother, a little old woman, nailed to her chair by rheumatism for over ten years. At midnight three policemen pulled me out of my home, and I woke up in the garrison, and that night I was twelve leagues from my town. . . . A month ago, I passed through my town with the army. . . . My mother was six feet under! . . . She lost her only comfort in life. . . . Now, no one needs me. But by God in heaven, these cartridges they make me carry will not be for the enemy. . . . And if I am granted this miracle (my Holy Mother of Guadalupe will grant it), if I get to join Villa . . . I swear by the sacred soul of my mother that these Federales will pay."

Another, who was young, very intelligent, but a chatterbox, a dipsomaniac and a marijuana smoker, called him aside and, looking at him straight in the face with his vague, glassy eyes, whispered in his ear: "*Compadre* . . . over there . . . on the other side . . . know what I mean? . . . They ride the very best the stables of the north and the interior have to offer, their horses' tack is heavy with pure silver. . . . What do we ride, bah! . . . Nags good for pulling buckets at an irrigation ditch . . . know what I mean *compadre?* Over there, they get paid in solid silver *pesos:* we get celluloid bills from the murderer's factory. . . . That's all I say. . . ."

And all of them confided in him, even a sergeant said naively: "I'm a volunteer, but I really put my foot in it. Today, what it'd take you a whole lifetime of working like a mule in peacetime, you can make in a few months running around the sierras with a rifle on your shoulder. But not if you're on this side *mano* . . . not on this side. . . ."

And Luis Cervantes, who already shared with the rank and file that surreptitious, implacable, mortal hatred for all noncoms, officers and all superiors, felt the last cobwebs fall from his eyes, and he saw clearly the end result of the struggle.

But behold, today, just when he meets his coreligionists, instead of greeting him with open arms, they lock him up in a pigsty!

Day came: the roosters crowed in their *jacales;* the chickens in the branches of the *huizache* in the corral stirred, opening their wings and fluffing their feathers, and landed in one fell swoop.

He observed his guards lying in the manure and snoring. The faces of the two men from the previous evening were revived in his imagination. One of

animal-like.

them, Pancracio, was blondish, freckled, had a hairless face, with a jutting chin, a flat sloping forehead, and ears glued to his skull, and was, on the whole, beastlike in his appearance. The other, Manteca, was skin and bones: sunken crossed eyes, with very straight hair falling on his neck, over his forehead and ears, his scrofulous lips eternally half open.

And he felt once again that he was getting gooseflesh.

VII

Sleepy still, Demetrio touched the curly tufts of hair that covered his humid forehead, parted against one ear, and opened his eyes.

Distinctly he heard the feminine, melodious voice that he had already heard in dreams, and turned toward the door.

It was day: the rays of the sun darted between the straws of the *jacal*. The same girl who had offered him a cup of deliciously cold water the night before (his dream all night long), now, equally sweet and tender, entered with a pot of milk brimming with foam.

"It's goat milk, but it's real good. . . . Go ahead, try it. . . ."

Grateful, Demetrio smiled, raised himself and taking the earthenware vessel began to take little sips, without taking his eyes off the girl.

Uneasy, she lowered her eyes.

"What's your name?"

"Camila."

"I like your name but I like your accent more. . . ."

Camila blushed, and as he tried to grab one of her hands she was frightened, took the empty vessel and escaped in a flash.

"Not like that, *compadre* Demetrio," Anastasio Montañés observed gravely, "you have to tame them first. . . . Hmm, when I think of the scratches women have left on my body! . . . I have a lot of experience when it comes to that. . . ."

"I feel good, *compadre*," Demetrio said, pretending not to hear, "looks like I had the chills; sweated a lot, and woke up refreshed. What's still bugging me is the damn wound. Call Venancio over so he can cure me."

"And what do you want us to do with the *curro* I caught last night?" Pancracio asked.

"That's right! . . . I forgot! . . ."

Demetrio, as always, thought and hesitated a good deal before making a decision.

"Let's see Codorniz, come over here. Look, ask about a chapel that is about three leagues from here. Go and steal the cassock from the priest."

"But, what are you going to do, *compadre?*" Anastasio asked stunned.

"If this *curro* has come to murder me, it's easy to get the truth out of him. I tell him I'm going to have him shot. Codorniz dresses up as a priest and hears his confession. If he has sinned, I shoot him; if not, I let him go."

"Hmm, that's a lot of trouble! . . . If it were up to me, I'd just blast him," Pancracio said with disdain.

At night Codorniz returned with the priest's cassock. Demetrio had the prisoner brought to him.

Luis Cervantes, who had not slept or eaten for two days, came in with a haggard face and bags under his eyes, his lips colorless and dry.

He spoke slowly and clumsily.

"Do what you want with me. . . . Surely I was wrong about you. . . ."

There was a long silence. Then:

"I thought you would gladly accept someone who comes to offer help, I may not be much help, but I do it for your sake. . . . What's it to me if the revolution wins or not?"

He was slowly livening up, and there were moments when the lassitude in his gaze would disappear.

"The revolution is for the benefit of the poor, the ignorant, those who have been slaves all their lives, the miserable ones who don't even know that they are miserable because the rich turn the tears, sweat, and blood of the poor into gold. . . ."

"Bah! . . . What's it all mean? I can't stand sermons!" Pancracio interrupted.

"I wanted to fight for the holy cause of the unfortunate. . . . But you don't understand me . . . you reject me. . . . Do with me as you like!"

"For now I'll just put this lariat round your neck. . . . Look what a chubby, white neck you have!"

"Yes, I know why you're here," Demetrio answered, bored, scratching his head. "I'm going to have you shot, see?"

Then turning to Anastasio:

"Take him away, . . . and if he wants to confess, get him a priest. . . ."

Anastasio, impassible as always, softly took Cervantes' arm.

"Let's go, *curro*. . . ."

A few minutes later when Codorniz showed up in a cassock, they all laughed until their sides hurt.

"Hmm! This *curro* is long-winded!" he exclaimed, "I even think he was laughing at me when I began to ask him questions."

"But he didn't spill anything?"

"Just what he said last night. . . ."

"I've got a feeling he didn't come to do what you fear, *compadre*," Anastasio said.

"Well then, give him something to eat and keep an eye on him."

VIII

The next day, Luis Cervantes could hardly get up. Dragging his wounded limb, he roamed from house to house looking for some alcohol, boiled water and rags. Camila, with her endless kindness, got him everything he needed.

When he began to wash, she sat beside him to see him dress the wound, with mountain girl curiosity.

"Hey, who taught you to tend to a wound? . . . And what's the water for? . . . And the rags, why'd you boil them? . . . Well look at that, such a fuss bout everything! . . . And what's that you put on your hands? . . . No! . . . *Aguardiente*, for real? . . . Go figure, and I thought *aguardiente* was only good for colic! . . . Ah! . . . Were you really gonna be a doctor? . . . Ha, ha, ha! . . . I'll die laughing yet! . . . Things you make up! . . . Animals in unboiled water! . . . Yuck! . . . Anyway, when I look I don't see nothing! . . ."

Camila went on asking questions, and with such familiarity, that before long she was calling him by his first name.

Absorbed in his thoughts, Luis Cervantes no longer heard what she said.

"Where are those splendidly armed and mounted men, who get paid in pure silver *pesos* minted by Villa in Chihuahua? Bah! A score of naked, louse-ridden wretches riding decrepit nags with sores from neck to tail. Could it be true, as the government press and he himself had asserted, that the so-called revolutionaries were nothing but a bunch of bandits who now had a magnificent pretext to satisfy their thirst for gold and blood? Was it all lies, what the sympathizers of the revolution said about them? But while newspapers were still loudly proclaiming triumph after triumph of the Federales, a paymaster who had recently come from Guadalajara let slip the rumor that Huerta's relatives and favorites were abandoning the capital and heading for the ports, even if he still kept howling and howling: 'I'll make the peace, no matter the cost.' Therefore, revolutionaries, bandits, whatever you wanted to call them, they were going to defeat the government; tomorrow belonged to them; therefore, you had to be with them and only them."

"No, so far at least, I haven't made a mistake," he said to himself, almost out loud.

"What are you saying?" Camila asked, "I was beginning to think the cat had gotten your tongue."

Luis Cervantes frowned and glared at that homespun-dressed monkey with bronze-colored skin, ivory teeth, and broad, flat feet.

"Hey, Curro, you good at telling stories?"

Luis grimaced and left without answering her.

She followed him with her eyes, dreamily, until his outline disappeared by the side of the brook.

She was so spellbound that she started when she heard the voice of her neighbor, one-eyed María Antonia, who, snooping from her hut, shouted:

"Hey you! . . . Give him a love potion. . . . Maybe he'll fall for you then. . . ."

"Bah! . . . Speak for yourself. . . ."

"I would, if I cared to! . . . But, yuck!, *curros* are disgusting. . . ."

IX

"Señá Remigia, lend me some eggs, my hen isn't laying. I have some men who want to have lunch."

Due to the change from the bright light of the sun to the darkness of the hut, made darker still by the thick smoke rising from the hearth, the neighbor's eyes opened wide. But after a few seconds she began to perceive clearly the outline of objects and in a corner the wounded man's stretcher that, near his head, touched the sooty and shiny thatch roof.

She squatted next to Señá Remigia and, glancing furtively at the place where Demetrio was resting, asked softly:

"How's the man doing? . . . Any better? . . . Good! . . . He's so young too! . . . But he's still very pale. . . . So the bullet wound is not closing? . . . Look, Señá Remigia, don't you want us to do a healing?"

Señá Remigia, naked from the waist up, stretches her thin, sinewy arms over the base of the *metate* and works the *tortilla* meal again and again with the roller.

"Who knows, it might not suit them," she answers without stopping her difficult labor, almost out of breath, "they've got their own doctor, see. . . ."

"Señá Remigia," another neighbor enters, bending her skinny backbone in order to make it through the door, "Don't you have some laurel leaves you can let me have so I can make a remedy for María Antonia? She got her cramps this morning. . . ."

And since it is really only a pretext to snoop and gossip, she turns her eyes to the corner where the sick man is, and winking, asks after his health.

Señá Remigia, lowers her eyes to signal that Demetrio is sleeping. . . .

"So, you're also here, Señá Pachita, . . . I didn't see you. . . ."

"God give you a good morning, Ña Fortunata. . . . How are you all this morning?"

"Well, María Antonia has 'the curse' . . . and, same as always, she has cramps. . . ." Squatting, she draws up next to Señá Pachita.

"I don't have laurel leaves, dear," Señá Remigia answers stopping her grinding for a moment; she pushes some hair away from her dripping face and then sinks her two hands into a bucket and brings out a handful of cooked corn, dripping yellowish, cloudy water. "I don't have any, but go to Señá Dolores: she always has herbs."

"Last night Ña Dolores went to the *cofradía*. I figure they came for her so she would get Tía Matías' girl out of trouble."

"Come now, Señá Pachita, you don't say! . . ."

The three old women form a lively circle, and speaking very softly, they get down to gossiping with great zest.

"As true as there is a God in heaven! . . ."

"Well, I was the first one to say it: 'Marcelina is fat as can be!' But nobody wanted to believe me."

"Poor child. . . . And worse yet if it turns out it's her uncle Nazario's! . . ."

"God have mercy on her! . . ."

"Her uncle Nazario, my eye! . . . A curse on the damn Federales! . . ."

"Then, she's yet another one they've ruined! . . ."

The *comadres'* racket finally woke up Demetrio.

They were silent for a moment, and a little later Señá Pachita, taking from her bosom a tender pigeon that was opening its beak gasping for air, said:

"Well, truth is I was bringing the gentleman here this remedy, . . . but I hear tell he's under a doctor's care. . . ."

"It doesn't matter, Señá Pachita; . . . it goes on him not inside him. . . ."

"Sir, excuse the bother, . . . I bring you this present," said the hag approaching Demetrio, "For blood hemorrhages there's nothing better than this remedy. . . ."

Demetrio agreed readily. They had already placed some pieces of bread soaked in *aguardiente* on his belly, and although he felt a lot of evaporation around his navel when they took them off, he still felt a lot of the heat.

"Go ahead, you know how to do it, Señá Remigia," the neighbors exclaimed.

From a reed sheath Señá Remigia pulled out a long and curved knife used to harvest cactus pears; took the pigeon in one hand, and running it along its belly, with the skill of a surgeon split it in half with one swipe.

"In the name of Jesus, Mary and Joseph!" Señá Remigia said making a blessing. Then quickly, she applied the two hot and dripping pieces of the pigeon to Demetrio's belly.

"You'll see, this'll bring you much relief. . . ."

Following Señá Remigia's instructions, Demetrio kept totally still, lying on one side.

Then Señá Fortunata spoke her piece. She liked the gentlemen of the revolution very much. Three months ago the Federales had stolen her only daughter, and ever since she was beside herself with grief.

At the beginning of her story, Codorniz and Anastasio Montañés, dug in like badgers at the foot of the stretcher, lifted their heads and listened with half-open mouths, but Señá Fortunata got into so many minute details that halfway through Codorniz got bored and went out to scratch himself in the sun, and by the time she solemnly finished: "I pray to God and the Most Holy Virgin Mary that you will not leave a single one of these infernal Federales alive," Demetrio, his face to the wall, feeling much relieved from the remedy on his belly, was going over an itinerary to invade Durango, and Anastasio Montañés was snoring like a trombone.

X

"Why don't you call the *curro* over to cure you, *compadre* Demetrio?" said Anastasio Montañés to his chief, who was suffering daily from chills and fevers. "You should see how he cured himself, and he's already so much better he doesn't even limp."

But Venancio, who had prepared the cans of lard and the strips of filthy rags, protested: "If anyone lays a hand on him, I won't answer for the results."

"*Compadre*, who says you're a doctor or nothin! . . . Betcha even forgot what you're doing here?" said Codorniz.

"Yes, I do remember, Codorniz, that you're with us because you stole a watch and some diamond rings," Venancio answered angrily.

Codorniz burst out laughing.

"At least! . . . Better'n running away from your town cause you poisoned your girlfriend."

"That's a lie!"

"Yes, you gave her Spanish fly to get her. . . ."

Venancio's cries of protest were drowned out by the roaring laughter of the others.

Demetrio, a sour look on his face, made them quiet down; then he began to complain and said:

"Well then, bring the student over."

Luis Cervantes came, he uncovered the leg, examined the wound carefully and shook his head. The blanket bandage was digging into the flesh; the swollen leg seemed ready to burst. Any movement made Demetrio suppress a moan. Luis Cervantes cut the bandage, washed the wound thoroughly, covered the thigh with large pieces of damp cloth and bandaged it.

Demetrio was able to sleep the whole afternoon and night. The next day he awoke very happy.

"This *curro* has a very light touch," he said.

Venancio remarked quickly:

"All right; but *curros* are like humidity, they seep in anywhere. It's because of *curros* that we've lost the benefits of previous revolutions."

And since Demetrio believed blindly in the barber's skill, the next day when Luis Cervantes came to cure him, he said:

"Listen, you do a good job, and when I am good and cured you can go home or wherever you want."

Luis Cervantes, discreetly, made no reply.

A week went by, two weeks; the Federales showed no sign of life. On the other hand, there were plenty of beans and corn in the neighboring villages. The people hated the Federales so much that they were happy to help the rebels. Demetrio's men, therefore, waited for their boss' complete recovery without impatience.

For many days, Luis Cervantes continued sad and silent.

"I'm beginning to think you're in love, Curro!" Demetrio joked one day, after the cure. He had begun to take a liking to him.

Little by little he took an interest in his comfort. He asked if the soldiers were giving him his ration of meat and milk. Luis Cervantes had to say that he ate only what the kind old women of the village gave him, and that people still looked on him as a stranger or an intruder.

"Curro, they're all good boys," Demetrio replied, "you just have to win them over. Starting tomorrow you'll have everything you need. You'll see."

Indeed, that very afternoon things began to change. Strewn on the stony ground, looking at sunset clouds that seemed like giant clots of blood, some of Macías' men heard Venancio's account of entertaining episodes from *The Wandering Jew*. Many, lulled by the barber's mellifluous voice, had begun to snore, but Luis Cervantes was attentive. After Venancio finished his account with strange anticlerical comments, he said emphatically: "Admirable! You have a beautiful gift!"

"I'm not half bad," Venancio replied, sure of himself, "but my parents died and I wasn't able to study for a profession."

"That doesn't matter. When our cause is victorious you will get a medical degree easily. Two or three weeks of visiting hospitals, a good recommendation from our *jefe* Macías . . . , and you will be a doctor. . . . You have such a knack for it that it will be child's play!"

After that night, Venancio was the only one who stopped calling him "*curro.*" It was Luisito this and Luisito that.

XI

"Hey, Curro, I wanna say something to you, . . ." said Camila one morning, when Luis Cervantes was going to her *jacal* to get boiling water to cure his foot.

The girl had been restless for some days, and her coyness and reticence bothered the young man. He interrupted his task abruptly, stood up, and staring at her replied:

"Well, . . . what is it you want to say to me?"

Camila then felt her tongue turn into a rag and she could not pronounce a word; her face turned as red as a bearberry, she shrugged her shoulders and bowed her head until it touched her bare breast. Then, motionless, her eyes fixed on the wound with idiotic obstinacy, she said in the weakest voice:

"Look how pretty it's healing, so quickly! . . . Just like the bud of a wild rose."

Luis Cervantes frowned angrily and resumed dressing his wound, ignoring her.

When he was done, Camila had disappeared.

For three days there was no sign of the girl anywhere. Señá Agapita, her mother, came when Luis Cervantes called and it was she who boiled the water and the bandages. He took great care not to ask any questions. But after three days, there was Camila again, more awkward and coy than ever.

Luis Cervantes had his mind on other things but his indifference encouraged Camila who spoke finally:

"Hey, Curro . . . I wanna say something to you. . . . Hey, Curro. I want you to help me learn *La Adelita*. . . . So's I. . . . Betcha can't guess why? . . . So's I can sing it often, often, when all of you leave, when you're no longer here, . . . when you're so far, far away . . . that you won't even remember me. . . ."

Her words had the same effect on Luis Cervantes as that of a steel point sliding down the side of a bottle.

Unaware, she continued as naïve as before:

"Well, Curro, why should I even tell you! . . . If you only knew how wicked that old man is who commands all of you. Just look what he did to me. . . . You know that Demetrio don't want anyone to cook for him except my mother, and don't want anybody but me to bring him his food. . . . Well, the other day I come in with the *champurrao,* and whatcha think that nasty old man did? Well, he grabs my hand and holds it hard, hard. Then he starts

pinching my legs. . . . But I slapped him good! . . . 'Stop it! . . . Let me be!
. . . Stop it you rude old man! . . . Let go of me, let go! . . . Shame on you!'
And then I pulled away from him and got loose, and ran out of there as fast
as I could. . . . Whatcha think, Curro?"

Never had Camila seen Luis Cervantes laugh with such joy.

"Is everything you're telling me really true?"

Thoroughly disconcerted, Camila could not reply. He laughed again uproariously and repeated his question. Feeling the greatest apprehension and
anxiety, she answered him in a broken voice:

"Yes, it's true. . . . And that's what I wanted to tell you. . . . Don't it make
your blood boil, Curro?"

Once more Camila beheld, spellbound, Luis Cervantes' fresh and radiant
face, the tender look in his green eyes, his cheeks, fresh and pink like those
of a porcelain doll, the smoothness of the white, delicate skin that showed
beneath his collar, and above the sleeves of a rough woolen shirt, the tender
blond color of his lightly curled hair.

"What are you waiting for, you silly girl? If the *jefe* likes you, what more
could you hope for?"

Camila felt something rise in her breast, something that came up to her
throat, made a knot at her throat. She shut her eyelids tightly to clear her
tearful eyes, then wiped her wet cheeks with the back of her hand, and as
she had done three days before, escaped with the nimbleness of a deer.

XII

Demetrio's wound had already healed. They were beginning to discuss plans
to go to the north, where they said the revolutionaries had triumphed all
along the Federal lines. An event took place that brought things to a head.
One day, Luis Cervantes was sitting on a crag of the sierra, in the cool of the
afternoon, his gaze lost in the distance, dreaming, killing time. At the foot
of the crest, stretched out among the reeds by the riverbank, Pancracio and
Manteca were playing cards. Anastasio Montañés, who was watching them
without much interest, suddenly turned his black-bearded face and sweet
eyes toward Luis Cervantes and said to him:

"Why're you sad, Curro? Why do you think so much? Come on over and
chat for a bit. . . ."

Luis Cervantes did not move, but Anastasio went over and sat by him to
be friendly.

"You miss the excitement of the city. It's clear you're the shiny shoes and
bow tie type. . . . Look, Curro, you see me here all dirty and ragged, I'm not
what I seem to be. . . . Bet you won't believe me? . . . I've no need to do this.

I own ten yoke of oxen. . . . It's true! . . . Just ask my *compadre* Demetrio. . . .
I have ten acres planted with crops. . . . Believe it or not. . . . Look, Curro,
I love to provoke the Federales, and that's why they can't stand me. The last
time, eight months ago (the time I've been here), I stuck a knife into a pretentious little captain (God forgive me), right about here, smack near the
belly button. . . . But, truly, I don't need to do this. . . . I'm here on account
of that business . . . and to give my *compadre* Demetrio a hand."

"Girl of my dreams!" shouted Manteca thrilled by the hand he was dealt.
He put a twenty-cent silver coin on the queen of spades.

"As you see, Curro, I can't stand gambling at all! . . . You want to place a
bet? . . . Go on, look. This little leather snake is still jingling!" said Anastasio shaking his belt and making the silver *pesos* ring.

Then Pancracio dealt the cards, the queen turned up and there was a
quarrel. Arguing, shouting, and then insults. Pancracio's stone face con-
fronted Manteca's snake-eyed look; he was convulsive like an epileptic.
Any moment now they would come to blows. Running out of sufficiently
wounding insults, they started naming fathers and mothers in richly embroidered obscenities.

But nothing came of it. After they ran out of insults, they called off the
card game, calmly put their arms around each others shoulders and walked
off in search of a drink of *aguardiente*.

"I don't like to fight with my tongue either. It's ugly, don't you think,
Curro? . . . The truth is, you see, that no one has ever insulted my family. . . .
I like to be respected. That's why you'll never see me going around picking a
fight. . . . Hey, Curro," Anastasio continued in a different tone of voice, placing a hand over his forehead and standing up, "What's all that dust rising over
there behind that hill? *Caramba!* I bet you they're *mochos!* . . . And here we
are caught off guard! . . . Come on, Curro, let's go report to the boys."

The report was met with great rejoicing:

"We're going to slam them!" said Pancracio first of all.

"We sure are going to slam them. What have they got that we ain't!" . . .

But the enemy turned out to be a bunch of burros and two drivers.

"Stop them. They're *arribeños* from the highlands and they're bound to
have news," said Demetrio.

And they had astounding news. The Federales had fortified El Grillo and
La Buja mountains in Zacatecas. They said it was Huerta's last stronghold,
and everyone was predicting the fall of the city. Families were leaving in a
rush, headed south. The trains were crammed with people; carriages and
wagons were scarce, and on the highways, many, seized by panic, traveled on
foot with their belongings on their backs. Pánfilo Natera was gathering his

people in Fresnillo, and the Federales were beginning to feel that "their pants were getting too big for them."

"The fall of Zacatecas is Huerta's *Requiescat in pace,*" Luis Cervantes declared with extraordinary vehemence, "We have to get there before the attack and join General Natera."

And noting the surprised looks that his words elicited from the faces of Demetrio and his companions, he realized that he was still a nobody there.

But the next day, when the men went out in search of good mounts to resume the march, Demetrio called Luis Cervantes over and said to him:

"Do you really want to come with us, Curro? . . . You're made of different stuff, and the truth is, I don't understand how you could like this sort of life. Do you think we're doing this just for fun? . . . True, why deny it, I like the excitement, but it's not only that. . . . Sit down, Curro, sit down, let me tell you a story. You know why I became an insurgent? You see, before the revolution, I had my land plowed and ready to sow, and if I hadn't had that run in with Don Mónico, Moyahua's *cacique,* by now I'd be rushing to yoke my oxen and get the planting done. . . . Pancracio, get me two bottles of beer, one for me and one for the *curro.* . . . By the sign of the Holy Cross . . . can't do me any harm now, can it? . . ."

XIII

"I'm from Limón, very near Moyahua, right by the Cañón de Juchipila. I had my house, my cows and a piece of land to farm. In other words, I lacked for nothing. Well it happens that we *rancheros* have the custom of going into town every eight days. You hear the mass, the sermon, then you go to the plaza, buy onions, tomatoes, and take care of all the errands. Then you go with your friends into Primitivo López' store to have an early lunch. You have a drink, sometimes to be polite you let them fill your glass more than you should, the drink goes to your head, and you feel great, you laugh, shout and sing, if you feel like it. Everything's fine because you don't bother anyone. But then they start picking on you. A policeman comes by again and again, puts his ear to the door. Then the chief of police or the deputies decide to spoil your fun. . . . Of course, you don't have lemonade in your veins! You have a soul inside your body, you get mad, and get up and tell them what's what! If they understand, well and good; they leave you in peace, and there it ends. But sometimes they want to talk tough and threaten . . . and a fellow's quick-tempered . . . and doesn't like dirty looks. . . . And, yes sir, out comes the knife, out comes the pistol. . . . And then it's head for the hills until they forget all about the poor stiff!"

"So, what happened with Don Mónico? That pompous ass! A lot less than with the others. Didn't even touch a hair on his head! I did spit on his beard for sticking his nose where he shouldn't, that's all. . . . Well that was enough for him to bring down the whole Federation on me. You probably know the story of what happened in Mexico City, where they killed Señor Madero and the other guy, what's his name Félix or Felipe Díaz, what do I know! . . . Anyway, Don Mónico went in person to Zacatecas to bring troops to grab me. Said I was a Maderista and was going to rise up in arms. But one has friends and someone warned me in time, and when the Federales came to Limón, I had cleared out. Later I was joined by my *compadre* Anastasio who took someone's life, and then Pancracio, Codorniz and many friends and acquaintances. After that more and more people joined us, and as you see, we fight as well as we can."

"*Mi jefe*," said Luis Cervantes after a few minutes of silence and meditation, "you already know that Natera's people are nearby, in Juchipila. It would be a good idea to join them before they take Zacatecas. We'll introduce ourselves to the general. . . ."

"I'm no good at that. . . . Following orders is not for me."

"But with only a few men over here, you will never be more than an unimportant insurgent leader. The revolution will win inevitably. When it's over, they will say to you, as Madero said to those who helped him: 'Friends, many thanks, now go back home. . . .'"

"That's all I want, to be left in peace to go back home."

"I'm getting to my point . . . I'm not done yet: 'To you, who raised me to the presidency of the Republic, risked your lives, in imminent danger of leaving your widows and orphans in dire poverty, now that I have reached my goal, I say: go pick up your hoes and shovels, return to your old way of barely living, always hungry and without clothes, just as before, while we, the ones on top, will make a few million *pesos*.'"

Demetrio shook his head and scratched himself smiling.

"Luisito has hit the nail right on the head!" Venancio the barber exclaimed with enthusiasm.

"As I was saying," Luis Cervantes continued, "When the revolution is over, it's over. What a shame so many lives were cut off, so many widows and orphans, so much blood spilled! And all for what? So that a few rascals can get rich and everything can be the same or worse than it was before? You are generous, and say: 'My only ambition is to return to my land.' But is it fair to deprive your wife and children of the fortune that the Divine Providence is now placing in your hands? Is it fair to forsake the motherland at that solemn moment when she will need the abnegation of her humble children to save her, to keep her from falling into the hands of her eternal oppressors and torturers, the *caciques?* . . . We must not forget that for a man the most sacred things in the world are the family and the motherland! . . ."

Macías smiled and his eyes twinkled.

"So you think, it's a good idea to join Natera, Curro?"

"Not only is it a good idea," Venancio proclaimed pointedly, "but indispensable, Demetrio."

"*Mi jefe*," Cervantes continued, "I liked you from the moment I met you, and I like you more and more, because I fully recognize your worth. Allow me to be totally frank. You don't yet understand your true, high and most noble mission. You, a modest man without ambition, fail to see the vital role you have to play in this revolution. It's not true that you are here because of the *cacique* Don Mónico. You have taken up arms against all the *caciques* who ravage our entire country. We are part of a great social movement whose goal is to make our country greater. We are the instruments of destiny who will vindicate the sacred rights of the people. We are not fighting to overthrow a miserable assassin, but to overthrow tyranny itself. That is what is known as fighting for our principles, our ideals. That is what Villa, Natera and Carranza fight for; that is why we fight."

"Yes, yes, that's what I think too," said Venancio with great enthusiasm.

"Pancracio, let me have two more beers. . . ."

XIV

"You should hear how well the *curro* explains things, *compadre* Anastasio," said Demetrio, still worried about what he had been able to gather from all of Luis Cervantes' words that morning.

"I did hear him," replied Anastasio, "It's true, he's a fellow who knows how to read and write, he understands things well. What I just don't get, *compadre*, is how you're going to present yourself to Señor Natera with such a small bunch as us."

"No problem! Starting today, we're going to do things different. I've heard tell that when Crispín Robles comes into a town he starts grabbing all the weapons and horses he finds; frees all the prisoners in jail, and before you know it, he has more men than he needs. You'll see. Truth is, *compadre* Anastasio, we've just been fooling around. Hard to believe it took this *curro* to set us straight."

"Just goes to show you what reading and writing does for you! . . ."

They both sighed sadly.

Luis Cervantes and many others came in to find out the date of departure.
"We leave tomorrow," Demetrio said without hesitation.

Then Codorniz suggested they bring musicians from the nearest village and have a farewell dance. And his idea was met with uncontrollable joy.

"We'll leave then," Pancracio exclaimed and he gave a howl, "but I'm not leaving alone. . . . I have my love and she's coming with me."

Demetrio said that he too would gladly bring along a girl who had caught his fancy, but he was keen on not leaving behind bitter memories like the Federales.

"You won't have to wait much; it can all be arranged when we return," Luis Cervantes whispered.

"What!" Demetrio said. "They say you and Camila? . . ."

"It's not true, *mi jefe;* she loves you . . . but she's afraid of you. . . ."

"Really, Curro?"

"Yes, but I agree very much with what you said: we must not leave behind bad impressions. . . . When we return triumphant, it will all be different. They'll even be grateful."

"Ah, Curro! . . . You're a sharp one!" answered Demetrio, smiling and patting his back.

As evening was falling, Camila, as usual, went down to the river for water. On the same path and headed in her direction came Luis Cervantes.

Camila felt her heart wanted to leap out of her.

Perhaps without noticing her, Luis Cervantes suddenly disappeared in a bend between boulders.

At that hour, as every day, the shadows softened the scorched rocks, the branches burned by the sun, and the dried-out moss to a matte tone. A warm wind blew, murmuring softly, making the spear-shaped leaves of the tender corn sway. It was the same as always, but in the rocks, the dried branches, in the fragrant air and in the swirling leaves, Camila now found something strange. As if all these things were very sad.

She turned at a giant and crumbling rock and came suddenly upon Luis Cervantes who was on top of a rock, with his legs hanging and his head bare.

"Hey, Curro, at least come say good-bye."

Luis Cervantes was pretty docile. He descended and came to her.

"You're so proud! . . . Did I serve you so badly you won't even speak to me? . . ."

"Why do you say that, Camila? You've been very good to me . . . more than a friend; you've cared for me like a sister. I leave full of gratitude to you and will always remember it."

"Liar!" Camila said transfigured with joy. "And if I hadn't spoken to you?"

"I was going to thank you tonight at the dance."

"What dance? . . . If there's a dance, I won't go. . . ."

"Why won't you go?"

"Cause I can't stand to look at that old man . . . that Demetrio."

"How silly you are!" . . . Look, he loves you a lot. Don't miss this opportunity that you will never have again in your whole life. Silly, Demetrio is going to be a general, he is going to be very rich . . . many horses, many jewels, very luxurious dresses, elegant homes and a lot of money to spend. . . . Imagine what it will be like to be with him!"

To keep him from seeing her eyes, Camila raised them to the blue sky. A dry leaf came loose from the heights of the cliff, and balancing slowly in the air, fell like a little dead butterfly at her feet. She bent over and took it in her fingers. Then, without looking him in the face, she whispered:

"Ay Curro . . . if you only knew how much it hurts to hear you say that to me! . . . It's you I love . . . only you. . . . Go away, Curro, go away. I don't know why I feel so ashamed. . . . Go away, go away!"

And she threw away the leaf she had shredded in her anxious fingers and covered her face with a corner of her apron.

When she opened her eyes again, Luis Cervantes had disappeared.

She followed the path of the *arroyo*. The water seemed dusted by the finest rouge, in its waves swirled a multicolored sky and the crags half light, half shade. A myriad luminous insects blinked in an eddy. And on the pebbled bottom she was reflected with her yellow blouse with green ribbons, her white, unstarched skirt, her head carefully combed, her eyebrows and forehead smooth, just as she had decked herself out to please Luis.

And she burst into tears.

Amid the reeds the frogs sang the implacable melancholy of the hour. Rocking on a dry branch, a dove also cried.

XV

At the dance there was much joy and very good mescal.

"I miss Camila," Demetrio declared out loud.

And their eyes searched for Camila.

"She's not feeling well, she has a headache," answered Señá Agapita, intimidated by the malicious looks they all gave her.

When the dance was over, Demetrio, a bit wobbly, thanked all the good village people for generously taking them in and promised that he would remember all of them when the revolution triumphed, "because in bed and in jail is where you know who your real friends are."

"God keep you in His holy hand," an old lady said.

"God bless you and guide your way," others said.

And María Antonia, who was very drunk:

"And come back soon . . . real soon! . . .

The next day María Antonia, who though pock-marked and with a veiled eye had a very bad reputation, so bad that it was generally said there wasn't a single man who had not had knowledge of her among the river reeds, shouted at Camila:

"Hey, you! . . . What's up? . . . What are you doing in that corner with your *rebozo* wrapped around your head? . . . Ooh! . . . Crying? . . . Look at your eyes! Now you look like a witch! . . . Come on . . . don't worry! . . . No pain that touches the soul ever lasts more than three days."

Señá Agapita scowled and muttered who-knows-what to herself.

Truth is that the women were saddened by the departure of Demetrio's people, and even the men, despite all the pretty offensive gossip that went around, regretted the loss of men who supplied the village with sheep and calves so they could eat meat every day. It's so nice to spend your life eating and drinking, sleeping away the hours in the shade of the rocks, while the clouds form and vanish in the sky!

"There they are again! Over there," shouted María Antonia, "They look like toys on a shelf."

In the distance, where the crags and the chaparral began to fuse into a single, velvety blue plane, you could see on a ridge near a summit the outline of Macías' men on their lean nags, against the sapphire light of the sky. A gust of hot air brought to the village the vague and fragmented strains of *La Adelita*.

Camila, who had come out to see them one last time when María Antonia shouted, could not restrain herself and went back in, drowning in sobs.

María Antonia guffawed and went away.

"Someone's given my daughter the evil eye," mumbled Señá Agapita, puzzled.

She meditated for a long time, and when she had thought enough, made a decision. From a stake nailed to one of the hut's posts, between the Holy Face of Jesus and the Virgin of Jalpa, she took down a rawhide strap her husband used to yoke the oxen, folded it and gave Camila a good thrashing to get all the evil out of her.

On his chestnut horse, Demetrio felt rejuvenated. His eyes recovered their particular metallic luster, and on his coppery, full-blooded Indian cheeks, the blood flowed again red and hot.

They all filled their lungs as if to breathe in the wide horizons, the vastness of the sky, the blue of the mountains and the fresh air, perfumed by the aromas of the sierra. And they made their horses gallop, as if through that unbridled race they could lay claim to the possession of all the land. Did any of them now remember the severe chief of police, the growling policeman and the conceited *cacique?* Did any remember the miserable *jacal,* where they lived like slaves, always under the vigilance of the master or the sullen and angry overseer, with the inexorable obligation of rising before the sun, shovel and basket in hand, or with the plow and goad, to earn their daily bowl of *atole* and plate of beans?

They sang, laughed and howled, drunk on sunlight, air and life.

Meco, prancing around, showed his white teeth, joked and clowned around.

"Hey, Pancracio," he asked very seriously, "in a letter my wife says it seems we have another son. How can that be? Haven't seen her since Señor Madero's time!"

"No, don't worry . . . she was on the nest when you left her!"

They all laugh raucously. Only Meco, with great gravity and indifference, sings in a horrible falsetto.

> *I gave her a penny*
> *And she said no . . .*
> *I gave her a nickel*
> *And she didn't take it.*
> *She insisted so much*
> *She got a dime out of me.*
> *Oh! Women are such ingrates,*
> *They have no consideration at all.*

The uproar ceased when the sun began to stun them.

All day long they made their way through the canyon, going up and down mountains, round, bare and dirty like scabby heads, mountains that followed upon mountains interminably.

At sunset, in the distance, amid blue hills, some little stone towers became visible, then the dusty road with white whirlwinds and the gray telegraph poles.

They advanced toward the highway, and in the distance they discovered the shape of a man crouching by the roadside. They got there. It was a ragged, ugly old man. With a dull blade he was laboriously mending a *huarache.* Near him a burro loaded with grass was grazing.

Demetrio asked:

"What are you doing here, grandpa?"

"I'm going to town to bring alfalfa to my cow."

"How many Federales are there?"

"Yeah . . . a few. At most a dozen."

Then the old man let loose. He said there were very serious rumors: that Obregón was already laying siege to Guadalajara, Carrera Torres had taken possession of San Luis Potosí, and Pánfilo Natera was in Fresnillo.

"All right then," said Demetrio, "you can go to your town, but make sure you don't say a word to anyone about what you've seen, or I'll shoot you. I'll find you even if you hide in the center of the earth."

"What do you say, boys?" Demetrio asked when the old man had gone.

"Let's hit them! . . . Let's not leave a single *mocho* alive!" they all exclaimed as one.

They counted cartridges and the hand grenades that Tecolote had made out of fragments of iron pipes and brass finials.

"Not much," Anastasio observed, "but we're going to swap them for carbines."

And they eagerly hurried forward, digging their spurs into the lean flanks of their worn-out mounts.

Demetrio's commanding voice stopped them.

They camped at the skirt of a mountain, protected by a thick grove of *huizache* trees. Without unsaddling, each one looked for a stone to use as a pillow.

XVI

At midnight, Demetrio Macías gave orders to march.

The town was one or two leagues away, and they had to hit the Federales at dawn.

The sky was cloudy, here and there a star was shining, and from time to time, the reddish blink of lightning lit the horizon.

Luis Cervantes asked Demetrio if it wouldn't be a good idea, to ensure the success of the attack, to get a guide or at least to obtain topographical information about the town and the location of the barracks.

"No, Curro," Demetrio answered, smiling with a look of disdain, "we fall on them when they least expect it, and that's it. We've done this many times. You ever seen ground squirrels poke their heads out of their nests when you flood them? Well, those unlucky *mochitos* are going to look just as dazed when they hear the first shots. They'll just be walking targets."

"What if the old man lied to us yesterday? What if there are fifty men instead of twenty? What if he was a spy planted by the Federales?"

"This *curro* is already afraid!" said Anastasio Montañés.

"Now you see that handling a rifle is different than applying poultices and giving enemas!" Pancracio observed.

"Mmm!" answered Meco, "Too much talk . . . over a dozen dazed rats!"

"It's time our mothers found out if they gave birth to men or what," added Manteca.

When they reached the edge of the town, Venancio went ahead and called at the door of a hut.

"Where are the barracks?" he asked the man who came out barefoot and with a poncho to cover his bare breast.

"The barracks are a tiny bit beyond the plaza, master," he answered.

But since no one knew where a tiny bit beyond the plaza was, Venancio forced him to walk at the head of the column to show them the way.

Trembling with fear, the poor devil exclaimed that what they were doing to him was a terrible thing.

"I'm a poor day laborer, *señor,* I have a wife and many small children."

"And I suppose mine are dogs?" replied Demetrio.

Then he ordered:

"All keep quiet, and go single file down the middle of the street."

Dominating the group of houses was the wide, square dome of the church.

"*Señores,* you see, in front of the church is the plaza, you walk just a tiny bit farther down, and right there are the barracks."

Then he got down on his knees and begged them to let him go back, but Pancracio, without answering, hit him on the chest with the butt of his rifle and made him go on.

"How many soldiers are there?" asked Luis Cervantes.

"Master, I don't want lie to your excellency, but truth is, the pure truth is, there's a whole mess of them."

Luis Cervantes turned to Demetrio who pretended not to hear.

Suddenly they came into a little plaza. A loud volley of rifle fire made them deaf. Shaking, Demetrio's chestnut horse hesitated on its legs, bent its knees and fell to the ground kicking. Tecolote gave a shrill scream and rolled off his horse that galloped wildly into the middle of the plaza.

A new volley, and the man who served as their guide opened his arms and fell over backwards, without uttering a cry.

Anastasio Montañés quickly picked up Demetrio and put him behind him on his horse. The rest had retreated already and sought the protection of the walls of the houses.

"*Señores, señores,*" a man from the town said, sticking his head out of a large entranceway, "you can get at them from behind the chapel . . . they're all there. Go back on this same street, turn left, then you'll find a little alleyway, keep going until you hit the very back of the chapel."

Just then they began to receive a heavy rain of pistol shots. The shooting came from the nearby rooftops.

"Mmm," said the man, "those aren't biting spiders! . . . It's the *curros* . . . Come in here until they leave. . . . They're even afraid of their shadows."

"How many *mochos* are there?" asked Demetrio.

"There were no more than a dozen, but last night they must have been afraid because they used the telegraph to call back more troops. It's anyone's guess how many they are! . . . But it doesn't matter if there's a lot of them. Most are conscripts of the *leva* and they'll turn, run and leave their officers at the first chance. My brother was picked for the damned *leva* and they are bringing him here. I'll come along with you, signal him and you'll see how they all come over to this side. And then we'll only have to finish off the officers. If the *señor* would give me a little weapon. . . ."

"No rifles left, brother, but this ought to help," said Anastasio Montañés handing him two grenades.

The head of the Federales was a very arrogant young man with blond hair and a turned-up mustache. As long as he'd had no clear idea of the number of attackers, he had been quiet and prudent in the extreme, but having just repulsed them with such success that they did not even have time to shoot back once, he was flaunting his courage and boldness in an outrageous manner. While all the soldiers scarcely dared to poke their heads from behind the parapets of the portico, his slender figure and his dragoon cape, which the air swelled from time to time, were outlined against the pale light of dawn.

"Ah, this reminds me of the coup!"

Since his military experience was limited to the adventure in which he was mixed up as a student at the military academy when it became clear that President Madero had been betrayed, whenever there was an opportunity he brought up the deeds at the Ciudadela.

"Lieutenant Campos," he ordered emphatically, "go down with ten men and flush those bandits out of their hiding places. . . . Scum! . . . They're only brave when it comes to eating cows and stealing chickens!"

At the small door, above the spiral staircase, a civilian appeared. He bore the message that the attackers were in a corral, where it would be easy to capture them immediately.

This was the report from the leading citizens of the town, who were posted on the rooftops and ready to make sure the enemy would not escape.

"I myself will finish them off," the officer said impetuously. But he soon changed his mind. When he reached the door of the spiral staircase he drew back:

"It's possible they're expecting reinforcements, and it wouldn't be prudent for me to abandon my post. Lieutenant Campos, you go and capture all of them alive, so that we can execute them today at noon, just when people are leaving the high mass. The bandits will see that I know how to make an example! . . . But if it's not possible, Lieutenant Campos, finish all of them off. Don't leave a single one alive. Do you understand?"

Satisfied, he began to stroll, meditating on the composition of the official report he would send. "General Aureliano Blanquet, Minister of War, Mexico City. My general, it is an honor for me to make known to you that in the early hours of the day . . . a group of five hundred commanded by rebel leader X . . . dared to attack this town. With the forcefulness called for by the situation, I made myself strong in the heights of the town. The attack began at dawn, lasting more than two hours of heavy fighting. Despite the numerical superiority of the enemy, I was able to inflict heavy losses, defeating them completely. There were twenty dead and many more wounded, to judge from the trails of blood they left behind in their hurried flight. On our side we were fortunate not to have a single casualty. It is my honor to congratulate you, the Minister of War, on the triumph of the Government forces. Long live General Victoriano Huerta! *Viva México!*"

"And later," he continued thinking, "I'll be promoted to major for sure." As he clasped his hands with joy, a detonation left his ears ringing.

XVII

"So, if we could cross this corral, we'd come out right into the alley?" Demetrio asked.

"Yes, except that there's a house past the corral, then another corral and a store further on," said the man from the town.

Demetrio thought and scratched his head. But he reached a decision quickly. "Can you get me a crowbar, a pick, something like that so as to make a hole in the wall?"

"Yes, we have everything . . . but. . . ."

"But what? . . . Where are they?"

"All the tools are there, but all these houses belong to the boss, and. . . ."

Without waiting to hear him, Demetrio headed for the room where all the tools were kept.

It was all done in a matter of minutes.

When they were in the alley, one after the other, close to the walls, they ran until they got behind the church.

They had to jump over a wall and then, right away, the rear wall of the chapel.

"God's will be done," thought Demetrio. And he was the first one to climb it.

Like monkeys, the others followed him, reaching the top with their hands streaked with dirt and blood. The rest was easier: footholds hollowed out in the masonry allowed them to climb the chapel wall easily, then the dome itself hid them from the soldiers.

"Hold on just a second," said the man from the town, "I'm going to see where my brother is. I'll signal you, . . . then you open fire on the officers, right?"

Except by then no one was paying attention to him.

Demetrio observed for an instant the black capes all along the parapet, in front and at the sides, and the towers crammed with people, behind the iron railings.

He smiled with satisfaction, and turning his face to his men, exclaimed: "Now!"

Twenty bombs exploded at the same time among the Federales, who, terror-stricken, got up with their eyes wide open. But before they could make sense of the situation, another twenty bombs burst loudly, leaving a heap of dead and wounded.

"Not yet! . . . Not yet! . . . I can't see my brother yet," begged the anxious man.

In vain an old sergeant insulted and swore at his soldiers, hoping that the restoration of order would save the day. They were no more than rats scurrying inside a trap. Some rush to the door of the spiral staircase only to be shot to rags by Demetrio. Others throw themselves at the feet of those twenty-some specters whose heads and chests are dark as iron, whose long white pants hang in tatters down to their *huaraches*. In the bell tower some try to escape from under the dead who have fallen on them.

"*Mi jefe!*" exclaims Luis Cervantes alarmed, "It's awful! . . . We're out of bombs and the rifles are in the corral!"

Demetrio smiles, takes out a knife with a long, shiny blade. Steel flashes instantly in the hands of his twenty soldiers, long and pointed, or wide as the palm of your hand, and many as heavy as machetes.

"The spy!" Luis Cervantes calls out triumphantly, "Didn't I tell you!"

"Don't kill me, *padrecito*," the old sergeant pleads at Demetrio's feet, who raises his weapon.

The old man lifts his Indian face that is full of wrinkles, not a gray hair on his head. Demetrio recognizes the man who deceived them the night before.

Frightened, Luis Cervantes abruptly turns his face away. The steel blade hits the ribs that go crack, crack, and the old man falls back with his arms spread and terror in his eyes.

"Not my brother! . . . Don't kill him, he's my brother!" the man from the town shouts terrified as he sees Pancracio jump on a Federal soldier.

It's too late. With a swipe of the blade Pancracio has sliced his neck, and two scarlet sprays gush as if from a fountain.

"Death to the *Juanes!* . . . Death to the *mochos!* . . ."

In the slaughter, Pancracio and Manteca distinguish themselves as they finish off the wounded. Exhausted, Montañés lets his hand drop; the sweet look is still on his impassive face, where the naïveté of the child and the amorality of the jackal shine.

"This one here's alive," Codorniz shouts.

Pancracio runs over. It's the little blond captain with the impressive mustache, white as wax, who, leaning against a corner near the entrance to the spiral staircase, has halted, lacking the strength to descend.

Pancracio shoves him all the way to the parapet. A knee to the hip, and something like a sack of stones falls twenty meters onto the floor of the church atrium.

"You're so stupid!" Codorniz exclaims, "Had I known, I wouldn't have told you. He had great shoes! I wanted them!"

The men bend over now and set to stripping the ones who have the best clothes. They put on their spoils and joke and laugh, enjoying themselves.

Demetrio, parting the long locks of sweat-soaked hair that have fallen over his forehead, covering his eyes, says:

"Now, let's get the *curros!*"

XVIII

Demetrio reached Fresnillo with a hundred men the same day that Pánfilo Natera began the advance of his forces on the city of Zacatecas.

The Zacatecan chief greeted him warmly.

"I know very well who you and your followers are! I heard of the whipping you gave the Federales from Tepic to Durango!"

Natera shook hands effusively with Macías, while Luis Cervantes declaimed:

"With men like my General Natera and my Colonel Macías, our country will be covered with glory."

Demetrio understood the impact of those words when he heard Natera call him "my colonel" repeatedly.

There was wine and beer. Demetrio clinked glasses many times with Natera. Luis Cervantes toasted: "To the triumph of our cause, which is the sublime triumph of Justice; may we soon see the realization of our dreams for the redemption of our noble suffering people, and may the same men who have watered the land with their blood be the ones who reap the fruits that are legitimately theirs."

Natera turned his stern face briefly to the chatterer, and then turning his back on him, began talking to Demetrio.

Little by little, one of Natera's officers had approached, paying close attention to Luis Cervantes. He was young and his expression was open and cordial.

"Luis Cervantes?" . . .

"Señor Solís?"

"From the moment you came in, I thought I recognized you. . . . And, now that I see you I still can't believe it!

"And yet, it's true. . . ."

"So then? . . . But let's have a drink, come along. . . ."

"Well!" Solís continued, offering Luis Cervantes a seat, "When did you become a revolutionary?"

"Two months ago."

"Oh, that explains why you still talk with the enthusiasm and faith we all did at the beginning!"

"Have you lost them already?"

"Look, *compañero,* don't think it strange if I confide in you right from the start. Here you long so much to talk to someone with common sense that when you do find him you need him like you need a jug of cold water after walking for hours with a dry mouth under the rays of the sun. . . . But, frankly, first I need you to explain . . . I don't understand how come the correspondent of *El País* in Madero's time, the same man who wrote furious articles in *El Regional,* the man who lavishly used the epithet *"bandidos"* for all of us, has now joined our ranks."

"The real truth is that they convinced me!" Cervantes replied emphatically.

"Convinced? . . ."

Solís let a sigh escape, filled the glasses, and they drank.

"Then, you're tired of the revolution?" Cervantes asked evasively.

"Tired? . . . I'm twenty-five, and as you see, healthy. . . . Disenchanted? Maybe."

"There must be a reason. . . ."

"'I thought to find a flowering meadow at the end of the road . . . and I found a swamp.' My dear friend: there are deeds and men who are nothing but pure bile. . . . And that bile falls drop by drop into your soul, and it embitters everything, poisons everything. Enthusiasm, hopes, ideals, joys, . . . you see! Then there is nothing left: you either become a bandit like them, or you leave the stage and hide behind the walls of a fierce and impenetrable egotism."

The conversation tortured Luis Cervantes; he suffered to hear phrases that were so out of place and out of date. In order to avoid taking an active part in it, he invited Solís to recount in detail the events that led him to such a state of disenchantment.

"Events? . . . Insignificant matters, mere nothings: gestures that most people don't notice; the sudden life of a line that contracts, of eyes that flash, of closing lips; the fleeting meaning of a phrase that is lost. But they're events, gestures and expressions whose cumulative logic and natural expression also make up the fearsome and grotesque grimace of a race . . . of an unredeemed race! . . ." He drank down another glass of wine, paused for a long time and then continued, "You might ask why I continue with the revolution. The revolution is a hurricane, and the man who gives himself to her is not a man anymore, he is the miserable dry leaf swept by the wind. . . ."

Solís was interrupted by the presence of Demetrio Macías, who approached them.

"We're leaving, Curro. . . ."

Fluently and with a tone of deep sincerity, Alberto Solís congratulated him effusively for his feats of arms, his adventures, that had made him famous even among the men of the powerful *División del Norte*.

And Demetrio, delighted, heard the account of his deeds, arranged and embellished in such a manner that he himself would not have recognized them. In fact, it sounded so good to him that he later told it the same way and even came to believe that it happened that way.

"What a charming man General Natera is!" observed Luis Cervantes as he returned to the inn. "On the other hand, that little Captain Solís . . . what a bore!"

Not hearing a word he said, Demetrio Macías, very happy, squeezed his arm and said softly:

"Curro, I'm a colonel for real now . . . and you're my secretary. . . ."

Macías' men also made many new friends that night, and "for the pleasure of having met," they drank plenty of mescal and *aguardiente*. Since not everyone gets along and sometimes alcohol is a bad adviser, naturally they had their differences, but it was all handled in good form outside the *cantina,* the inn, or the brothel, without bothering friends.

The next morning they found some dead: an old prostitute with a bullet hole in her navel and two of Colonel Macías' recruits with holes in their skulls. Anastasio Montañés reported this to his chief, and shrugging his shoulders Demetrio said:

"Bah! . . . So, bury them. . . ."

XIX

"Here come the *gorrudos,*" the people of Fresnillo called out in amazement when they learned that the revolutionaries' assault on Zacatecas had failed.

The chaotic mass of men was returning, sunburnt, filthy and almost naked, their heads covered by high-crowned hats made of palm leaves with immense brims that hid half their faces.

They called them "gorrudos." And the *gorrudos* came back as happy as when they marched off to combat days before, sacking each town, each *hacienda,* each village and even the poorest *jacal* they passed.

"Who'll buy this machine off me?" one was calling out, flushed and tired of carrying his loot.

It was a new typewriter that attracted everyone with its dazzling chrome fittings.

The "Oliver" had changed owners five times in a single morning. At first it was worth ten *pesos* and was devalued one or two *pesos* each time it changed owner. Truth was it weighed too much and no one could stand carrying it more than a half hour.

"I'll give you a quarter *peso* for it," offered Codorniz.

"It's yours," answered the owner, handing it over quickly, fearing that the buyer would repent.

For twenty-five cents Codorniz had the pleasure of taking it in his hands and then throwing it against the rocks where it broke noisily.

It was like a signal: all those who were carrying heavy or cumbersome objects began to get rid of them, smashing them against the rocks. Crystal and china objects flew; heavy mirrors, brass candlesticks, fine statuettes, vases, and all the day's loot considered redundant were left, smashed to pieces by the roadside.

Demetrio, who did not share in that joy unrelated to the results of military operations, called Montañés and Pancracio aside and said to them:

"They don't have the guts. It's not so hard to take a city. Look, first you open up like this, . . . then you slowly close in, close in . . . until zap! . . . That's it!"

Meanwhile with a broad gesture, he opened his strong, sinewy arms, then brought them together little by little, matching the gesture to his words, until they were pressed against his chest.

Anastasio and Pancracio found the explanation so simple and clear that they answered convinced:

"That ain't nothing but the truth! . . . They just ain't got guts! . . ."

Demetrio's men were lodged in a corral.

"You remember Camila, *compadre* Anastasio?" exclaimed Demetrio sighing, as he lay on the dung, where all of them, already stretched out, were yawning with sleep.

"Camila who, *compadre?*"

"The one who used to cook for me over in the village. . . ."

Anastasio made a gesture that meant: "I don't want to talk about women."

"I can't forget," continued Demetrio, talking with the cigar in his mouth, "I was doing real bad. I had just drunk a jug of blue, very cool water. 'Don'tcha want more?' asked that little cinnamon girl. . . . Well, then the fever knocked me out, and all I could see was a gourd of blue water and hear that little voice: 'Don'tcha want more?' . . . But what a voice, *compadre,* to my ears it was like a silver street organ. . . . Hey, Pancracio, what do you say? Shall we go to the village?"

"Look here, *compadre* Demetrio, believe it or not, I got a lot of experience when it comes to skirts. . . . Women! . . . Lot's of experience . . . and what experience! . . . When you consider all the sores and scratches they've left on my hide! To hell with 'em! They're the devil incarnate. Really, *compadre,* believe it or not. . . . That's why you won't see. . . . Anyway, I got a lot of experience when it comes to that."

"When are we going to the village, Pancracio?" insisted Demetrio, blowing a mouthful of gray smoke.

"Just say the word. . . . You know I left my love there. . . ."

"Your love, . . ." said Codorniz sleepily.

"Yours . . . and mine too. Hope you take pity on us and really bring her," mumbled Manteca.

"Yes, Pancracio, bring that one-eyed María Antonia, it's cold here," shouted Meco from a distance.

And many broke into laughter, while Manteca and Pancracio began their tournament of insults and obscenities.

XX

"Here comes Villa!"

The news spread with the speed of lightning.

Ah, Villa! . . . The magic word. The great man appears; the unvanquished warrior who even from a distance can charm like a boa.

"Our Mexican Napoleon!" exclaims Luis Cervantes.

"Yes, 'The Aztec eagle, who has cleaved the head of that snake Victoriano Huerta with his steel beak' . . . That's what I said in a speech in Ciudad Juárez," said Alberto Solís, Natera's aide, in a somewhat ironic tone.

They were seated at the bar of a *cantina,* drinking beer.

And the *gorrudos,* with scarves around their necks, coarse leather shoes, and calloused cowboy hands, ate and drank without stopping; they spoke only of Villa and his troops.

The stories of Natera's men left Macías's men open-mouthed with admiration.

Oh, Villa! . . . The battles of Ciudad Juárez, Tierra Blanca, Chihuahua, Torreón!"

But deeds witnessed were worth nothing. You had to hear the account of his prodigious feats, where a surprisingly magnanimous act would be followed by the most bestial deed. Villa is the indomitable lord of the sierra, the eternal victim of all governments who hunt him like a beast. Villa is the reincarnation of the old legend: the providential bandit, who passes through the world with the luminous torch of an ideal: steal from the rich and make the poor rich! And the poor turn him into a legend that time will embellish so that it will live on from generation to generation.

"But I can tell you, my friend Montañés," said one of Natera's men, "that if my General Villa likes you, he will give you a *hacienda,* but if you rub him the wrong way, . . . he'll have you shot! . . ."

"Ah, Villa's troops! Real northern men, well-outfitted, Texan hats, brand new khaki suits, and four-dollar U.S. shoes."

And when they said this, Natera's men looked at each other disconsolately, painfully aware of their big palm-leaf *sombreros,* rotted by the sun and the wet, and the tattered trousers and shirts that half covered their dirty lice-ridden bodies.

"There's no hunger there. . . . They bring railroad cars jam-packed with oxen, sheep, cows. Boxcars full of clothes; whole trains full of ammo and weapons, and enough food for all to burst."

Then they talked about Villa's airplanes.

"Ah, the aeroplanes! Down on the ground, close up, you wouldn't even know what they are; they look like canoes, they look like rafts; but when they start to go up, my friend, it's a racket that will stun you. Then something like an automobile going real fast. And then picture a big bird, real big, which all of a sudden doesn't even seem to budge. And here comes the good part: inside that bird, there's a gringo with thousands of grenades. Just try and picture that! Come fighting time, and it's like you was feeding corn to chickens, there go handfuls and handfuls of lead for the enemy. . . . And you have yourself a cemetery: dead men here, dead men there, and dead men everywhere!"

And when Anastasio Montañés asked his interlocutor if Natera's men had ever fought side by side with Villa's, it became clear that everything they were talking about was only hearsay, since not one of them had ever seen Villa's face.

"Well, when it comes to that, man to man we're all the same! . . . Far as I'm concerned no man is worth more than another. To fight, all you need is just a bit of pride. I don't need to be a soldier! But truth is I don't need to. . . ."

"I have my ten yoke of oxen! . . . Bet you don't believe it?" said Codorniz behind Anastasio, mimicking him and bursting into laughter.

XXI

The thunder of rifle fire abated and became distant. Luis Cervantes made bold to take his head out of his hiding place, amid the debris of some fortifications at the summit of a hill.

He could scarcely tell how he had gotten there. He never knew when Demetrio and his men disappeared from his side. He suddenly found himself alone, and then dragged along by an avalanche of infantry he was knocked off his horse, and when he got up all trampled, a rider hoisted him behind him on the horse. But shortly, horse and riders were flung to the ground, and not knowing what became of his rifle, his revolver, or anything, he found himself in the middle of the white cloud of smoke with bullets whistling all around. And that hole and the piles of broken adobes seemed a safe shelter.

"*Compañero!* . . ."

"*Compañero!* . . ."

"My horse threw me; I was jumped; they thought I was dead and they took my weapons. . . . What could I do?" explained Luis Cervantes, embarrassed.

"No one threw me . . . I'm here as a precautionary measure, . . . understand?"

Alberto Solís' festive tone made Luis Cervantes blush.

"*Caramba!*" the former exclaimed, "Your *jefe* is quite a little macho! What daring and serenity! He left not only me, but a lot of other veterans with our mouths open."

Confused, Luis Cervantes didn't know what to say.

"Ah! You weren't there? Bravo! You found a safe place early on! . . . Look, *compañero,* let me explain. Let's go there behind that crag. You see that little slope at the foot of the mountain, what we have before us is the only route of access. To the right, the drop is straight down and any maneuver is impossible on that side. It's more or less the same on the left: the climb is so dangerous, that just one false step means tumbling down and being torn to shreds by the razor-sharp edges on the rocks. Well then, part of Moya's brigade lay on the slope with our chests to the ground, determined to advance on the first Federal trench. Projectiles buzzed over our heads. The battle was in full swing. Then they stopped shooting at us. We assumed they were being attacked vigorously from the rear. Then we hurled ourselves on the trench. But oh, *compañero*, look! . . . The bottom half of the slope is a real carpet of corpses. That's the work of the machine guns; they literally swept us off. A few of us managed to escape. The generals were pale and hesitated to order a new charge with the reinforcements that had just come to us. That's when Demetrio Macías, without waiting or asking anyone for orders, shouted:

'*Arriba, muchachos!* . . .'

'What a madman!' I exclaimed, amazed.

"The commanders, caught by surprise, didn't say a word. Macías' horse climbed over the crags, as if it had the claws of an eagle instead of hooves. '*Arriba, arriba!*' his men shouted and followed him like deer, over the rocks, men and horses as if they were one. Only a boy slipped and fell to the abyss; the rest appeared at the summit in a matter of seconds, swarming over the trenches and knifing soldiers. Demetrio was lassoing machine guns, roping them as if they were wild bulls. It wouldn't last, though. They were outnumbered and would be wiped out quicker than it took them to get there. But we took advantage of the momentary confusion, and with dizzying speed we hurled ourselves on the enemy positions and dislodged them easily. Ah, what a soldier your *jefe* is!"

From the mountaintop one could see a side of the Bufa with its rocky summit, like the plumed headdress of a proud Aztec king. Its six hundred-meter slope was covered with the dead, their hair tangled, their clothes stained with dirt and blood, and on that pile of warm corpses, ragged women, like starving coyotes, were rummaging and looting.

Amid the white smoke of the rifle fire and the black clouds spewing from burning buildings, the sun was shining on houses with large doors and multiple windows, all closed. The streets wound back and forth in picturesque patterns, climbing the neighboring hills. And over the cheery group of houses rose a stately building with slender columns and the towers and domes of the churches.

"How beautiful the Revolution is even in its savagery!" declared Solís, moved. Then in a low and vaguely melancholic voice:

"What a shame that what is coming won't be the same. We have to wait a bit. Until there are no more combatants, until the only shots heard are those of the mobs given over to the delights of looting. Until shining diaphanously, like a drop of water, we can see the psychology of our race condensed in two words: steal, kill! . . . My friend, what a disappointment, if we who offered all our enthusiasm, our very lives to overthrow a miserable assassin, instead turn out to be the builders of an enormous pedestal so that a hundred or two hundred thousand monsters of the same species can raise themselves! . . . A nation without ideals, a nation of tyrants! . . . All that blood spilled, and all in vain!"

Many fugitive Federal soldiers were climbing, fleeing the soldiers with large palm *sombreros* and baggy white trousers.

A bullet whistled by.

Alberto Solís, who with arms crossed was lost in thought after his last words, was suddenly startled and said:

"*Compañero,* I'm not enjoying these damn buzzing mosquitoes. Would you mind if we move a little farther?"

Luis Cervantes' smile was so scornful that Solís, intimidated, sat down calmly on a rock.

His smile drifted again as he followed the spirals of the rifle smoke and the dust clouds of each collapsing house and sinking roof. And he thought he had found a symbol of the revolution in those clouds of smoke and those clouds of dust that rose fraternally and embraced, became one, and vanished into nothing.

"Ah!" he exclaimed suddenly, "Yes, now I see! . . ."

And his outstretched hand pointed to the railway station. The trains puffing furiously, hurling thick columns of smoke, the railroad cars crammed with people escaping at full steam.

He felt a dull little blow in his belly, and as if his legs had become rags, he slid off the rock. Next his ears buzzed . . . then, darkness and silence eternal. . . .

Part Two

I

To the champagne whose bubbles refract the lamplight, Demetrio Macías prefers the limpid tequila of Jalisco.

Men stained with dirt, smoke and sweat, with curly beards and matted hair, covered with grimy rags, group around the tables of a restaurant.

"I killed two colonels," claims one in a harsh, guttural voice, a short, fat fellow with a braid-trimmed hat, a suede jacket, and a reddish-purple silk scarf at his neck. "They couldn't run, their bellies were so huge: they stumbled on stones, and climbing the hill they turned red as tomatoes and their tongues hanging out a mile! . . . 'Don't run so much, *mochitos*,' I shouted, 'Stop, I don't like frightened chickens. . . . Stop, *pelones*, I'm not going to hurt you! . . . Give yourselves up!' Ha, ha, ha! . . . They fell for it. . . . Bang, bang! One for each . . . and then they really rested!"

"One of the big shots got away from me," said a soldier with a grimy face, who was sitting in a corner of the room between the wall and the counter, with his legs stretched out and the rifle between them. "He had gold all over, damn him! The braid on his epaulettes and cape sparkled. And what did I do? . . . I'm so dumb, I let him go! He took out his handkerchief and he gave me the password, and I stood there with my mouth open. But as soon as he turns the corner, he starts shooting and shooting! . . . I let him finish a round of bullets. . . . Here I come! . . . Holy Mother of Jalpa, don't let me miss this son of . . . a bad word! Nothing doing, he made a break for it! . . . Some horse he had! Flashed before my eyes like lightning. . . . Some poor bastard coming up the same street paid for it. . . . Did I make him do a flip!"

They constantly interrupt each other, and while they heatedly recount their adventures, women with olive skin, flashing eyes, and ivory teeth, with revolvers at their waists, cartridge belts across their chests, and huge palm *sombreros* on their heads, come and go between the groups like stray dogs.

A girl with rouge-smeared cheeks, very dark neck and arms, and of the coarsest appearance, jumps on the *cantina* bar, near Demetrio's table.

He turns his face to her and meets lascivious eyes under a small forehead, framed by wiry hair.

The door opens wide and Anastasio Montañés, Pancracio, Codorniz and Meco come in one after the other, open-mouthed and dazzled.

45

Anastasio gives a shout of surprise and rushes to greet the short, fat *charro* with the braided hat and the reddish-purple scarf.

They are old friends and have just recognized each other. And they hug so hard their faces turn purple.

"*Compadre* Demetrio, I have the pleasure of introducing you to Güero Margarito . . . a real friend! . . . Ah, how I love this *güero!* You'll get to know him, *compadre*. . . . He's a sly one! . . . Güero, remember the Escobedo Penitentiary, over in Jalisco? . . . A year together!"

Demetrio, who remained silent and unsociable amid the general hubbub, without removing the cigar from his mouth, muttered as he put out his hand:

"Pleasure. . . ."

"So you're Demetrio Macías?" burst in the girl on top of the bar who was swaying her legs and touching Demetrio's back with her coarse leather shoes.

"At your service," he answered, barely turning his face.

Indifferent, she continued to move her legs, showing off her blue stockings.

"Hey, Pintada! . . . What you doing around these parts? . . . Come down from there and have a drink," said Güero Margarito.

The girl immediately accepted the invitation, impudently made room for herself and sat in front of Demetrio.

"So you're the famous Demetrio Macías who saved the day at Zacatecas?" asked Pintada.

Demetrio nodded his head yes, while Güero Margarito let out a laugh and said amused: "Pintada, you devil, you don't miss a trick! . . . You're already itching to try out a general! . . ."

Demetrio, who didn't understand, raised his eyes to her; they faced each other like two strange dogs sniffing each other warily. Unable to hold the girl's fiercely provocative gaze, Demetrio lowered his eyes.

From their tables, some of Natera's officers started to tease Pintada with obscene remarks.

Without batting an eyelid, she said:

"General Natera is gonna give you a little eagle. . . . Come on, put it there! . . ."

And she vigorously held out her hand to Demetrio and gave him a manly handshake.

Flattered by the congratulations showered on him, Demetrio ordered champagne.

"No, I don't want wine now, I'm not feeling well," Güero Margarito said to the waiter, "just bring me a glass of ice water."

"I'll eat anything you got so long as it ain't chili peppers or beans," said Pancracio.

Officers kept coming in, and little by little the restaurant got full. It teemed with stars and bars on hats of every shape and color, large silk scarves at the neck, rings with chunky diamonds, and heavy gold watch chains.

"Hey, waiter," shouted Güero Margarito, "I asked you for ice water. . . . You understand I'm not asking for charity. . . . See this wad of bills: I'll buy you and . . . even your wife, you understand? . . . I don't care if you ran out or why you ran out. . . . You figure out how to get it for me. . . . I warn you I have a temper! . . . I told you I don't want explanations, I want a glass of ice water. . . . Are you going to bring it or not? . . . No? . . . Then take that. . . ."

A resounding slap knocks down the waiter.

"That's the way I am, General Macías. Notice I don't have a single hair left on my face. You know why? Because I have a temper and when there's no one to vent my rage on, I pull out my hairs until the rage dies down. You have my word of honor, General, if I didn't do it, I would die of a fit!"

"It's very bad to swallow your rage," a man with a straw hat like the roof of a *jacal* affirms very seriously. "In Torreón, I killed an old woman who didn't want to sell me a plate of enchiladas. Everyone wanted them. I didn't get to eat them, but at least it calmed me down."

"I killed a shopkeeper in Parral because he gave me some Huerta bills in the change," said another one with a little star, whose black, calloused fingers glittered with jewels.

"In Chihuahua, I killed a guy, cause I kept running into him at the same table and at the same time when I was going to lunch. . . . It shocked me a lot! . . . What do you want! . . ."

"Well . . . I killed. . . ."

It's an endless subject.

Near dawn, when the restaurant is full of joy and spittle, when the dark-faced, ashen northern women mix with the garishly painted young girls from the shantytowns, Demetrio takes out his jewel-encrusted, chiming gold watch and asks Anastasio Montañés what time it is.

Anastasio looks at the face of the watch, then sticks his head out a window, and looking at the starry sky says:

"The Seven Sisters are hanging low, *compadre;* won't be long before sunrise."

Outside the restaurant the shouts, the laughter and the songs of the drunkards continue. Soldiers ride by on runaway horses, whipping the sidewalks. From every part of the city you hear rifles and pistols being fired.

And down the middle of the street, headed for the hotel, walk Demetrio and Pintada, stumbling with their arms around each other.

II

"What idiots!" exclaimed Pintada laughing loudly. "Where'd you come from? Soldiers don't stay at inns anymore. Where *have* you been? Anywhere you are, thing to do is pick the house you like and you grab it. No need to ask anyone's permission. Who's the revolution for? For the fancy-pants? Well, now the fancy-pants is us. . . . Hey, Pancracio, let me have your machete. . . . Damn rich people! . . . Keep everything under lock and key."

She dug the steel point into the crack above a drawer, and pushing the handle down she broke the lock and lifted the splintered lid of the desk.

The hands of Anastasio Montañés, Pancracio and Pintada sank into the pile of letters, prints, photographs and papers scattered all over the rug.

Pancracio showed his anger at not finding something to his liking by flinging a framed portrait into the air with the tip of his *huarache;* its glass shattered against the central chandelier.

They drew their empty hands from the papers, cursing.

But Pintada continued to break the locks on drawer after drawer tirelessly, until there was no place she had not scrutinized.

They did not notice the silent rolling of a small box covered in gray velvet, that came to a stop by Luis Cervantes' feet.

He, who looked on everything with an air of profound indifference, while Demetrio seemed to sleep spread-eagled on the rug, brought the little box closer to himself with the tip of his foot, bent over, scratched his ankle and deftly picked it up.

He was dazzled: two sparkling, clear diamonds in a filigree setting. Swiftly, he hid it in his pocket.

When Demetrio awoke, Luis Cervantes said to him:

"General, look what a mess the boys have made. Wouldn't it be better to keep them from doing this?"

"No, Curro. . . . Poor fellows! . . . It's the only fun they have after running at the bullets with their bellies."

"Yes, General, but I wish they wouldn't do it here. . . . You see, this discredits us, and what is worse, discredits our cause . . ."

Demetrio fixed his eaglet eyes on Luis Cervantes. He tapped his teeth with the nails of two fingers and said:

"Don't turn red. . . . Look, you don't have to tell me anything! . . . Finders, keepers. You got the little box, fine; I got my gold chiming watch."

Then in perfect harmony they showed each other their loot.

Meanwhile, Pintada and her comrades were searching the rest of the house.

Codorniz came into the parlor with a twelve-year-old girl whose forehead and arms were already marked by copper-colored stains. Both stood amazed when they beheld piles of books on the rug, tables and chairs, mirrors unhung and broken, print and portrait frames destroyed, furniture and bibelots dashed to pieces. With avid eyes, holding his breath, Codorniz sought his prey.

Outside, in a corner of the patio and surrounded by choking smoke Manteca was roasting ears of corn; he fed the embers with books and papers that burst into flames.

"Hah!" Codorniz shouted suddenly, "Look what I found me! . . . What a saddlecloth for my mare! . . ."

And with one tug he tore down a plush curtain that came crashing down, rod and all, on top of the finely carved back of an armchair.

"Hey, look at all these naked women!" yelled the young girl with Codorniz, amused by the illustrations of a deluxe edition of the *Divine Comedy.* "This one's for me; I'm taking it."

And she began to tear off the engravings she liked best. Demetrio got up and took a seat next to Luis Cervantes. He asked for beer, handed a bottle to his secretary and downed his in one gulp. Then, feeling drowsy, he half-closed his eyes and went back to sleep.

"Excuse me," a man spoke to Pancracio in the entrance way, "when may I speak to the general?"

"You can't talk to him; he has a hangover," answered Pancracio. "What do you want?"

"I want him to sell me some of those books they're burning."

"I can sell 'em to you"

"How much for them?"

Perplexed, Pancracio knit his brow:

"Five cents for the ones with pictures, and the rest . . . you can have for free if you buy the whole lot off me."

The man came back for the books with a bushel basket.

"Demetrio, hey, Demetrio, wake up already!" shouted Pintada, "Stop sleeping like a fat pig! Look who's here! . . . Güero Margarito! You don't know how great this *güero* is!"

"General Macías, I have the greatest respect and admiration for you, and I've come to tell you that I like you and your manners. So, if you don't object, I want to transfer to your brigade."

"What's your rank?" asked Demetrio.

"First captain, General."

"Come on then . . . I'll make you a major."

Güero Margarito was a little round man with a handlebar mustache and truly evil blue eyes that disappeared between his cheeks and his forehead when he laughed. A former waiter of Delmonico's in Chihuahua, he now wore three brass bars, the insignia of his rank in the División del Norte.

Güero heaped praise on Demetrio and his men, and this was reason enough for a whole case of beer to be emptied in a jiffy.

Pintada appeared suddenly in the middle of the parlor, wearing a splendid silk dress with gorgeous lace.

"You only forgot the stockings!" exclaimed Güero Margarito, splitting his sides with laughter.

Codorniz' girl also burst out laughing.

But Pintada didn't care; she made a gesture of indifference, flung herself on the rug and kicked off the white satin slippers, pleased to wiggle her naked toes numbed by the tight shoes, and said:

"Hey, you, Pancracio! . . . Go and bring me some blue stockings from my loot."

The parlor was filling with new friends and old campaign comrades. Demetrio, who was now becoming lively, began to refer in detail to some of his most notable feats of arms.

"What's that noise?" he asked, surprised by the tuning of string and brass instruments in the patio of the house.

"My General," Luis Cervantes said solemnly, "it is a banquet that your old friends and *compañeros* offer in your honor, to celebrate your feat of arms in Zacatecas and your well-deserved promotion to general."

III

"General Macías, allow me to introduce my future wife," Luis Cervantes pronounced emphatically, escorting a girl of rare beauty into the dining room.

All turned to her, and she opened her large blue eyes in amazement.

She was fourteen at most; her skin was as fresh and soft as a rose petal; her hair blond; and the expression in her eyes had a trace of wicked curiosity, but mostly there was a vague, childish fear.

Luis Cervantes noticed that Demetrio fixed his bird of prey gaze on her and he felt satisfied.

They made room for her between Güero Margarito and Luis Cervantes, across from Demetrio.

Amid the crystal, porcelain and vases of flowers, there were plenty of bottles of tequila.

Meco came in sweaty and complaining, carrying a case of beer.

"You still don't know this Güero," said Pintada, noticing that he did not take his eyes off Cervantes' fiancée, "he's so quick; I've never seen anyone in this world as clever."

She gave him a lewd look and then added:

"That's why I can't even stand to look at him!"

The orchestra broke into a catchy bullfighting march. The soldiers roared with joy.

"What a wonderful *menudo,* General! . . . I swear I've never had a better tripe stew in my life," said Güero Margarito, and then reminisced about Delmonico's in Chihuahua.

"You really like it, Güero?" Demetrio replied. "Then serve him more until he's stuffed."

"That's just what I like," confirmed Anastasio Montañés, "and it's real fun, if I like a stew, I eat and eat until I burp."

This was followed by loud chewing and swallowing noises. They drank copiously.

At the end, Luis Cervantes took a glass of champagne and stood:

"My General. . . ."

"Oh!" Pintada interrupted, "Now he's gonna give a speech, that always bores me. I'd rather go to the corral, anyway, there's nothing more to eat."

Luis Cervantes held up the black cloth patch with a little brass eagle, during a toast that no one understood, but that they all applauded uproariously.

Demetrio took in his hands the insignia of his new rank, and very flushed, his eyes shining and his teeth flashing, said with great naïveté:

"And now what am I supposed to do with this buzzard?"

"*Compadre,*" Anastasio Montañés, who had just stood, said tremulously, "I don't have to tell you. . . ."

Whole minutes passed; the damned words did not want to come to *compadre* Anastasio's summons. His red face filled with pearls of sweat on his grime-encrusted forehead. Finally he decided to end his toast:

"Thing is, I don't have to tell you . . . 'cause you already know I'm your *compadre.* . . ."

And since all had applauded Luis Cervantes, Anastasio himself, when he finished, gave the cue, clapping with great seriousness.

But it all worked out and his clumsiness encouraged others. Manteca and Codorniz offered toasts.

It was going to be Meco's turn, when Pintada burst in shouting triumphantly. Clicking her tongue, she was trying to get a beautiful jet-black mare into the dining room.

wants to be part of it.

"My loot! My loot!" she exclaimed, patting the arched neck of the gorgeous animal.

The mare resisted going past the door, but a pull on the halter and a lash on the haunch made her enter with great spirit and noise.

The soldiers, stunned, beheld the rich prize with ill-concealed envy.

"I don't know what it is about this darn Pintada, she always beats all of us to the best loot!" exclaimed Güero Margarito. "That's how it's been since she joined us in Tierra Blanca."

"Hey, you, Pancracio, go get me a bundle of alfalfa for my mare," Pintada ordered curtly.

Then she handed the rope to a soldier.

Once more they filled their glasses and goblets. Some were beginning to nod and close their eyes; most shouted jubilantly.

And among them, Luis Cervantes' girl, who had spilled all her wine on a handkerchief, looked this way and that with her large blue eyes full of fear.

"*Muchachos,*" shouts Güero Margarito standing, his high, guttural voice rising above the clamor, "I'm tired of life and I feel like killing myself now. I'm fed up with Pintada . . . and this little cherub from heaven won't even look at me. . . ."

Luis Cervantes noted that the last words alluded to his fiancée, and was greatly surprised that the foot he felt between the girl's feet was not Demetrio's but belonged to Güero Margarito.

And indignation boiled in his breast.

"Mind me now, boys!" Güero continued with his revolver on high, "I'm going to shoot myself smack in the forehead!"

And he aimed at the large mirror at the end of the room, where he appeared full-length.

"Don't budge, Pintada! . . ."

The mirror shattered into large, pointed fragments. The bullet had grazed Pintada's hair, who didn't even blink.

fearless.

IV

At sundown, Luis Cervantes awoke, rubbed his eyes and got up. He was on the hard ground, among the flower pots in the garden. Near him, breathing noisily, sound asleep, were Anastasio Montañés, Pancracio and Codorniz.

His lips felt swollen, his nose, hard and dry; he saw blood on his hands and shirt, and instantly remembered what had happened. Then, he got up and walked to a bedroom, pushed the door several times, without managing to open it. He hesitated for a few seconds.

Then it was all true; he was sure it wasn't a dream. He had left the dining room table with his girl and led her to the bedroom, but before he closed the door, Demetrio, drunk and stumbling, rushed to follow them. Then Pintada followed Demetrio, and they began to struggle. Demetrio, his eyes glowing like embers and with crystalline threads on his coarse lips, avidly searched for the girl. Pintada, shoving hard, made him move back.

"What are you doing! . . . What! . . ." howled Demetrio, annoyed.

Pintada placed her leg between his, tripped him, and Demetrio fell full-length outside the room.

He got up furious.

"Help! . . . Help! . . . She's gonna kill me! . . ."

Pintada caught Demetrio's wrist vigorously and turned aside the barrel of his pistol.

The bullet drilled into the bricks. Pintada kept bellowing. Anastasio Montañés approached Demetrio from behind and disarmed him.

Like a bull in the middle of the ring, Demetrio turned his wild eyes on them. He was surrounded by Luis Cervantes, Anastasio, Manteca and many others.

"Idiots! . . . You took away my gun! . . . As if I need a gun to handle the likes of you!"

He opened his arms, and in seconds threw the first person he grabbed face down onto the brick floor.

And after that? Luis Cervantes couldn't remember anything else. Most likely they had all fallen asleep right there, thoroughly battered. Most likely his fiancée, afraid of all the brutes, had taken the wise precaution of locking herself in.

"Perhaps this bedroom connects with the parlor and I can enter that way," he thought.

His steps woke Pintada, who was sleeping near Demetrio, on the rug at the foot of a love seat piled with alfalfa and corn where the black mare was dining.

"What you looking for?" the girl asked, "Oh, yeah, I know what you want! . . . Shame on you! . . . See here, I locked up your fiancée 'cause I couldn't hold this damned Demetrio any more. Take the key; it's on the table."

In vain Luis Cervantes looked in every hiding place in the house.

"All right, Curro, what's the story with that girl"

Luis Cervantes kept looking nervously for the key.

"What's eating you; I'll get you the key. But tell me . . . I like to hear about these things. That *currita* is just like you. . . . She's not a hick like the rest of us."

"There's nothing to tell. . . . She's my fiancée and that's that."

"Ha, ha, ha! Your fiancée and . . . all right! Look here, Curro, I'm way ahead of you, these aren't baby teeth. Manteca and Meco dragged that poor girl out her house; I knew that . . . but you must've given them something for her . . . some gold-plated cufflinks . . . a miraculous picture of Our Lord of la Villita. . . . Am I right, Curro? . . . Sure there are people like that! . . . Tough part is finding them! . . . Right?"

Pintada rose to give him the key, but she too couldn't find it and was quite surprised.

She thought for a while.

Suddenly she started running toward the bedroom door, placed an eye on the keyhole and stayed still until she got used to the darkness in the room. Suddenly, without taking her eye from the keyhole, she muttered:

"Güero . . . son of a! . . . Come take a peek, Curro!"

And she walked away, laughing.

"I tell you; never seen a man quicker than him!"

Next morning, Pintada watched for the moment Güero came out the bedroom to feed his horse.

"You poor young thing! . . . Hurry, go home! . . . Before these men kill you! . . . Hurry, run! . . ."

And she threw Manteca's lice-ridden blanket on the young girl with the big blue eyes and the face of a virgin, who was only wearing a nightgown and stockings, took her by the hand and led her out to the street.

"God Almighty!" she exclaimed, "Yes sir . . . How I love that Güero!"

V

Like ponies whinnying and gamboling when the thunder first comes in May, that's how Demetrio's men go through the sierra.

"On to Moyahua, *muchachos!*"

"Home of Demetrio Macías."

"Home of the *cacique* Don Mónico!"

The landscape grows bright, the sun peers from a scarlet sash over the diaphanous sky.

Gradually the mountain ranges emerge like monstrous lizards with angular vertebrae; mountains that seem like colossal heads of Aztec idols, like the faces of giants, fearsome and grotesque grimaces, that now make you smile, now fill you with a vague terror, a mysterious foreboding.

At the head of the troops goes Demetrio Macías with his general staff: Colonel Anastasio Montañés, Lieutenant Colonel Pancracio, and Majors Luis Cervantes and Güero Margarito.

In a second row follow Pintada and Venancio, who courts her with many compliments and poetically recites the desperate verses of Antonio Plaza.

When the sun's rays tint the walls of the village, four by four, bugles blaring, they enter Moyahua.

The crowing of the roosters was deafening and the dogs barked the alarm; but the townspeople gave no sign of life anywhere.

Pintada spurred her black mare and in one leap was alongside Demetrio. She proudly wore a silk dress and large gold earrings. The pale blue of the dress accentuated the olive tone of her face and the coppery stains of venereal disease. Sitting astride, her skirt rode up to her knees, revealing the faded stockings with many holes. She wore a revolver on her chest and had a cartridge belt across the saddle.

Demetrio, too was luxuriously dressed: an embroidered *sombrero,* chamois pants with silver buttons down the side and a short jacket embroidered with gold thread.

You could now hear doors being forced open. The soldiers had already spread through the village and were collecting arms and mounts.

"We're going to pay a morning call on Don Mónico," Demetrio announced gravely, dismounting and handing the reins of his horse to a soldier, "We're going to have lunch at Don Mónico's . . . a friend who loves me very much. . . ."

His staff makes a sinister smile.

And noisily dragging their spurs on the sidewalks, they headed for a large pretentious house, that was unquestionably the home of a *cacique.*

"It's locked, airtight, said Anastasio Montañés pushing the door with all his might.

"But I know how to get it open," replied Pancracio quickly aiming his rifle at the lock.

"No, no," Demetrio said, "first knock."

Three blows with the butt of the rifle, three more and no one answers. Pancracio becomes insolent and disregards further orders. He shoots, blows the lock and the door opens.

They see skirt hems, children's legs, all scattering into the depths of the house.

"I want wine! . . . Wine, over here! . . ." Demetrio asks in a commanding voice, pounding on the table.

"Sit down, *compañeros.*"

A woman appears, then another and another, and between their black skirts, the heads of frightened children. One of the women, trembling, walks toward a cupboard, takes out glasses and bottles and serves wine.

"What weapons do you have?" Demetrio asks harshly.

"Weapons? . . ." the woman answers, her tongue clinging to the roof of her mouth. "What weapons do you expect lone, decent women to have?"

"Alone, then! . . . And Don Mónico? . . ."

"He's not here sir. . . . We only rent the house. . . . We only know Don Mónico by name."

Demetrio orders a search.

"No sir, please. . . . We ourselves will bring you all we have, but for the love of God, don't hurt us. We are decent girls and all alone!"

"And the kids?" asks Pancracio brutally. "Did they pop out of the ground?"

The women leave precipitously and return moments later with a splintered shotgun, covered with dust and cobwebs, and a rusty, broken pistol.

Demetrio smiles:

"Well, let's see the money. . . . "

"Money? . . . What money do you expect poor girls to have?"

And they turn their pleading eyes to the nearest soldier, but then horrified shut them tight: he looks just like the henchman who is crucifying Our Lord Jesus Christ in the stations of the cross at the parish church! . . . They have seen Pancracio!

Demetrio orders the house searched.

At once the women rush out again and return immediately with a motheaten purse, with a few bills issued by Huerta.

Demetrio smiles, and without further ado, has his men enter the house.

Like hungry dogs that have caught scent of their prey, the mob penetrates, trampling the women who try to block the entrance with their bodies. Some faint, others run away; the children scream.

Pancracio gets ready to break the lock on a large wardrobe, when the doors open and a man jumps out with a rifle in his hands.

"Don Mónico!" they exclaim surprised.

"Please, Demetrio! . . . Don't do anything to me! . . . Don't hurt me! . . . I'm your friend Don Demetrio! . . ."

Demetrio Macías smiles sarcastically and asks him if it's proper to greet friends with a rifle in one's hands.

Don Mónico, confused, stunned, throws himself at his feet, hugs his knees, kisses his feet:

"My wife! . . . My children! . . . Dear friend, Don Demetrio! . . ."

His hand trembling, Demetrio puts his revolver back in his belt.

A painful silhouette passes through his memory. A woman with her child in her arms, crossing the rocks of the sierra at midnight by the light of the moon . . . a burning house. . . .

everyone for themselves

"Vámonos! . . . Everyone out!" he calls out somberly.

His staff obeys; Don Mónico and the women kiss his hands and weep gratefully.

Out in the street the happy and boisterous mob is waiting for the General's permission to loot the *cacique's* house.

"I know where they hide the money, but I'm not telling," says a boy with a basket under his arm.

"Ha! I know where it is!" replies an old woman who is holding a jute bag to gather anything God may send her way. "Up in the attic, there's a lot of junk and in the middle of all that junk there's a satchel with a shell design. . . . That's where the good stuff is! . . ."

"That's not true," says a man, "they're not that dumb to leave their silver lying around like that. I think it's buried in a leather bucket in the well."

And the crowd mills about, some have ropes to tie up their bundles, other have trays, the women stretch out their aprons or the ends of their shawls, to see how much will fit. Waiting, they all thank God Almighty for the part of the loot they expect.

When Demetrio announces that he won't give permission and orders all to retire, the disconsolate townspeople obey and scatter right away, but among the soldiers there is a dull murmur of disapproval and no one moves from their spot.

Irritated, Demetrio again orders them to leave.

A young boy, a recent recruit with a little *aguardiente* in him, laughs and walks fearlessly toward the door.

But before he crosses the threshold, a shot fells him instantly, like when a wounded bull is finished off at the ring.

Demetrio, smoking pistol in hand, immutable, waits for the soldiers to leave.

"Set the house on fire," he orders Luis Cervantes when they get to the barracks.

And Luis Cervantes, with rare solicitude, did not transmit the order, but executed it in person.

Two hours later, when the small plaza was blackened by smoke and huge tongues of fire rose from Don Mónico's house, no one understood the general's strange behavior.

VI

They were lodged in a large, somber house that had also belonged to Moyahua's *cacique*.

Their predecessors on that farm had left vigorous traces of their occupancy on the patio, that they had turned into a dung heap, on the walls where the missing patches of plaster showed the bare adobe, on the floors, wrecked by the hooves of animals, in the garden, now a scattering of withered leaves and dry branches. From the moment you entered you tripped on the legs of furniture, chair bottoms and backs, all soiled by dirt and refuse.

At ten in the evening Luis Cervantes yawned, very bored, and said goodbye to Güero Margarito and Pintada, who were drinking nonstop on a bench in the plaza.

He went to headquarters. The only furnished room was the parlor. He walked in and Demetrio, who was lying on the floor staring at the ceiling with blank eyes, stopped counting the beams and turned his face.

"Is it you, Curro? . . . What's up? . . . Come on in, sit down."

Luis Cervantes first went over to trim the candle, then dragged over a backless chair whose cane bottom had been replaced by burlap. The legs of the chair creaked and Pintada's black mare snorted and moved in the darkness, her round terse haunch describing an elegant curve.

Luis Cervantes sank into the chair and said:

"General, I've come to deliver your commission . . . here it is. . . ."

"But Curro . . . that's not what I wanted! . . . Moyahua is almost my home. . . . People will say that's why I joined the revolution! . . ." Demetrio replied as he looked at the bag bursting with coins that Luis was handing him.

He left his seat to crouch by Demetrio. He stretched a serape on the floor and on it emptied the bag of *hidalgos* that glowed like gold embers.

"First of all, General, only you and I know about this. . . . Furthermore, you have to make hay while the sun shines. . . . Today the sun is shining, but tomorrow? . . . You have to look ahead. A bullet, a rearing horse, even a ridiculous cold . . . and your widow and orphans will be destitute! . . . What about the government? Ha, ha, ha! . . . Go to Carranza or Villa, or any of the other principal leaders and talk to them about your family. . . . If they reply with a kick . . . you know where, consider yourself lucky. . . . And they're right, General. We didn't rise up in arms to make Carranza or Villa president of the Republic; we fight for the sacred rights of the people, that have been trampled by vile *caciques*. . . . And just like neither Villa nor Carranza nor anyone else is going to come to ask our permission to compensate themselves for the services they are rendering the fatherland, neither do we need to ask anyone's leave."

Demetrio raised himself a bit, took a bottle near his head, tipped it back and then filling his cheeks, spat a mouthful far from him.

"Curro, you really are long-winded!"

Luis suddenly felt queasy. The sprayed beer seemed to have stirred the fermentation of the trash heap on which they were resting: a carpet of orange and banana peels, fleshy watermelon rinds, fibrous mango pits and chewed sugarcane stalks, all mixed with the chili-stained corn husks from tamales, and all damp from people relieving themselves.

Demetrio's calloused fingers went back and forth over the shiny coins, counting them.

When he recovered, Luis Cervantes took out a small can of Fallières Phosphatine and spilled out charms, rings, earrings and many other valuable jewels.

"Look, General, if as seems likely, this thing is going to keep on going, if the Revolution doesn't end, we already have enough to go abroad and enjoy ourselves for a while." Demetrio shook his head no. "You wouldn't do that? . . . Well, why would we stay now? . . . What cause will we fight for?"

"I can't explain, Curro, but men just don't do that . . ."

"Take what you want, General," said Luis Cervantes exhibiting the jewels in a row.

"You keep it all. . . . Really, Curro . . . truth is, I don't love money! . . . You want the truth? Long as I don't run out of drink and have a girl I like, I'm the happiest man in the world."

"Ha, ha, ha! . . . The things you say, General! . . . Then, why do you put up with that serpent, Pintada?"

"Curro, I'm fed up with her; but that's me for you. I can't get around to telling her. . . . I don't have the courage to send her to. . . . That's me, that's my character. See, the moment I like a woman, I get tongue-tied, and if she doesn't break the ice . . . I can't manage to do anything," and he sighed. "There's Camila, the one in the village. . . . That girl's ugly; but I can't get enough of her. . . ."

"General, just say the word, and we'll bring her here."

Demetrio winked mischievously.

"I swear, I'll do right by you, General. . . ."

"Really Curro? . . . If you do that for me, I'll give you the watch, gold chain and all, since you like it so much."

Luis Cervantes' eyes shone. He took the Phosphatine can, which was again full, stood and said, smiling:

"*Hasta mañana*, General. . . . Sleep well tonight."

VII

"What do I know? Same as you. The General said: 'Codorniz, saddle your horse and my black mare. You're going on a mission with Curro.' So, that's how it was: we left here at noon and by nightfall we were at the village. One-eyed María Antonia put us up. . . . She wanted to know how you were, Pancracio. . . . Near daybreak, Curro woke me up: 'Codorniz, Codorniz, saddle the horses. Leave me my horse and you go back to Moyahua and take the general's mare with you. I'll catch up to you in a while.' The sun was already high when he arrived with Camila on his saddle. He got her off and we put her on the black mare."

"Well, what about her, how'd she feel about it?" one of them asked.

"Her? She was running at the mouth, she was so happy! . . ."

"And Curro?"

"Quiet, same as always; you know how he is."

"I think," Venancio ventured gravely, "that if Camila was in Demetrio's bed this morning, it was by mistake. We drank a lot. . . . Remember! . . . The alcoholic spirits went to our heads. We all passed out."

"What alcoholic spirits are you talking about? . . . Curro and the general planned the whole thing."

"Of course! If you ask me that Curro is no more than a . . . !"

"I don't like to talk about friends behind their backs," said Güero Margarito, "but I will say that I've known him to have two girlfriends, and I got one . . . and the General got the other. . . ."

And they burst out laughing.

When Pintada realized what had happened, she sweetly went over to console Camila.

"Poor little thing, tell me what happened!"

Camila's eyes were swollen from crying.

"He lied to me, he lied to me! . . . He came to the village and said: 'Camila, I've come for you. Will you go with me?' Well, what do you think, of course I wanted to go with him! I love him, love him, and love him to bits. . . . Just look at me, I'm nothing but skin and bones, 'cause the only thing I do is think about him! Sun comes up and I don't even feel like grinding corn in the *metate*. . . . My mother calls me to lunch and the *tortilla* turns to dust in my mouth. . . . And it hurts so bad! . . . it hurts! . . ."

And she began to cry again, and she covered her mouth and nose with a corner of her *rebozo* so they wouldn't hear her sobs.

"Look, I'm gonna get you out of this fix. Don't be silly, stop crying. Don't think about Curro. . . . You know what that Curro is? . . . I swear it's true! . . . That's what the general uses him for! . . . Silly! . . . All right, you wanna go home?"

"Holy Virgin of Jalpa protect me! . . . My mother'll beat me dead!"

"She'll do nothing of the kind. Listen to me. The troops have to leave any moment now. When Demetrio tells you to get ready to leave with us, tell him you hurt all over, and you feel like you had a beating, and stretch out and yawn a lot. Then touch your forehead and say: 'I'm burning with fever.' Then I'll tell Demetrio to leave us both behind, cause I'm staying to cure you and when you're well we'll catch up to him. And what we'll do is I'll get you home safe and sound."

VIII

The sun had already set and the village was wrapped in the gray sadness of its old streets and the terrified silence of its inhabitants who had retired early, when Luis Cervantes arrived at Primitivo López' store to break up a spree that was promising to get out of hand. Demetrio was there getting drunk with his old comrades. You couldn't fit one more person at the bar. Demetrio, Pintada and Güero Margarito had left their horses outside, but the rest of the officers had brutally entered on horseback. Their embroidered hats with colossal concave brims were perpetually swaying; the horses' haunches moved back and forth, and they constantly moved their fine heads with their large black eyes, trembling noses and small ears. Through the infernal drunken din you could hear the snorting of the horses, the coarse sound of their hooves on the pavement, and from time to time a brief and nervous neigh.

When Luis Cervantes arrived, they were commenting on a banal occurrence. A man with a bloody little black hole on his forehead was lying on his back in the middle of the road. Although opinions on the subject were divided at first, now they reached a consensus thanks to a convincing argument put forth by Güero Margarito. The poor devil, who was lying there very dead, was the sexton of the church. But what an idiot! . . . It was his fault. . . . Who told him to wear matching pants, jacket and cap? Pancracio can't stand to see an aristocratic dandy!

Eight wind musicians, their faces red and round like suns, their eyes popping out, their lungs winded from blasting their brass instruments since daybreak, stop playing on Cervantes' command.

"General," he said, making his way among the horsemen, "an urgent message just arrived. You are ordered to go after the Orozquistas immediately."

All faces, which had darkened for a moment, shone with joy.

"On to Jalisco, *muchachos!*" shouted Güero Margarito, slapping the counter.

"Get ready, Jalisco girls, I'm coming!" shouted Codorniz, curling his hat.

All brimmed with joy and enthusiasm. Demetrio's friends, excited by the liquor, offered to join his ranks. Demetrio was so happy he could hardly talk. "Give the Orozquistas a beating! . . . Finally we go after real men! . . . No more killing Federales; it's like killing rabbits or turkeys!"

"If I catch Pascual Orozco alive!" said Güero Margarito, "I'll flay the soles of his feet and make him walk the sierra for twenty-four hours."

"That the guy who killed Señor Madero?" asked Meco.

"No," replied Güero solemnly, "but he slapped my face when I was a waiter at Delmonico's in Chihuahua."

"The black mare for Camila," Demetrio ordered Pancracio who was already saddling horses.

"Camila can't go," Pintada said quickly.

"Who asked your opinion?" Demetrio replied harshly.

"Camila, ain't it right you woke up aching all over and now have a fever?"

"Who, me? . . . me? . . . Whatever Don Demetrio says. . . ."

"Oh, what a ninny! . . . Say you can't, say you can't," Pintada whispered in her ear uneasily.

"Thing is, he's growing on me. . . . Can you believe it?" Camila answered, also softly.

Pintada became furious and puffed out her cheeks; but she said nothing and went over to mount the mare Güero Margarito was saddling for her.

IX

The whirlwind of dust that stretched for a good bit along the road broke abruptly into diffuse and violent shapes, and you could make out swelling chests, wild manes, trembling noses, impetuous oval eyes, legs that spread and drew together as they ran. The men with bronze faces and ivory teeth, flaming eyes, brandished their rifles or lay them across their saddles.

Bringing up the rear and at a slow pace came Demetrio and Camila. She still looked tremulous, with her lips white and dry; he was in a bad mood because of the futile operation. No trace of the Orozquistas, no combat. A few scattered Federales and a poor devil of a priest with a hundred deluded followers, all gathered under an old banner that said "Religion and Rights." The priest was left there swaying, hanging from a mesquite, and scattered all over the field were the dead with little red felt badges on their breasts that read "Stop! The Sacred Heart of Jesus is with me!"

"Truth is I'm caught up for all my back pay," said Codorniz, showing the gold watches and rings that he had taken from the priest's residence.

"It's a pleasure to fight this way," exclaimed Manteca, larding every phrase with obscenities. "At least you know why you're risking your neck!"

And with the same hand he held the reins, he grasped a shining halo that he had torn from the statue of Christ the Divine Prisoner at the church.

When Codorniz, who was an expert in these matters, covetously examined Manteca's loot, he laughed solemnly:

"Your halo is made of tin! . . ."

"Why are you dragging around that fleabag?" Pancracio asked Güero Margarito, who was one of the last to arrive, bringing a prisoner.

"You want to know why? Because I've never had the chance to get a really good look at the face a fellow makes when you squeeze his neck with a lasso."

The prisoner, who was very fat, had a hard time breathing; his face was red, his eyes bulged and his forehead was dripping sweat. He was tied by the wrists and had been made to walk.

"Anastasio, lend me your *reata;* this dude will snap my halter rope. . . . But, now that I think of it, no. . . . My Federal friend, I'm going to kill you once and for all; you've suffered a lot. You see, the mesquites are still too far away and there isn't even a telegraph pole anywhere near to hang you from."

And Güero Margarito drew his pistol, placed the barrel over the prisoner's left nipple and slowly drew back the trigger.

The Federal became as pale as a corpse, his face became drawn and his glassy eyes broke. His chest throbbed violently and his whole body shook as if from a great chill.

Güero Margarito kept his pistol there for eternal seconds. His eyes shone in a strange way, and his pudgy face, his swollen cheeks, glowed with supreme sensual pleasure.

"No, my Federal friend!" he said pulling the weapon away and returning it to its holster, "I don't want to kill you yet. . . . You're going to continue being my assistant . . . You'll see if I have a wicked heart or not!"

And he winked wickedly at those who were near him.

The prisoner had become like an animal; he only made swallowing noises; his mouth and throat were dry.

Camila, who had been left behind, spurred her mare and caught up to Demetrio.

"What an evil man that Margarito is! . . . If you saw what he's doing to a prisoner!"

And she told him what she had just witnessed.

Demetrio frowned, but said nothing.

Pintada called Camila over.

"Hey you, what stories you telling Demetrio? . . . Güero Margarito's my true love. . . . Get that into your head! . . . See . . . if anyone messes with him, they have to mess with me. I'm warning you! . . ."

Thoroughly frightened, Camila rejoined Demetrio.

X

The troops camped on a plain, near three lonely little houses in a row, whose white walls stood out against the purple band of the horizon. Demetrio and Camila went toward them.

In the corral, a man wearing a white shirt and pants stood, avidly sucking on a corn husk cigarette. Near him, sitting on a tile, another man was removing the kernels from the corn by rubbing together the ears between his hands; one of his legs was dry and twisted and had something like a goat's hoof on its end. From time to time he shook it to frighten away the chickens.

"Hurry up, Pifanio," said the one who was standing, "the sun already set and you haven't led the animals down to the water."

A horse neighed outside and the two men raised their heads, surprised.

Demetrio and Camila were looking over the rail of the corral.

"All I want is lodging for me and my woman," Demetrio said to calm them down.

And since he explained that he was the head of an army unit that was going to camp nearby overnight, the man who was standing, who was the owner, ushered them in with great courtesy. And he ran for a bucket of water and a broom, and swept and watered the best corner of the barn so as to decently lodge such honorable guests.

"Pifanio, go unsaddle our guests' horses."

The man who was separating the kernels from the ears of corn stood up with difficulty. He was wearing a tattered shirt and vest, and ragged pants whose lifted flaps hung from the waist.

He walked, and his step marked a grotesque beat.

"*Amigo,* can you really work?" Demetrio asked, refusing to let him remove the saddles.

"Poor fellow," his master shouted from inside the barn, "he's not strong! . . . But does he ever earn his pay! . . . He works from the crack of dawn! . . . Been a while since the sun set . . . and there he is still working!"

Demetrio went out with Camila to take a walk around the camp. The plain of golden furrows, shorn even of bushes, stretched out immense in its desolation. The three large ashes in front of the little houses seemed a miracle, with their dark green tops, round and undulating, and their rich foliage that reached down, kissing the ground.

"What is it about this place that makes me feel so sad!" said Demetrio.

"Yes," Camila answers, "me too."

By the bank of a stream, Pifanio is pulling roughly on the rope of a windlass. An enormous pot was spilling over a pile of fresh grass, and in the fading light of the evening the crystal spray poured onto the trough where a skinny cow, a saddle-bruised horse, and a burro drank noisily.

Demetrio recognized the lame peon and asked him, "How much you earn a day, *amigo?*"

"Sixteen cents, *jefe*. . . ."

He was a little man, blond and scrofulous, with straight hair and blue eyes. He cursed his boss, the farm, and his rotten luck.

"Son, you sure earn your pay," Demetrio interrupted gently, "You complain and complain but work and work."

And turning to Camila, "There's always others worse off than we are in the sierra, right?"

And they kept on walking.

The valley was lost in shadows and the stars hid.

Demetrio embraced Camila lovingly around the waist, and who knows what words he whispered in her ear.

"Yes," she answered weakly.

Because "he was growing on her."

Demetrio slept badly, and very early he went out of the house.

"Something's gonna happen to me," he thought.

It was a silent and discreetly joyous dawn. A thrush was singing timidly in the ash tree; the animals were rooting in the garbage in the corral; the pig was grunting off his sleep. The orange tint of the sun made its appearance, and the last star went out.

Demetrio was walking slowly to the camp.

He was thinking about his yoke of oxen: two dark, young oxen that had barely worked two years in his well-fertilized two acres. The face of his young wife was faithfully reproduced in his memory: her features, which were sweet and infinitely docile to her husband, were defiant and proud toward strangers. But when he tried to reconstruct the image of his son, all his efforts were in vain; he had forgotten him.

He reached the camp. Stretched out between the furrows, the soldiers slept, and among them their horses lay with fallen heads and closed eyes.

"The spare horses are exhausted, *compadre* Anastasio; we should stay and rest at least one day."

"Ay! *compadre* Demetrio! . . . How I wish we were already in the sierra! You know . . . believe it or not . . . I just can't get used to this place. . . . It's so sad, so gloomy! . . . Something's missing, something's wrong here! . . ."

"How many hours from here to Limón?"

"It's not a question of hours: it's a three days' journey, and long days too, *compadre* Demetrio."

"You see! . . . I want to see my wife!"

It didn't take long for Pintada to go off looking for Camila.

"Too bad, too bad! . . . Just that Demetrio's going to ditch you. He told me, that's who. . . . He's gonna bring his real wife . . . and she's very pretty, very white. . . . What cheeks she has! . . . But if you don't wanna go; they might even hire you: they have a baby and you can take care of it. . . ."

When Demetrio came back, Camila, in tears, told him everything.

"Don't pay attention to that crazy woman. . . . They're lies, all lies. . . ."

And since Demetrio did not go to Limón nor remember his wife again, Camila was happy and Pintada became a scorpion.

XI

Before daybreak they set out for Tepatitlán. Spread along the road and the plowed fields, their silhouettes undulated softly to the monotonous and regular step of their horses, fading in the pearly tone of the waning moon that bathed the whole valley.

Very far away you could hear dogs bark.

"Today by noon we'll get to Tepatitlán, tomorrow Cuquío, and then . . . the sierra," said Demetrio.

"General, wouldn't it be a good idea," Luis Cervantes whispered at his ear, "to get to Aguascalientes first?"

"What are we going to do there?"

"We are running out of funds. . . ."

"What! . . . Forty thousand *pesos* in eight days?"

"This week alone, we've recruited close to five hundred men, and we've used up everything for their advances and bonuses," Luis Cervantes whispered back.

"No. We're going straight to the sierra. . . . We'll see. . . ."

"To the sierra! . . . To the sierra! . . . There's nothing like the sierra."

The plains still oppressed their hearts; they spoke of the sierra with enthusiasm and rapture, and they thought of the sierra as a desired lover whom they hadn't seen in a long time.

It became daylight. Later, a cloud of red dirt rose toward the east, against an immense curtain of flaming purple.

Luis Cervantes held back the reins of his horse and waited for Codorniz.

"What will it be then, Codorniz?"

"Curro, I already told you: two hundred just for the watch. . . ."

"No, I'll buy the whole lot: watches, rings and all the little jewels. . . . How much?"

Codorniz hesitated, became pale; then burst out: "Gimme two thousand bills for everything."

But Luis Cervantes gave himself away; his eyes gleamed with such obvious greed that Codorniz backed out and said quickly:

"No, just kidding, I'm not selling nothing. . . . Just the watch, and only cause I already owe Pancracio two hundred *pesos*. He beat me again last night."

Luis Cervantes took out four new bills with "two faces" and put them in Codorniz' hand.

"Really," he said, "I'm interested in the whole lot. . . . No one will give you more for it than I."

When they began to feel the sun, Manteca suddenly shouted:

"Güero Margarito, your assistant wants to kick the bucket. Says he can't walk anymore."

The prisoner had let himself drop, exhausted, in the middle of the road.

"Shut up!" yelled Güero Margarito going back. , "So you're tired already, sunshine? You poor thing! I'm going to buy a glass case just to keep you in a corner of my house, like a statue of the Christ Child. But first we have to get to town, and I'm going to help you."

And he took out his saber and hit the wretch several times.

"Let's see that *reata*, Pancracio," he said then, with a strange glow in his eyes.

But since Codorniz pointed out that the Federal moved neither hand nor foot, he guffawed and said:

"How stupid of me! . . . Just when I had finally trained him not to eat! . . ."

"This is it, we're in Little Guadalajara," Venancio said, discovering the pretty village of Tepatitlán, lying softly on a hillside.

They were overjoyed to enter the town; blushing faces and beautiful dark eyes peered from the windows.

The schools became barracks. Demetrio lodged in the sacristy of an abandoned chapel.

Then, as always, with the pretext of looking for weapons and horses, the soldiers spread out in search of loot.

In the afternoon some of Demetrio's men were sprawled before the church portico, scratching their bellies. Bare-chested and with great seriousness, Venancio was removing fleas from his shirt.

A man came up to the wall asking permission to talk to their commander.

The soldiers raised their heads, but no one answered.

"I am a widower, gentlemen; I have nine children and I work for a living. . . . Don't be cruel to the poor!

"If it's a woman you want, no problem," said Meco, who was greasing his feet with the end of a tallow candle, "there's Pintada, and we'll sell her to you at cost price."

The man smiled bitterly.

"Only thing wrong with her," observed Pancracio, who lay on his back looking at the blue sky, "is soon as she sees a man, she's ready for him."

They had a good laugh over that, but Venancio, very seriously, showed the man the door to the sacristy.

The man entered timidly and made his complaint to Demetrio. The soldiers had just "cleaned him out." They hadn't left him a single grain of corn.

"Why'd you let them?" answered Demetrio indolently.

Then the man went on wailing and whining, and Luis Cervantes was going to throw him out rudely. But Camila intervened:

"Come on, Don Demetrio, don't you be heartless too; give him an order so they'll give him his corn back! . . ."

Luis Cervantes had to obey; he wrote a few lines, and Demetrio wrote a scrawl under them.

"God bless you, girl! . . . God in Heaven will reward you. . . . Ten bushels of corn, hardly enough food for this year," exclaimed the man, weeping with gratitude. And he took the piece of paper and kissed everyone's hands.

XII

They were reaching Cuquío, when Anastasio Montañés approached Demetrio and said:

"Why, *compadre*, I haven't even told you . . . what a real rascal that Güero Margarito is! You know what he did to that man who complained we had taken his corn to feed our horses? Well, he took the order you gave him and went to the barracks. 'Yes, *amigo*,' said Güero, 'come on in; it's only fair to return what's yours. Come in, come in. . . . How many bushels did we steal? . . . Ten? Are you sure it's not more than ten? . . . Yes, that's right; about fifteen, more or less. . . . Sure it wasn't twenty? . . . Try to remember. . . . You're so poor, you have so many children to feed. Yes, that's what I said, about twenty; that's about right. . . . Come over here; I'm not going to give you fifteen or twenty. You just start counting . . . one, two, three . . . and when you don't want more, just say enough.' And he takes out his saber and he gave him a thrashing that made him beg for mercy."

Pintada almost fell down laughing.

And Camila, unable to contain herself, said:

"Damn that old man, he's rotten to the core! . . . No wonder I can't stand the sight of him!"

Instantly, Pintada's face was contorted.

"What's it to you?"

Camila was frightened and made her mare run ahead.

Pintada shot off on hers and, rapidly overtaking Camila, grabbed her by the head and undid her braid.

Spooked by the blow, Camila's mare reared up. As the girl let go of the reins to brush the hair out of her face, she hesitated, lost her balance and fell on some rocks, cutting her forehead.

Laughing uncontrollably, Pintada galloped and caught the runaway mare with great skill.

"There you go, Curro, a job for you!" said Pancracio when he saw Camila riding on Demetrio's saddle with a bloody face.

Luis Cervantes pompously ran over with his medicine kit, but Camila stopped sobbing, wiped her eyes and said in a muffled voice:

"You? . . . Even if I was dying . . . I wouldn't take water from you! . . ."

In Cuquío Demetrio received a message.

"Back to Tepatitlán, General," said Luis Cervantes, quickly scanning the communiqué. "You'll have to leave your people there and go to Lagos to take the Aguascalientes train."

There were heated protests; some *serranos* swore that they would abandon the column, and there was grunting, grousing and grumbling.

Camila cried all night, and the next morning she asked Demetrio permission to return home.

"Guess I haven't grown on you! . . ." Demetrio answered gruffly.

"You have, Don Demetrio, you have too grown on me, . . . but you seen how things are. . . . That woman! . . ."

"Don't you worry, I'll get rid of her before the day is over. . . . My mind's made up."

Camila stopped crying.

They were all saddling already. Demetrio approached Pintada, and speaking very softly said:

"You can't come with us anymore."

"What do you mean?" she asked confused.

"You can stay here or go where you want, but not with us."

"What're you saying?" she exclaimed astonished, "You kicking me out? Ha, ha, ha! . . . What the . . . ? I can't believe you swallow the stories that . . . tells you!"

And Pintada insulted Camila, Demetrio, Luis Cervantes, and whoever crossed her mind, with such energy and originality that the troops heard curses and obscenities they didn't even know existed.

Demetrio waited a long time patiently, but when she gave no sign of stopping, he calmly told a soldier:

"Throw that drunk out."

"Güero Margarito! My darling Güero! Come defend me from these . . . ! Please my sweet Güerito! . . . Come and show them you're a real man and they're nothing but a bunch of sons of . . . !"

And she gesticulated, kicked and screamed.

Güero Margarito appeared. He had just woken up; his blue eyes were lost behind his swollen lids and his voice was hoarse. He found out what was going on, and approaching Pintada, said gravely:

"Yes, I think it's a good idea for you to go to . . . ! We're all fed up with you!"

Pintada's face became granite. She tried to talk, but her muscles were rigid.

The soldiers were laughing it up; Camila, very frightened, was holding her breath.

Pintada eyed everyone around her. And it all happened in the blinking of an eye; she bent over, took a sharp and shining blade from between her leg and her stocking and jumped Camila.

A strident scream and a body falls, spurting blood.

"Kill her!" Demetrio shouted beside himself.

Two soldiers fell on Pintada, who held them off brandishing her knife.

"Not you, you scum! . . . *You* kill me Demetrio!" She walked up, handed him her weapon, thrust out her chest and let her arms drop.

Demetrio raised the bloodstained knife, but his eyes clouded, he hesitated, he stepped back.

Then in a faded, hoarse voice he yelled:

"Get out of here! . . . Now! . . ."

No one dared to stop her.

Silent and somber, she slowly walked away.

And the silent spell was broken by the high guttural voice of Güero Margarito:

"Ah, what a relief! . . . Finally got rid of that bedbug! . . ."

XIII

In the middle of my body
A dagger he plunged,
Why I don't know
I just don't know . . .
He did know,
But I did not . . .

And from that mortal wound
My blood did flow,
Why I don't know
I just don't know . . .
He did know,
But I did not . . .

Head drooping, hands crossed on the saddle, Demetrio melancholically hummed the obsessive tune.

Then he would be quiet; for long minutes he would remain sadly silent.

"When we get to Lagos, I'll get rid of your blues, General. Plenty of pretty girls for us to enjoy there," said Güero Margarito.

"Only thing I want to do now is get good and drunk," Demetrio replied.

And he rode away from them again, spurring his horse, as if he wanted to abandon himself wholly to his sadness.

After many hours of riding, he called Luis Cervantes over:

"Listen, Curro, now that I think of it, what the hell am I supposed to do in Aguascalientes?"

"General, you are going to vote for the provisional president of the Republic."

"Provisional president? . . . Well, then, what's Carranza like? . . . Truth is I don't understand these here politics. . . ."

They reached Lagos. Güero wagered that he would make Demetrio laugh out loud before the night was over.

Spurs dragging, goat-skin chaps sagging below his waist, Demetrio entered "El Cosmopolita," with Luis Cervantes, Güero Margarito and his assistants.

"Why are you running away, *curros?* . . . We don't eat people!" Güero exclaimed.

The townspeople, caught just as they were trying to escape, stopped. Some inconspicuously returned to their tables and resumed drinking and talking, and others hesitatingly went up to pay their respects to the commanders.

"General! . . . Such a pleasure! . . . Major! . . ."

"That's more like it! . . . That's how I like my friends, polite and decent," said Güero Margarito.

"Vamos, *muchachos,*" he added jovially taking out his revolver, "here's a firecracker for you to dodge."

A bullet ricocheted from the cement, passing between the legs of the tables and the legs of the dandies, who jumped around like ladies frightened by mice under their skirts.

Blanching, they smile to humor the major. Demetrio barely parts his lips while his retinue doubles up with laughter.

"Güero, that one who's going out was stung by the wasp; look, he's limping," observes Codorniz.

Without paying attention or even turning around to look at the wounded man, Güero affirms enthusiastically that at a distance of thirty paces and on the draw, he can hit a tequila shot glass.

"Let's see, hold it there *amigo*," he says to the waiter of the *cantina*. Then he leads him by the hand to the entrance of the hotel's patio and places a shot glass full of tequila on his head.

Terrified, the poor devil resists, wants to run away, but Güero prepares his gun and aims.

"Get back to your place . . . you piece of jerky! Or I'll really shoot a hot one into you."

Güero returns to the opposite wall, raises his weapon and takes aim.

The glass shatters, bathing the boy's face in tequila; he's as pale as a corpse.

"This time it's for real!" he shouts as he runs to the *cantina* for a new glass, that he places on top of the boy's head.

He returns to his place, whirls on his feet and fires on the draw.

Except that this time he has shot off an ear instead of the glass.

Holding his stomach from laughing so much, he says to the boy:

"Here boy, take these bills. It's nothing a little arnica and brandy won't heal!"

After drinking a lot of liquor and beer, Demetrio speaks:

"Güero, you pay . . . I'm leaving. . . ."

"I don't have any more cash, General, but no problem. . . . What do we owe you, *amigo?*"

"A hundred and eighty *pesos,* boss," the *cantina* owner replies courteously.

Güero quickly jumps on the bar, and with two sweeps of the hand knocks down all the bottles and glasses.

"Don't forget to send the bill to your father Pancho Villa, you hear?"

"Hey, *amigo*, where can we find some whores?" Reeling from the liquor, he asks a short, well-dressed man who is shutting down a tailor's shop.

The man solicitously gets off the sidewalk to let him pass. Güero stops and looks at him with impudence and curiosity:

"Hey, *amigo,* you really are cute and little! . . . What's that, you don't agree? . . . You calling me a liar? . . . That's more like it. . . . You know how to do the dwarf dance? . . . What do you mean, you don't! . . . Sure you do! . . . I saw you do it in a circus! And you're good at it too! I'll show you! . . ."

Güero takes out his pistol and begins to shoot at the tailor's feet; being very fat and very short he gives a little hop at every shot.

"Now you see, you do know how to do the dwarf dance!"

And throwing his arms around his friends' shoulders, he heads for the red-light district, marking his progress by shooting the street lamps at every corner, door or house in the town. Demetrio leaves him and returns to the hotel, humming through his teeth:

> *In the middle of my body*
> *A dagger he plunged,*
> *Why I don't know*
> *I just don't know . . .*

XIV

Cigar smoke, the pungent smell of sweaty clothes, liquor stench and the breath of the crowd; packed tighter than a cattle car full of pigs. Most wear Texan hats, braided hatbands, and dress in khaki.

"Gentlemen, a well-dressed gentleman stole my bag at the Silao station . . . the savings of a lifetime of work. I can't feed my boy."

The voice was high, shrill and whiny; but it faded quickly in the uproar of the car. "What did the old woman say?" asked Güero Margarito as he came in looking for a seat.

"Something about a bag . . . a decent boy, . . ." answered Pancracio, who had already found a place to sit on the laps of some peasants.

Demetrio and the others elbowed their way through. And since those who were holding up Pancracio preferred to give up their seats and stand, Demetrio and Luis Cervantes were happy to take them.

A woman who had been standing since Irapauto with a child in her arms fainted. A peasant quickly picked up the child. No one else noticed a thing. The army women were each taking up two or three seats with their luggage, dogs, cats and parrots. On the other hand, the men wearing Texan hats had a good laugh about the plump thighs and limp breasts of the fainted woman.

"Gentlemen, a well-dressed gentleman stole my bag at the Silao station . . . the savings of a lifetime of work. I can't even feed my boy."

The old woman speaks quickly and sighs and sobs automatically. Her sharp eyes look all around. She gets a bill here and farther on another. They rain on her. She collects her money and advances a few seats:

"Gentlemen, a well-dressed gentleman stole my bag at the Silao station. . . ."

The effect of her words is swift and predictable.

"A well-dressed gentleman! A well-dressed gentleman who steals a bag! That's unspeakable! It elicits a general feeling of indignation. What a shame that well-dressed gentleman isn't there, on hand, so that at the very least each one of the generals present could have him shot!"

"If there's something I can't stand it's a thieving *curro*," says one, bursting with indignation.

"To steal from a poor woman!"

"To steal from a wretched, defenseless woman!"

And they all express the tenderness of their hearts in words and deeds: an insult for the thief and five *pesos* in revolutionary currency for the victim.

"Tell you the truth, I don't think killing is bad, because when you kill it's always in a fit of rage; but stealing? . . ." exclaims Güero Margarito.

They all seem to agree with this weighty reasoning, but after a brief silence and some moments of reflection, a colonel ventures:

"Truth is, when you come down to it, it all depends. There's nothing like the truth, right? And the real truth is I've stolen . . . and if I say that all of us here have done it too, I don't figure I'll be lying. . . ."

"Boy, did I steal sewing machines in Mexico City," a major exclaimed, "I made more than five hundred *pesos,* and I sold them at fifty cents apiece!"

"In Zacatecas I stole such fine horses that I thought: 'You are all set, Pascual Mata, no more worries for the rest of your living days,'" said a grayhaired, toothless captain. "Bad thing was that General Limón liked my horses and he stole them from me."

"Well! Why deny it! I've stolen also," agreed Güero Margarito, "but here are my *compañeros,* ask them how much I've saved. What I like is spending it with friends. A drunken spree with all my friends is more fun than sending a cent to the women back home. . . ."

Although the "I stole" topic seems inexhaustible, it fades out when decks of cards appear on every bench, drawing officers to them like mosquitoes to light.

The thrill of gambling quickly absorbs all and it makes the air hotter and hotter; it smells like a barracks, a jail, a brothel and even a pigsty.

And over the general uproar you can hear, way in the other car:

"Gentlemen, a well-dressed gentleman stole my bag. . . ."

The streets of Aguascalientes had become garbage dumps. The men dressed in khaki, like bees at a hive's entrance, swarmed at the doors of restaurants, lunch stands and taverns, at tables full of slop, and outdoor stands where a pile of pieces of filthy cheese rose next to a tray of rancid pork rinds.

The smell of fried food stirred Demetrio's appetite and that of his companions. They pushed their way into a cheap restaurant, and a disheveled and revolting old woman served them earthenware plates of pork bones swimming in a watery chili broth and three leathery, burned *tortillas*. They paid two *pesos* for each, and when they left Pancracio swore that he was hungrier than before they went in.

"Now," said Demetrio, "we are going to get advice from General Natera."

And they followed a street to the house where the northern commander was staying.

A mixed and agitated group of people blocked their progress at a street corner. Lost in the crowd, a man called out in a singsong and with an unctuous accent something that sounded like a prayer. They approached so that they could see him. The man, who was wearing a white shirt and trousers, repeated: "All good Catholics who recite with devotion this prayer to the Crucified Christ will be free from storms, plagues, wars and famine. . . ."

"This guy's got a good thing going," said Demetrio smiling.

The man waved a fistful of printed sheets above his head and said:

"Fifty cents for the prayer to the Crucified Christ, fifty cents. . . ."

Then he would disappear for an instant and resurface holding a snake fang, a starfish, the skeleton of a fish. And in the same prayerful accent he would expound on the medicinal properties and rare virtues of each item.

Codorniz, who did not trust Venancio, asked the hawker to pull a tooth; Güero Margarito bought the kernel of a certain fruit with the power to protect its owner from lightning and any misfortune, and Anastasio Montañés bought a prayer to Crucified Christ, that he carefully folded and with great piety stored inside his shirt.

"As there's a God in Heaven, *compañero*, the ball keeps rolling! Now it's Villa against Carranza!" said Natera.

And Demetrio, silent, wide-eyed, awaited further explanation.

"What I mean," Natera continued, "is that the Convention does not recognize Carranza as *primer jefe* and is going to elect a provisional president of the Republic. . . . Understand, *compañero?*"

Demetrio nodded to indicate that he did.

"So, what do you say to that, *compañero?*" asked Natera.

Demetrio shrugged his shoulders.

"Looks like we're supposed to keep on fighting. So, we'll go at it. You know you can count on me, General."

"Fine, so who are you with?"

Demetrio, thoroughly perplexed, raised his hands to his hair and scratched briefly.

"Look, I'm not a schoolboy so don't ask me questions. . . . You're the one who gave me this little eagle I wear on my hat. . . . So, all you gotta say is: 'Demetrio, do this and that . . . end of story!' "

Part Three

I

El Paso, Texas, May 16, 1915

Dear Venancio:

I have not been able to answer your kind letter from January because my professional responsibilities take up all my time. As you know, I received my degree in December. I regret the fate of Pancracio and Manteca, but I can't say I'm surprised they knifed each other after a card game. It's a shame; they were so brave! I deeply regret not being able to communicate with Güero Margarito to extend my warmest congratulations; the noblest and most beautiful act of his life was his suicide!

I think it would be difficult, my dear friend Venancio, for you to obtain the medical degree you so desire here in the United States, even if you have amassed enough gold and silver to buy it. I esteem you, Venancio, and believe you deserve better in life. I have an idea that might be of mutual interest and that would further your ambition to change your social station. If you and I became partners, we could do well for ourselves. While it is true that for the time being I don't have any reserve funds, because I spent everything on my studies and obtaining my degree, I do have something that is worth much more than money: my perfect knowledge of this place, its needs, and the best business ventures one could undertake. We could start a genuine Mexican restaurant; you would be the nominal owner and we would split the profits at the end of each month. There is something else regarding a matter of great interest to both of us, your change of social milieu. I remember that you play the guitar rather well, and I think it would be easy, given my contacts and your musical knowledge, to secure your admission to the Salvation Army, a most respectable organization that would give you the status you desire.

Don't hesitate, dear Venancio, bring your funds and we will be rich before long. Please convey my affectionate greetings to the General, Anastasio and my other friends.

Your friend who values you,

Luis Cervantes

Venancio finished reading the letter for the hundredth time, and sighing, repeated his comment:

"That Curro, he really knew what he was doing!"

"But what I really can't get through my head," observed Anastasio Montañés, "is how come we gotta keep on fighting. . . . Didn't we lick the Federales?"

Neither the General nor Venancio answered; but those words kept hitting their coarse brains like a hammer on an anvil.

Pensive and crestfallen, they ascended the slope at the slow pace of their mules. Anastasio, restless and stubborn, went over and made the same remark to other groups of soldiers who laughed at his naïveté. Because if you've got a rifle in your hands and your cartridge belts are full, it's because you're going to fight. Against whom? For whom? No one ever cares about that!

The undulating, endless dust cloud stretched either way on the trail, in a swarm of palm *sombreros,* filthy old khaki uniforms, dirty blankets and the black swirl of horses.

The men were burning with thirst. Not a puddle, well or a brook with water along the way. A breath of fire rose from the white barren ground of a ravine, throbbed over the curly heads of the *huizaches* and the sea-green leaves of the nopal cactus. And, as if to mock them, the cactus flowers were blooming. Some were fresh, succulent and bright, others waxlike and diaphanous.

By noon they stumbled upon a hut that clung to the ridges of the sierra, then on three poor houses scattered along the banks of a river of burning sand, but all was silent and abandoned. As the troops approached, people slipped away to hide in the canyons.

Demetrio was indignant:

"Anyone you find hiding or running away, grab them and bring them to me," he ordered his soldiers, his voice breaking.

"What! . . . What do you mean?" exclaimed Valderrama surprised, "Grab the *serranos?* These brave mountain people who haven't imitated the chickens who are now nesting in Zacatecas and Aguascalientes? Our own brothers, who defy storms clinging to their rocks like moss? I protest! . . . I protest! . . ."

He dug his spurs into the flanks of his miserable nag and caught up to the general.

"The *serranos,*" he said emphatically and solemnly, "are flesh of our flesh and bone of our bones. . . . 'Os ex osibus meis et caro de carne mea.' . . . *Serranos* are made of the same stuff we are . . . the strong stuff heroes are made of. . . ."

And with brave and sudden familiarity he hit the general's chest with his fist; the general smiled benevolently.

Valderrama, vagabond, madman and half-poet, was he right?

When the soldiers got to a village and swarmed desperately around the empty huts and houses, they did not find a single stale *tortilla*, a rotten chili pepper or even some grains of salt to put on their detested fresh beef. From their hideouts their peaceful brothers watched, some with the stony impassibility of Aztec idols, others more human, with sordid tight smiles on their hairless faces. They saw how these fierce men, who a month before had made their remote and miserable homes tremble with fear, now came out of their huts, where the ovens were cold and the water jars were dry. They were despondent, their heads bowed, humiliated like dogs kicked out of their own homes.

But the general did not change his mind and some soldiers brought him four tightly bound fugitives.

II

"Why do you hide?" Demetrio asked the prisoners.

"We're not hiding, *jefe;* we're headed home."

"Where?"

"Our land . . . Nombre de Dios, Durango."

"Is this the road to Durango?"

"*Pacíficos* can't use the roads now. You know that, *jefe.*"

"You aren't *pacíficos;* you're deserters.

"Where are you coming from?" Demetrio continued watching them with a sharp eye.

The prisoners became confused, looked at each other perplexed, and found no ready answer.

"They're *carranclanes!*" one of the soldiers remarked.

That instantly restored the prisoners' presence of mind. It resolved the terrible enigma that had haunted them since they had run into these unknown troops.

"Carrancistas?" one of them answered proudly, "We'd rather be pigs! . . ."

"It's true, we're deserters," said another, "we quit on my General Villa this side of Celaya, after the whipping they gave us."

"General Villa, defeated? . . . Ha, ha, ha!"

The soldiers had a good laugh about that.

But Demetrio frowned as if something very dark had passed over his eyes.

"The son of a . . . hasn't been born yet, who can defeat my General Villa!" exclaimed indignantly a copper-faced veteran with a scar from forehead to chin.

Undaunted, one of the deserters kept staring at him and said:

"I know you. When we took Torreón, you were with General Urbina. In Zacatecas you were already with Natera and then you joined the troops from Jalisco. . . . Am I lying?"

The effect was sudden and decisive. The prisoners were then able to give a full account of Villa's colossal defeat at Celaya.

A stunned silence met their account.

Before they continued their march, they lit fires to roast bull meat. Anastasio Montañés, who was looking for firewood among the *huizaches,* saw at some distance, poking behind some rocks, the shorn head of Valderrama's nag.

"Loco, you can come back now, there ain't going to be any shooting after all!" he began to shout.

Because Valderrama, a romantic poet, always disappeared for the whole day whenever there was any talk of executions.

Valderrama heard Anastasio's voice and must have been convinced that the prisoners had been set free, because moments later he was near Venancio and Demetrio.

"Have you heard the news?" Venancio said gravely.

"I haven't heard anything."

"It's serious! A disaster! Villa defeated in Celaya by Obregón. Carranza is victorious everywhere. We're ruined!"

Valderrama's gesture was one of solemn disdain like that of an emperor:

"Villa? . . . Obregón? . . . Carranza? . . . X . . . Y . . . Z . . . ! What's it to me? . . . I love the Revolution like I love an erupting volcano! The volcano because it's a volcano, and the Revolution because it's the Revolution! . . . But what do I care what stones wind up on top or on the bottom after the cataclysm? . . ."

And since the rays of the midday sun reflected on his forehead the glare from a white bottle of tequila, he turned his horse around, and with his soul full of joy charged at the bearer of such a marvel.

"I really like that *loco,*" said Demetrio smiling, " 'cause sometimes he says things that get you thinking."

They continued on their way, and their anxiety was translated into a gloomy silence. The other catastrophe was taking shape, quietly but relentlessly. Villa defeated was a fallen god. And fallen gods aren't gods; they're nothing.

When Codorniz spoke, his words caught faithfully what they all felt:

"That's it, *muchachos* . . . now it's everyone for himself! . . ."

III

That little town, like all parishes, *haciendas* and villages, had emptied into Zacatecas and Aguascalientes.

Therefore, the finding of a barrel of tequila by one of the officers was an event tantamount to a miracle. It was a well-kept secret, and the troops left mysteriously at dawn under the command of Anastasio Montañés and Venancio. When Demetrio awoke to the sound of music, his staff, now made up mostly of young ex-Federal officers, revealed the discovery, and Codorniz, interpreting the thoughts of his colleagues, said sententiously:

"Times are bad and we have to seize the opportunity, because 'some days a duck can swim, but some he can't even get a drink of water.'"

The string instruments played all day and they solemnly did justice to the barrel; but Demetrio was very sad, "Why I don't know, I just don't know," repeating the refrain to himself again and again.

That afternoon they had cockfights. Demetrio and his leading officers sat in the shade of the porch of the municipal building, in front of a large grass-invaded plaza, with an old, rotting kiosk and lonely adobe houses.

"Valderrama!" Demetrio called, bored of looking at the cockpit, "Come and sing me 'The Gravedigger.'"

But Valderrama didn't hear him, because instead of waiting for the cockfight he was engaged in an extravagant monologue, watching the sun set behind the hills and declaiming with solemn gestures:

"Master, it is good for us to be here, and let us make three tabernacles; one for thee, and one for Moses, and one for Elias."

"Valderrama!" Demetrio shouted again, "Sing me 'The Gravedigger.'"

"Loco, the general is talking to you," called one of the officers who was closer.

And Valderrama with his eternally complacent smile on his lips, came over then and asked the musicians for a guitar.

"Quiet!" shouted the players.

Valderrama stopped tuning. In the arena, Codorniz and Meco were setting loose two cocks with long, extremely sharp spurs. One was dark red, with beautiful obsidian highlights; the other was gold, with feathers like copper scales blazing with fire.

The fight was very brief, and in its ferocity it was almost human. As if moved by a spring, the roosters leaped on each other. Raised feathers on their curving necks, eyes like corals, combs erect, their legs tense, for an instant they didn't even touch the ground, their plumage, beaks and claws all confused into one; the dark-red one broke loose and was thrown, legs up, beyond the line. His cinnabar eyes went out, the leathery lids closing slowly, and his fluffed feathers trembled convulsively in a pool of blood.

Valderrama, who had not repressed a gesture of violent indignation, began to tune. His anger disappeared with the first few melancholy chords. His eyes glowed like those eyes that shine with the glow of madness. As his gaze wandered over the plaza, the ruined kiosk, the old houses, with the sierra in the background and the sky burning like a roof, he began to sing.

He put so much soul into his voice and played the guitar strings with such expression that when he finished, Demetrio turned his face away so no one could see his eyes.

But Valderrama threw himself in his arms, and embraced him strongly, and with his typical, sudden, universal and always timely intimacy, whispered in his ear:

"Drink them! . . . Those are very beautiful tears!"

Demetrio asked for the bottle and gave it to Valderrama.

Valderrama avidly drank half the bottle, almost in one gulp; then he turned to those present and adopting a dramatic pose and his declaiming tone, exclaimed with his eyes full of tears:

"Behold how the great pleasures of the Revolution are resolved in one tear! . . ."

Then he went on talking crazy, but totally crazy, to the dusty grass, the rotting kiosk, the gray houses, and the haughty mountain and the immeasurable sky.

IV

Juchipila appeared in the distance, white and bathed by the sun amid the foliage, at the foot of a high, arrogant mountain, pleated like a turban.

Seeing the little towers of Juchipila, some soldiers sighed with sadness. Their march through the canyons was now the march of a blind man without a guide; they felt already the bitterness of the exodus.

"That town is Juchipila?" asked Valderrama.

Valderrama, during the first stage of his first drinking binge of the day, had been counting the crosses scattered all over the roads and trails, in the rock escarpments, in the winding arroyos, on the banks of the river. Crosses of recently varnished black wood, crosses made with two logs, crosses made by piles of stones, crosses painted with whitewash on crumbling walls, humble crosses traced with charcoal on the faces of the rocks. The trail of blood of the first revolutionaries of 1910, murdered by the government.

With Juchipila already in sight, Valderrama dismounts, bows, genuflects and solemnly kisses the ground.

The soldiers pass without stopping. Some laugh at the *loco* and others make some wisecrack.

Valderrama, aloof, recites his prayer solemnly:

"Juchipila, cradle of the 1910 Revolution, blessed land, land irrigated by the blood of martyrs, by the blood of dreamers . . . the only good ones! . . ."

"Because they didn't have time to be bad," an ex-Federal officer brutally completes the phrase as he passes by.

Valderrama stops, thinks, frowns and lets go a loud laugh that echoes in the rocks, mounts his horse and runs after the officer to ask him for a drink of tequila.

Soldiers who are maimed, lame, rheumatic and consumptive speak ill of Demetrio. Armchair warriors now join the ranks and wear officer's bars on their hats, before they have even learned how to hold a rifle. While veterans seasoned in a hundred combats, now unfit for work, veterans who began as buck privates are still buck privates.

And the few remaining leaders, Macías' old comrades, are indignant because vacancies in his staff are filled with young perfumed dandies from the capital.

"But worst of all," says Venancio, "is that we're getting full of ex-Federales."

Even Anastasio, who ordinarily feels that everything Demetrio does is just fine, now joins the malcontents and exclaims:

"Look, *compañeros*, I'm a straight talker . . . and I'm gonna tell my *compadre* that if we're gonna let Federales in here, we're in bad shape. . . . It's true! Believe it or not . . . I always speak my mind, I swear on my mother's life, that's what I'm gonna tell my *compadre* Demetrio."

And he told him. Demetrio listened benevolently, and when he stopped talking, replied:

"*Compadre,* you got that right. We're in bad shape: soldiers badmouth the noncoms, noncoms badmouth the officers and the officers badmouth us. . . . And we are just about ready to send both Villa and Carranza to . . . to have themselves a good time. . . . But I'm thinking that we're kind of like that *peón* in Tepatitlán. Remember, *compadre?* He never stopped grousing about his boss, but he also never stopped working. That's just like us: we grumble and grumble and we fight and fight. . . . But don't go around saying that, *compadre.* . . ."

"Why, *compadre* Demetrio?"

"Well, I don't know. . . . Just because. . . . Understand? What I need you to do is raise the morale of the men. I've received orders to go back and stop a detachment coming from Cuquío. In just a few days we need to have a run-in with the *carranclanes,* and this time we've got to beat the living daylights out of them."

Valderrama, the vagabond of the highways, who joined the troops one day, though no one could remember where or when, caught wind of what Demetrio was saying, and since as they say, even a madman won't eat fire, that same day he went as he had come.

V

They entered the streets of Juchipila as the bells of the church were pealing happily, noisily and with that special tone that moved the hearts of all the canyon dwellers.

"*Compadre,* it feels like we're back in the days when the revolution was just starting, when we used to arrive at a town and they rang and rang the bells for us, and people would meet us with music, flags, and cheered us and even shot fireworks," said Anastasio Montañés.

"Now, they don't love us," replied Demetrio.

"Of course, since we're licked for sure," observed Codorniz.

"That's not it. . . . They can't even stand the sight of the others either."

"But, how could they love us, *compadre?*"

And they said nothing else.

They were coming out to a plaza, in front of the octagonal church, rough and massive, reminiscent of colonial times.

The plaza must have been a garden, to judge from the thin, mangy orange trees, interspersed amid the ruins of iron and wood benches.

Again they heard the loud and joyous pealing. Then, with melancholic solemnity, the sweet voices of a feminine choir escaped from the interior of the church. To the beat of a bass guitar, the maidens of the town were singing the "Mysteries of the Rosary."

"What holy day is it today, *señora?*" Venancio asked a gnarled old woman who was rushing to church.

"The Sacred Heart of Jesus!" answered the pious old woman, half choking.

They recalled that a year ago they had taken Zacatecas. And they all became sadder still.

Just like all the other towns they had passed through since Tepic, as they made their way through Jalisco, Aguascalientes and Zacatecas, Juchipila was in ruins. The black traces of fire were visible in the roofless houses, in the charred walls. Closed houses, and here and there an open store sarcastically showing its naked shelves, reminiscent of the white skeletons of horses scattered over all the roads. The fearsome grimace of hunger was already on the dirt-colored faces of the people, in the luminous flame of their eyes which, when they came to rest on a soldier, burned with the fire of a curse.

The soldiers roam the streets in vain looking for food and bite their tongues with rage. Only one miserable lunch stand is open and soon it's jam-packed. There are no beans, no *tortillas:* only chopped chiles and salt. In vain the leaders show their pockets bursting with bills; in vain they threaten.

"Pieces of paper, yes! . . . That's all you bring! . . . Well, you can eat them! . . ." says the owner, an insolent old woman, with a huge scar on her face, who says that "she's already slept in a coffin so she ain't afraid to die."

And in the sadness and desolation of the town, while the women sing in the church, the birds keep twittering in the trees, and the song of the *currucas* is heard from the dry branches of the orange trees.

VI

Demetrio's wife, mad with joy, went out to meet him on the sierra trail, leading the boy by the hand.

It's been almost two years!

They embraced and remained silent; she overwhelmed by sobs and tears.

Demetrio, stunned, saw that his wife had aged, as if ten or twenty years had already gone by. Then he looked at the boy, who fixed his eyes on him, amazed. And his heart skipped a beat when he noticed the duplication of the same steel lines of his face and the fiery gleam of his eyes And he wanted to draw him near and embrace him; but the little boy, who was very scared, sought the refuge of his mother's bosom.

"It's your father, son! . . . It's your father! . . ."

Still the boy hid his head shyly between the folds of the skirt.

Demetrio, who had given his horse to an orderly, was walking slowly with his wife and son along the rough mountain trail.

"Now that you're here at last, God be praised! . . . You'll never leave us again! You'll stay with us now, right? . . ."

Demetrio's face darkened.

And they both stood silent and distressed.

A black cloud was rising behind the sierra, and they heard muffled thunder. Demetrio repressed a sigh. Memories swarmed to his mind like bees to a hive.

Rain started to fall in big drops and they had to take refuge in a rocky grotto.

The downpour was unleashed noisily and shook the white San Juan flowers, clumps of stars hanging from trees, on the rocks, in the weeds, amid the *pitahayo* cactus and all over the sierra.

Below, at the bottom of the canyon and through the gauze of the rain, you could see straight swaying palms; they slowly rocked their angular heads, and when the wind blew they opened like fans. And the sierra was everywhere: waves of hills that follow upon hills, more hills surrounded by mountains, and these enclosed by a wall of mountains so high that their blue summits were lost in the sapphire sky.

"Demetrio, for the love of God! . . . Don't go! . . . My heart tells me something will happen to you now! . . ."

And she shakes as she again abandons herself to her sobbing.

The boy, frightened, cries and screams, and she has to contain her terrible sorrow to comfort him.

The rain is stopping; a swallow with a silver belly and angular wings obliquely crosses the crystal threads, lit suddenly by the evening sun.

"Why are you still fighting, Demetrio?"

Frowning, Demetrio takes a pebble absentmindedly and throws it to the bottom of the canyon. He remains lost in thought looking at the cliff, and says:

"See how that pebble can't stop. . . ."

VII

It was a real wedding morning. On the eve, it had rained all night and the morning sky was covered with white clouds. Wild ponies with unruly manes and tense tails trotted on the summits of the sierra, as proud as the peaks that raise their heads to kiss the clouds.

The soldiers walk along the rough stony mountainside, infected by the joy of the morning. No one thinks about the treacherous bullet that might be waiting up ahead. The happiness of departure hinges precisely on the unforeseen. And that is why the soldiers sing, laugh and talk wildly. The souls of the old nomadic tribes stir in their souls. It doesn't matter where they are going or where they are coming from; what matters is to walk, to keep walking always, never stop; to be masters of the valley, the plains, the sierra and all that the eye can see.

Trees, cacti and ferns, everything seems freshly washed. The rocks, their ochre looking like the rust of old armors, drip large drops of transparent water.

Macías' men are silent for a moment. It seems they have heard a familiar sound: the bursting of a distant rocket, but a few minutes go by and nothing more is heard.

"In this very sierra," says Demetrio, "I, with only twenty men, inflicted more than five hundred casualties on the Federales. . . ."

And when Demetrio begins to recount that famous feat of arms, the men realize the grave danger they are in. What if the enemy weren't two days' travel away? What if they turned out to be hiding in the brush of that formidable gully along whose bottom they have ventured? But who's going to say he's afraid? When did Demetrio's men ever say: "We won't go there?"

And when the shooting breaks out up ahead, where the vanguard is, no one is surprised. The recruits turn tail and desperately seek the exit to the canyon.

A curse escapes from Demetrio's dry throat:

"Shoot them! . . . Shoot any who run away! . . ."

"Drive them from the high ground!" he then roars like a beast.

But the enemy, hiding by the thousands, unleash their machine guns, and Demetrio's men fall like sheaves cut by a sickle.

Demetrio sheds tears of rage and pain when Anastasio slides slowly from his horse, without uttering a complaint, and lies motionless. Venancio falls by his side, his chest horribly torn by a machine gun, and Meco falls over the edge and rolls to the bottom of the abyss. Suddenly Demetrio finds himself alone. The bullets buzz in his ears like hail. He dismounts, crawls over the rocks until he finds cover, places a rock to protect his head, and chest to the ground, he begins to fire.

The enemy fans out, in pursuit of the few fugitives who are still hiding in the chaparral.

Demetrio aims and he doesn't miss a single shot. . . . Paf! . . . Paf! . . . Paf!

His famous marksmanship fills him with joy; wherever he aims the bullet finds its mark. He empties a clip and he inserts another. And aims. . . .

The smoke of the rifles still has not dissipated. The cicadas intone their imperturbable and mysterious song; the doves coo sweetly from the nooks of the rocks; the cows browse peaceably.

The sierra is wearing its best; over its inaccessible summits the whitest fog is falling like a white veil on a bride's head.

And at the foot of a crevice, enormous and sumptuous like the portico of an ancient cathedral, Demetrio Macías, his eyes forever fixed, continues to aim with the barrel of his rifle. . . .

Appendix

Historical and Literary Context of
The Underdogs

The Mexican Revolution

My purpose here is not to give a nuanced, detailed account of the Mexican Revolution. Many historians have done this and I list several useful works in the Recommended Readings that follows this Appendix. My aim, rather, is to provide those readers unfamiliar with the confusing military and political process known as the Mexican Revolution with an orientation sufficient for understanding many of the events and historical figures mentioned in Azuela's novel. In this regard the glossary should be of help. It is also useful to contextualize the action depicted in *The Underdogs* within the larger canvas of the Revolution.

Porfirio Díaz (1830–1915) entered Mexican history as the hero of the Cinco de Mayo. As a young general in President Benito Juárez' army, his decisive action helped inflict the first defeat on the invading French army on May 5, 1862, during the defense of the city of Puebla. A *mestizo* of humble origin, Díaz was associated originally with President Benito Juárez' liberal reforms. Although Díaz first ran for the presidency with a "No Reelection" slogan, he served as president of Mexico from 1876–1880 and then from 1884–1911, being reelected again and again without real opposition. His long regime ushered in an era of modernization and foreign investment that brought prosperity to the upper and middle classes but left the masses of the people in grinding poverty. Any protests were crushed by the federal army and the *rurales*. In 1906, for example, when the miners at the Cananea Consolidated Copper Company went on strike, the American owner of the mine was allowed to bring United States troops from Arizona who put a bloody end to the strike. The Díaz regime favored the rich over the poor and foreigners over Mexicans.

The challenge to Porfirio Díaz' dictatorship came from an unexpected source—not from a peasant or a factory worker but from the scion of one of Mexico's richest families, the liberal and idealistic Francisco Madero. The initial form that challenge took was also unusual—not conspiracy or armed revolt but the publication of a book. In *The Presidential Succession of 1910*, published in January 1909, Francisco Madero bluntly described Mexico's ills and proposed a solution. As Mexican historian Enrique Krauze puts it:

> For Madero, the Mexican sickness—a natural consequence of the militarism that had devastated the country throughout the nineteenth century—was absolute power in the hands of one man. Such power could not support any genuine progress, nor was there any infallible man who could wield it with balance. . . . [T]he balance sheet on his [Díaz'] thirty years of administration—in the ways that most mattered—placed the Porfiriato solidly in the red.
>
> On the slim credit side, Madero acknowledged material progress, at the cost of freedom; and advance in agriculture, though not without importing grains; buoyant industry, though monopolistic and subsidiary; and unquestionably peace—at the price of sacrificing all political life. The liabilities, on the other hand, were "terrifying": the slavery of the Yaqui people, the repression of workers in Cananea and Río Blanco, illiteracy, excessive concessions to the United States, and a ferocious centralization of politics. Economic, social, and political wounds translated into something worse. For Madero, absolute power had corrupted the Mexican soul, inciting "a disinterest in public life, disdain for the law, and a tendency toward cunning, cynicism, and fear."[1]

The solution Madero proposed was a return to democracy without reelections; he sent a copy of his book to President Díaz. The response of the Díaz regime was to harass the Madero family, to attempt to thwart Madero's growing antireelectionist movement, and eventually to jail him. In July, Díaz was reelected and Madero escaped from prison in San Luis Potosí.

In October 1910, Francisco Madero initiated a revolution against Porfirio Díaz' unconstitutional government with the proclamation of the Plan of San Luis Potosí, which called on all Mexicans to rise up in arms against Díaz on November 20. There were popular uprisings throughout the country and with the help of many local leaders, among them Pancho Villa and Pascual Orozco in the north and Emiliano Zapata in the south, the revolutionaries won numerous victories. On May 25, 1911, Díaz went into exile.

On November 6, 1911, Madero was elected president. Madero's inexperience in politics, his desire to avoid the authoritarianism of Porfirio Díaz,

---

[1] Enrique Krauze, *Mexico: Biography of Power*, p. 252.

and paradoxically his restoration of democracy all helped to undermine his administration. He unwisely kept many of Díaz' appointees in power and the new political freedom was employed by labor and peasant groups to demand reforms. Madero did not have a clear political plan beyond opposing Díaz' dictatorship and a firm stance against presidential reelection. Madero's revolution was political rather than social, but his Plan de San Luis Potosí talked about tyranny and oppression, and criticized the Díaz regime for promoting the prosperity of a small group rather than that of the country.[2]

Although Madero had no plan for labor or agrarian reform, his vague statements were interpreted by many among the bourgeoisie and the peasantry to promise far more than he probably intended. This misunderstanding contributed to Madero's downfall because the very sectors of society that helped defeat Díaz felt betrayed when the economic and social reforms they expected did not materialize. First among these former supporters to rebel was Emiliano Zapata, whose November 1911 Plan de Ayala called for the immediate restitution of communal lands that had been usurped over the years by landowners in southern Mexico. Zapata's rebellion was put down by Madero's army. In the north Madero's army also had to quell uprisings by General Bernardo Reyes and by Emilio Vásquez Gómez in Chihuahua. In March 1912, Pascual Orozco, who had put down the Vásquez Gómez revolt, in turn rebelled against Madero. The Orozquistas were a serious threat to the government until they were contained by General Victoriano Huerta in May 1912.

The resultant disorders and apparent danger to life and property of foreigners caused American ambassador Henry Lane Wilson to become an enemy of the Madero administration.[3] In February 1913, part of the army rebelled against President Madero in Mexico City.[4] On February 18, Victoriano Huerta, commanding general of the Madero government's troops, joined the rebels, and with the aid of Ambassador Wilson forced Madero's resignation and assumed the presidency. On February 22, as they were being taken to prison, President Madero and Vice President Pino Suárez were shot, either on Huerta's orders or those of his coconspirators.

The army coup and Madero's assassination set off uprisings to restore constitutional government in three northern states: by Venustiano Carranza in

---

[2] Michael C. Meyer and William L. Sherman, *The Course of Mexican History,* p. 498.

[3] Ibid., p. 520.

[4] This is the incident alluded to by a character in the novel (Part I, Chapter XVI), the young blond Federal captain who constantly brags about his participation as a cadet in the coup against Madero.

Coahuila, Pancho Villa in Chihuahua, and Álvaro Obregón in Sonora. Meanwhile, in the south Emiliano Zapata continued to lead an Indian peasant rebellion for agrarian reform.

The Constitutionalists, as those who opposed Huerta were called, gained the support of Woodrow Wilson, the new president of the United States. Wilson allowed the Constitutionalists to buy munitions in the United States and imposed an embargo on Huerta. In April 1914, the U.S. Navy seized Veracruz to keep Huerta from receiving German arms. A series of Constitutionalist victories, culminating in Pancho Villa's capture of the city of Zacatecas, forced Huerta to go into exile in July 1914.[5]

In November 1914, the Aguascalientes convention failed to resolve differences between the Constitutionalist factions.[6] Once Huerta was gone, divisions sharpened between the Constitutionalists about what direction the Revolution should take. In discussions at the Convention, a clear rift emerged between Villistas and Zapatistas, who favored immediate agrarian reform, and Carrancistas who favored a more gradual approach. In December 1914, civil war broke out with Villa and Zapata forming an alliance and Obregón supporting Carranza.

The turning point of this civil war came on April 15 at the battle of Celaya where General Obregón, who had been studying reports from the war in Europe, employed new tactics which defeated Pancho Villa's cavalry with well-placed machine guns, barbed wire, and devastating artillery.[7] By the end of 1915 Carranza controlled most of Mexico, and then served as president until 1920. Carranza did not carry out the promised land and labor reforms. Zapata resisted until he was assassinated in 1919. In 1920, Obregón overthrew Carranza, who was assassinated on May 23. Pancho Villa came to terms with President Obregón, agreeing to stay out of politics in exchange for a large ranch. In Durango, Villa was murdered under mysterious circumstances on July 20, 1923.

Although the Cristero Rebellion, a conservative Catholic revolt against the revolutionary government's anticlerical measures, again rocked Mexico with civil war from 1926 to 1929, the military phase of the Mexican Revolution

---

[5] It is in the battle of Zacatecas that Azuela's protagonist Demetrio Macías distinguishes himself and acquires legendary status. His approach reflects that of Villa, whose northern army was famous for its effective cavalry charges. See Part I, Chapter XXI.

[6] In Part II, Chapter XI, Azuela describes how Cervantes convinces Demetrio to attend the convention at Aguascalientes.

[7] See Part III, Chapter II, where Demetrio and his men learn of Villa's defeat at Celaya.

came to an end with the assassination of Carranza and the rise to power of Álvaro Obregón, the general whose modern tactics had defeated Villa at the battle of Celaya. In Mexican historiography, however, the term *Mexican Revolution* also applies to the political process that has continued to the present day.

The Underdogs in the Context of the Revolution

Despite its fame as the epic novel of the Mexican Revolution, the action of *The Underdogs* is rather limited in terms of space, time, and protagonists. Azuela's novel deserves its reputation as an epic work because it is timeless and archetypal, and yet it is set in a specific region and period of the Revolution.

Geographically all the events of the novel take place in the five states of Jalisco, Aguascalientes, Zacatecas, Durango, and Nayarit. Although some of the towns they pass are not mentioned by name in the novel, it is possible to plot the itinerary of Demetrio and his men on a map with a degree of certainty. Their progress through the cities mentioned (Juchipila, Tepic, Durango, Fresnillo, Zacatecas, Moyahua, Tepatitlán, Cuquío, Lagos de Moreno, Aguascalientes), describes a large circle and a smaller circle (see map, p. xvi). The large circle plotted by Juchipila–Tepic–Durango–Fresnillo–Zacatecas–Moyahua would seem to indicate a triumphant homecoming since Moyahua is the large town near Demetrio's home near Juchipila. At that point, Demetrio is ordered to go to Guadalajara to pursue a band of Orozquistas; however, he makes it only as far as Tepatitlán. They decide to return to their home in the mountains but progress only as far as Cuquío where Demetrio receives orders to participate in the Aguascalientes Convention, traveling via Tepatitlán and Lagos de Moreno. This leg of his campaign describes a small loop. From Aguascalientes Demetrio's band returns to Juchipila, presumably retracing their steps.

Azuela takes some pains to suggest that Demetrio and his men are actually not making progress but going around in circles. That geographic pattern may be of literary significance because the action of the novel itself begins and ends in the same location, the Juchipila Canyon, and most critics have taken the novel's circularity as Azuela's statement about the futility of the Revolution.[8]

ineffectiveness.

---

[8] Azuela also followed part of this itinerary during his campaign as a medical officer with the troops of Julián Medina, witnessing a combat in the Juchipila Canyon. See Stanley Robe's excellent account of Azuela's military service in *Azuela and the Mexican Underdogs* (Berkeley: University of California Press, 1979), especially pp. 55–59.

The novel's time frame is just as clear. Since the closing episodes of the novel take place in the aftermath of the battle of Celaya and the narrator indicates that Demetrio and his wife have not seen each other for almost two years, in chronological terms *The Underdogs* depicts a period between 1913 and 1915. Demetrio's men begin fighting Huerta's troops, the Federales, who are referred to insultingly as *mochos* and *pelones* (allusions to the draftees' short regulation haircuts) and wind up siding with Villa and fighting the Carrancistas whom they call *carranclanes* (a word that sounds a bit like *alacranes,* Spanish for "scorpions").

Throughout the novel Azuela makes allusion to events and leading figures of the Revolution. These references help to contextualize the events depicted in the novel, but they also almost invariably reveal the ignorance and confusion of Demetrio and his men with respect to the historical process in which they are participating. In the following passage, Güero Margarito fantasizes about what he would like to do if he captured General Orozco:

> "If I catch Pascual Orozco alive!" said Güero Margarito, "I'll
> flay the soles of his feet and make him walk the sierra for
> twenty-four hours."
> "That the guy who killed Señor Madero?" asked Meco.
> "No," replied Güero solemnly, "but he slapped my face
> when I was a waiter at Delmonico's in Chihuahua." (p. 62)

The scene reveals Meco's ignorance; it was generally assumed that it was Victoriano Huerta who had Madero shot.[9] It also reveals, besides his characteristic sadism, that Güero Margarito's motivation is not revolutionary but personal.

Likewise Demetrio, who as leader of the band could be expected to be better informed than Meco, says to his assistant Cervantes: "You probably know the story of what happened in Mexico City, where they killed Señor Madero and the other guy, what's his name Félix or Felipe Díaz, what do I know! . . ." (p. 25). Félix Díaz, Porfirio Díaz' nephew, was involved in the coup against Madero; Demetrio is thinking of Pino Suárez, Madero's vice president. Azuela's point is that this revolutionary leader has a hazy notion of the events of the Revolution. In that passage Demetrio is in fact explaining to Cervantes that he became a revolutionary because he was persecuted

---

[9] In Part I, Chapter VI, a Federal soldier, who is obviously better informed than Meco, refers to Huerta as "the murderer" in a conversation with Cervantes.

by Don Mónico, a powerful landowner and political boss. He, like Güero Margarito, has personal reasons for doing what he does.

At two other key moments in the novel, Demetrio reveals his confusion and apathy regarding major revolutionary decisions. Once is when they are on their way to the Convention in Aguascalientes:

> After many hours of riding, he called Luis Cervantes over:
> "Listen, Curro, now that I think of it, what the hell am I supposed to do in Aguascalientes?"
> "General, you are going to vote for the provisional president of the Republic."
> "Provisional president? . . . Well, then, what's Carranza like? . . . Truth is I don't understand these here politics . . ." (p. 71)

The other time is when General Natera, his commander, asks him whether he intends to side with Villa or Carranza:

> "As there's a God in Heaven, *compañero,* the ball keeps rolling! Now it's Villa against Carranza!" said Natera.
> And Demetrio, silent, wide-eyed, awaited further explanation.
> "What I mean," Natera continued, "is that the Convention does not recognize Carranza as *primer jefe* and is going to elect a provisional president of the Republic . . . Understand, *compañero?*"
> Demetrio nodded to indicate that he did.
> "So, what do you say to that, *compañero?*" asked Natera.
> Demetrio shrugged his shoulders.
> "Looks like we're supposed to keep on fighting. So, we'll go at it. You know you can count on me, General."
> "Fine, so who are you with?"
> Demetrio, thoroughly perplexed, raised his hands to his hair and scratched briefly.
> "Look, I'm not a schoolboy so don't ask me questions. . . . You're the one who gave me this little eagle I wear on my hat. . . . So, all you gotta say is: 'Demetrio, do this and that . . . end of story!'"(pp. 75–76)

Demetrio's response is totally consistent with his rudimentary understanding of the Revolution. If in the first instance he joined the uprising because he was being hunted down by Federal troops at the behest of a landowner, now he continues to fight because his commanding officer tells him that

↗ a lack of agency.

"the ball keeps rolling." He joins the Villistas because Natera, the man who made him a general ("gave me this little eagle I wear on my hat") is joining them. Azuela deftly dramatizes the *caudillismo*[10] which vitiated the revolutionary process.

In other cases Azuela introduces necessary information in a credible manner. For instance, Demetrio and his men learn of Villa's defeat at the battle of Celaya when they run into a group of men whom they accuse of being with Carranza:

> "Carrancistas?" one of them answered proudly, "We'd rather be pigs! . . ."
> "It's true, we're deserters," said another, "we quit on my General Villa this side of Celaya, after the whipping they gave us.
> "General Villa, defeated? . . . Ha, ha, ha!"
> The soldiers had a good laugh about that. (p. 79)

The incredulous laughter of Demetrio's troops serves as an indicator of the legend of invincibility that had grown around Villa and his División del Norte.

The Mexican Revolution was the first major war of the twentieth century, and many of the technological advances and horrors of modern warfare were first experienced by Mexican combatants. It was also a war in which old and new tactics clashed. Although some revolutionary units were well equipped, generally it was Huerta's troops, the Federales, who had uniforms and standard modern equipment. In *The Underdogs* we see that Demetrio's band is hardly equipped for the struggle. To encourage them Demetrio recounts the bravery and improvisation of other rebels:

> "God willing," Demetrio said, "tomorrow or even tonight we'll look the Federales in the eyes. We'll show them around, what do you say, *muchachos?*" [. . .] "We don't know how many they are." Demetrio observed, searching their faces. "In Hostotipaquillo, Julián Medina and half a dozen field hands with knives sharpened on their *metates* stood up to all the cops and Federales in the town and kicked them out. . . ." (p. 4)

This appeal to their pride is effective and his men enthusiastically respond to the challenge:

---

[10] *Caudillismo* refers to the tendency to follow the lead of strong men because of personal allegiance rather than political conviction.

"What do Medina's men have that we don't?" said a strong, compact man with thick, black eyebrows and beard and a sweet look in his eyes.

"All I know is," he added, "my name ain't Anastasio Montañés if tomorrow I ain't got a Mauser rifle, a cartridge belt, trousers, and shoes. I mean it! . . . (pp. 4–5)

Through Anastasio's reply Azuela shows that the revolutionaries acquired their equipment from the enemy dead. In their first engagement with the enemy in the Juchipila Canyon, however, there aren't enough weapons for everyone and Demetrio's men have to take turns:

"Anastasio, don't be mean! . . . Gimme your carbine. . . . *Ándale,* just one little shot! . . ."

Manteca, Codorniz and the others who had no weapons pleaded, they begged as a great favor to take just one shot. [. . .] The comrades now shared weapons, picking targets and making hefty bets.

"My leather belt if I don't hit the one on the dark horse on the head. Lend me your rifle, Meco. . . ." (pp. 6–7)

When they assault a town occupied by the Federales, they are still improvising with homemade weapons and banking on the rifles of the enemy dead:

They counted cartridges and the hand grenades that Tecolote had made out of fragments of iron pipes and brass finials.

"Not much," Anastasio observed, "but we're going to swap them for carbines" (p. 31).

When all else fails, Demetrio and his men fall back on hand-to-hand combat. In the same engagement, when they have run out of bombs and left their rifles behind, Cervantes panics but "Demetrio smiles, takes out a knife with a long, shiny blade. Steel flashes instantly in the hands of his twenty soldiers, long and pointed, or wide as the palm of your hand, and many as heavy as machetes" (p. 35). A blood bath, graphically described by Azuela, follows.

Machine guns were one of the major armament innovations in the Mexican Revolution. At the battle of Zacatecas, Solís, a revolutionary officer, describes how they attacked the Federal trenches on a hill and were mown down by machine gun fire. In this instance Demetrio's wild and unexpected cavalry charge up the hill works and his men knife the Federales as "Demetrio was lassoing machine guns, roping them as if they were wild bulls"(p. 43). Historically, however, we know that by the time of the battle of Celaya the boldness and bravery of Villa's cavalry was useless against

Obregón's concerted machine gun crossfire and artillery barrages. War evolved during the course of the Mexican Revolution, and Azuela's novel chronicles that change.

Another innovation recorded by Azuela in this novel is the first use of airplanes in war. Huerta used airplanes to conduct bombing raids against Villa's troops in the north.[11] In a passage in which a revolutionary soldier vaunts the superiority of Villa's División del Norte, Azuela gives a wonderful description of the Villista airplanes in action:

> "Ah, the aeroplanes! Down on the ground, close up, you wouldn't even know what they are; they look like canoes, they look like rafts; but when they start to go up, my friend, it's a racket that will stun you. Then something like an automobile going real fast. And then picture a big bird, real big, which all of a sudden doesn't even seem to budge. And here comes the good part: inside that bird, there's a gringo with thousands of grenades. Just try and picture that! Come fighting time, and it's like you was feeding corn to chickens, there go handfuls and handfuls of lead for the enemy. . . . And you have yourself a cemetery: dead men here, dead men there, and dead men everywhere!" (pp. 41–42)

The effectiveness of Azuela's description lies in his ability to make his readers see the airplane through the eyes of peasants. The similes used by the speaker are taken from the likely frame of reference of rural life. The airplane is first compared to a canoe, then to the only machine most peasants are likely to have seen—an automobile, and finally the bombing itself is compared to feeding chickens.

Subsequently, Anastasio finds out that his interlocutor has never fought alongside Villa's troops and that this is all hearsay. Azuela's irony is not lost on his readers, but airplanes did play a role in the revolutionary campaigns. This passage in which one of Natera's men brags about the exploits of Villa's army to a member of Demetrio's band is an example of how Azuela turns the intimate story of a small group of revolutionaries into what reads like an epic account of the Revolution. Villa and his legendary División del Norte never appear in the pages of the novel except in this account, but the reader's concept of the war is enriched by that account. This economical narrative device makes Azuela's novel, which is actually rather limited in scope, seem panoramic. Likewise, Natera's brief conversation with Demetrio about whether to side with Carranza or Villa stands for the whole Convention of

---

[11] See Meyer and Sherman. *The Course of Mexican History,* p. 525.

Aguascalientes. Azuela is a master of synecdoche and knows how to make a snippet represent the whole. *The Underdogs* achieves its epic effect paradoxically by focusing on a small group of men and following their itinerary.

It is not uncommon to read descriptions of *The Underdogs* as an epic work. As far as covering the scope of events those readings are inaccurate, but they are right in the sense that like all epics it is a foundational work.[12] As the best-known literary work written during and about the Revolution, Azuela's novel has helped to define a watershed moment in the history of modern Mexico in the imagination of the Mexican people and helped in the fashioning of their national identity.

Azuela's main focus in the novel is not trained on the vast historical sweep or ideological intricacies of the Revolution; his deepest interest is in its most humble protagonists. This becomes clear from the moment we read the title he chose for his novel: *Los de abajo: Cuadros y escenas de la revolución actual.* The title of the novel in Spanish, *Los de abajo,* literally means "those below" as opposed to *los de arriba* or "those on top." Hence it bears witness to a consciousness of class that is largely absent from *The Underdogs,* the title used in all translations of this novel. As Anita Brenner pointed out in her 1929 review of the first English translation of *Los de abajo* done by Enrique Munguía:

> Unhappily, the sentimental English version of the Spanish title helps to give . . . [an] erroneous impression. "The Under Dogs" was written as a simple descriptive account of the mass in revolution, a mass then by no means the under dog, but rather the deepest and hottest fire of the volcano to which Azuela's mad poet compares the upheaval.[13]

Brenner is right: whatever they may have been before, by the time we meet them, Demetrio Macías' men are anything but underdogs. They have come from the bottom of society but are now fighting for their interests and they are on the winning side. Demetrio's band is made up of men who have risen up in arms against the injustices they have experienced, not in the abstract but personally.

---

[12] See Carlos Fuentes, "The Barefoot Iliad," and Seymour Menton, "Epic Textures of *Los de abajo,*" in Azuela, *The Underdogs,* trans. Fornoff.

[13] From Anita Brenner, "Blood and Struggle of Mexico Incarnate in *Underdogs* Azuela Etches Scenes Brutally Realistic," Anita Brenner's review of the Munguía translation of *Los de abajo. New York Evening Post,* August 31, 1929. See Related Texts.

The novel's subtitle, *Cuadros y escenas de la revolución actual* (Pictures and Scenes from the Present Revolution), underscores Azuela's desire to eschew a comprehensive panoramic view of the Revolution in favor of a fragmentary approach that will convey an immediacy and lack of historical perspective. Azuela paints portraits and scenes from the Revolution he himself witnessed, but there are no portraits of the famous leaders of the Revolution: Villa, Carranza, Obregón, Zapata.

Many of the leaders of the Revolution whose names appear in history books are mentioned, but they never appear as characters in the pages of the novel. Even in the case of the one historical figure to appear as a character in the novel, Azuela evades description. The only description Azuela gives of Pánfilo Natera, Demetrio's commander, who was actually one of Villa's generals, is: "Natera turned his stern face briefly to the chatterer, and then turning his back on him, began talking to Demetrio" (p. 37). Azuela is clearly not interested in drawing his portrait. By contrast, the novel is full of detailed descriptions of "los de abajo." Their faces, expressions, actions, thoughts, hopes, and fears fill the pages of the novel. In this respect Anita Brenner says of Azuela's novel: "It is almost exactly a parallel in literature of José Clemente Orozco's monumental series of black-and-white scenes of the revolution—dramatic, rapid, passionately realistic."[14]

But *The Underdogs* truly outdoes José Clemente Orozco, David Alfaro Siqueiros, and Diego Rivera in terms of realism. The peasants depicted by the Mexican muralists are airbrushed abstractions in comparison. No Mexican muralist represented revolutionaries with Azuela's disregard for pious stereotypes. Demetrio's men fight bravely and the author makes it clear that right is on their side, but he does not mince words in describing them:

> [Cervantes] observed his guards lying in the manure and snoring. The faces of the two men from the previous evening were revived in his imagination. One of them, Pancracio, was blondish, freckled, had a hairless face, with a jutting chin, a flat sloping forehead, and ears glued to his skull, and was, on the whole, beastlike in his appearance. The other, Manteca, was skin and bones: sunken crossed eyes, with very straight hair falling on his neck, over his forehead and ears, his scrofulous lips eternally half open. (pp. 13–14)

---

[14] Brenner, "Blood and Struggle of Mexico Incarnate in *Underdogs* Azuela Etches Scenes Brutally Realistic." See Related Texts. Here Brenner is not talking about murals but about drawings that are a closer pictorial equivalent of Azuela's prose.

Compare this portrait of two members of Demetrio's band with the idealized representations of peasant revolutionaries that grace the murals commissioned by the revolutionary government.

Azuela's unsentimental, unflinching realism has not always been universally praised. After the rediscovery of the novel in 1924, many critics accused him of being antirevolutionary because of what they considered his unflattering portraits of the revolutionaries. In a lecture he gave in 1945, the novelist had this to say about political interpretations of his novel:

> I owe to my novel *The Underdogs* one of the greatest satisfactions I have enjoyed in my life as a writer. The celebrated French novelist Henri Barbusse, an eminent communist, had it translated and published it in *Monde,* the Paris magazine he directed. *L'Action française,* the organ of the monarchists and the extreme right in France, received my novel with praise. This occurrence is very meaningful for an independent writer and needs no comment.[15]

His fragmentary approach to the depiction of the Revolution and his focus on the deeds and misdeeds of a band of revolutionaries also came under attack, and his reply in that same lecture is biting:

> I have been accused of not having understood the Revolution; of seeing the trees but not the forest. True, I never could glorify scoundrels nor sing the praises of their swindles. I envy those who did see the forest and not the trees, because that perspective is very advantageous economically.[16]

Azuela interprets the phrase "seeing the trees but not the forest" as seeing the faults but not the virtues of the Revolution, and "seeing the forest but not the trees" as ignoring the abuses and benefiting personally from the Revolution. His response, given the context of the corruption of the institutionalized revolutionary government that held power for decades in Mexico, demonstrates that he is indeed an independent writer, unwilling to bend to the official sanitized version of the Revolution. Although its name changed over the years, the Partido Revolucionario Institucional, or PRI (Institutional Revolutionary Party), held power in Mexico from 1929 when Plutarco

---

[15] From a 1945 lecture given by Azuela cited in J. Ruffinelli, "La recepción crítica de *Los de abajo,*" in Mariano Azuela, *Los de abajo,* Edición crítica, coordinador, Jorge Ruffinelli (Colección Archivos, 1988), p.280. The translation of the quotation is mine.

[16] Ibid., p. 294. My translation.

Elías Calles founded the National Revolutionary Party, its first avatar, until 2000 when Vicente Fox, the candidate of the Partido de Acción Nacional, or PAN (National Action Party), won the presidential election. A major theme in the literature about the Mexican Revolution from Azuela to Usigli to Fuentes is how the revolutionaries betrayed the Revolution when they became generals and then politicians.

The Place of *The Underdogs* in Mexican Culture

Few literary works have had as inauspicious a beginning and as resounding and long-lasting an impact as Mariano Azuela's novel *The Underdogs*. Now universally hailed as the most important novel of the Mexican Revolution and a foundational work of modern Mexican and Latin American literature, it drew little attention when it was first published in 1915. Dr. Mariano Azuela, who had served as a medical officer with the revolutionary forces of Jalisco's Julián Medina, had fled the growing chaos of a revolution that had degenerated into a civil war and crossed the border to El Paso, Texas. Among the few assets Azuela brought with him was the unfinished manuscript of a novel he had begun to write during the campaign. In El Paso, Azuela finished the novel and managed to sell it to a publisher for about twenty dollars. It appeared in installments in the newspaper *El Paso del Norte* and was published in book form by the same newspaper in December of 1915, although the date on the title page is 1916.[17] Appearing as it did in a frontier town and amid the turmoil of the Revolution, it is hardly surprising that it scarcely attracted critical attention. Rediscovered in 1924 and touted as an example of the promise of the Mexican novel during a polemic about the sad state of Mexican fiction, it has never been out of print since then.[18]

As a work of literature that depicted and sought to interpret the events of a revolution that was still raging, Azuela's novel has continued to live at the crossroads between history and literature. Viewed as a historical chronicle of the Mexican Revolution, it played a key role among the foundational works of art that contributed to the postrevolutionary redefinition of Mexican identity. *The Underdogs,* and the stream of novels about the Revolution that it inspired, contributed to that construction of a new national identity as

---

[17] See Robe, *Azuela and the Mexican Underdogs*, p. 93.

[18] For the history of the rediscovery of the novel see John E. Englekirk, "The Discovery of *Los de abajo* by Mariano Azuela," *Hispania,* 18 (1935), 53–62. See also Jorge Ruffinelli, "From Unknown Work to Literary Classic," in Azuela, *The Underdogs,* trans. Fornoff. For a detailed history of the different editions of *Los de abajo* see Robe, *Azuela and the Mexican Underdogs.*

much as did the works of the great Mexican muralists Rivera, Orozco, and Siqueiros; José Vasconcelo's *The Cosmic Race* (1925); Rodolfo Usigli's depiction of the betrayal of the Mexican Revolution by its very leaders in his scathing play *The Impostor: A Play for Demagogues* (1944); and Octavio Paz' influential and controversial collection of essays about the Mexican national character, *The Labyrinth of Solitude* (1950). The legacy of *The Underdogs* is in strong evidence in the novels of the subgenre known as the novel of the Mexican Revolution and in major works of contemporary Mexican literature: Juan Rulfo's collection of short stories, *The Burning Plain* (1953), and his novel *Pedro Páramo* (1955); Elena Poniatowska's *Here's to you, Jesusa!* (1969); and Carlos Fuentes' *The Death of Artemio Cruz* (1962) and *Old Gringo* (1985).

Viewed strictly as a work of fiction, *The Underdogs* troubled and dazzled readers with its (for the time) brutally frank depiction of violence, sex, and other human passions. Azuela's clipped, staccato prose, with its frequent use of the present tense and abrupt changes in tenses, disoriented and challenged early readers and has continued to earn the admiration of generations of writers in Mexico and Latin America. None of Azuela's nineteen other novels has gained anywhere near as much attention and admiration as *The Underdogs*.

Literary Considerations

Mariano Azuela's *The Underdogs* is a novel full of bewildering contrasts and contradictions. It is at times brutal and tender, revolting and beautiful, exhilarating and depressing, aestheticist and journalistic, revolutionary and counterrevolutionary. *The Underdogs*, like the Revolution that gave birth to it, is also a novel with one foot in the nineteenth century and another in the twentieth century. These contradictions have kept the novel dynamic and enigmatic even as the centenary of its publication approaches.

Because Azuela was writing *The Underdogs* while serving in the revolutionary army, it literally was born in the midst of the Mexican Revolution, but it was also born in the heyday of *modernismo,* the most important literary movement Latin America had known. Although modernists varied in their approach, many made a cult of beauty and wrote about exotic lands, though typically not their own. They were influenced by European literary movements of the late nineteenth century. In imitation of the writings of the French Parnassians, symbolists, and decadents, many Latin American *modernistas* introduced Greek, Roman, and Germanic mythology into their works, wrote about exotic faraway places, and often set their works in the distant past. They cultivated a prose and poetic style that sought to be musical and stressed the beauty of the words. Two compatriots of Azuela, Manuel Gutiérrez Nájera and Amado Nervo, were among the leading *modernistas*. A characteristic *modernista* trait is the description of nature in terms of jewels. Although it will be clearly apparent to any reader that Azuela is by no stretch of the imagination a *modernista*, some of his descriptions of nature reveal clear aestheticist tendencies. The following are good examples:

> When he reached the summit, the sun was bathing the plateau in a lake of gold. Toward the ravine you could see enormous sliced rocks, promontories that rose like fantastical African heads, *pitahayo* cactus like the fossilized fingers of giants, trees leaning toward the bottom of the abyss. And amid the arid boulders and dry branches, the fresh San Juan roses shone like a white offering to the star whose gold threads were already gliding from rock to rock. (p. 4)

And:

> The landscape grows bright, the sun peers from a scarlet sash over the diaphanous sky.
> Gradually the mountain ranges emerge like monstrous lizards with angular vertebrae; mountains that seem like colossal heads of Aztec idols, like the faces of giants, fearsome and grotesque grimaces, that now make you smile, now fill you with a vague terror, a mysterious foreboding. (p. 54)

Both descriptions owe a debt to *modernismo* but it is interesting that the first one, which occurs earlier in the novel, is closer to that style than the second. The first description enlists a precious metal, the sun "bathes the plateau in a lake of gold" and "the fresh San Juan roses shone like a white offering to the star whose gold threads were already gliding from rock to rock," and exotic elements, rocks "like fantastical African heads," cactus "like the fossilized fingers of giants," to compose this dawn landscape. The second description is more restrained. There is the aestheticist phrase "the sun peers from a scarlet sash over the diaphanous sky" but the mountain ranges that "emerge like monstrous lizards with angular vertebra" and the "mountains that seem like colossal heads of Aztec idols" are at least decidedly Mexican. In the third part of the novel, however, Azuela still resorts to Orientalism to describe a Mexican landscape: "Juchipila appeared in the distance, white and bathed by the sun amid the foliage, at the foot of a high, arrogant mountain, pleated like a turban" (p. 82). *Modernista* influence dies hard.

Nature in *The Underdogs* is represented with great sensitivity and beauty even when the landscape is stark and hostile. For example:

> The men were burning with thirst. Not a puddle, well or a brook with water along the way. A breath of fire rose from the white barren ground of a ravine, throbbed over the curly heads of the *huizaches* and the sea-green leaves of the *nopal* cactus. And, as if to mock them, the cactus flowers were blooming. Some were fresh, succulent and bright, others waxlike and diaphanous. (p. 78)

It will also be noticed from the previous descriptions that personification of the landscape is a frequent feature of Azuela's writing. Furthermore, personification is generally employed to suggest that nature has a hostile intent against Macias' men or at the very least is meant to leave the reader with a sense of foreboding.

These beautifully painted landscapes stand in marked contrast to other descriptions that even today require a strong stomach. It is difficult to imagine the impact of the following passage on a readership accustomed to the exquisite world of *modernista* literature:

> Demetrio raised himself a bit, took a bottle near his head, tipped it back and then filling his cheeks, spat a mouthful far from him.
> "Curro, you really are long-winded!"
> Luis suddenly felt queasy. The sprayed beer seemed to have stirred the fermentation of the trash heap on which they were resting: a carpet of orange and banana peels, fleshy watermelon rinds, fibrous mango pits and chewed sugarcane stalks, all mixed with the chili-stained corn husks from tamales, and all damp from people relieving themselves. (pp. 58–59)

This description is an example of Azuela's gritty realism, which was revolutionary for the Mexican novel at this time; but what purpose does it serve?

At first sight this incident seems to be demonstrating the coarseness and savagery of the peasant versus the sensibility of the middle-class intellectual. Upon closer analysis it becomes clearer whom Azuela considers truly disgusting. Demetrio Macías, the hero of Zacatecas, is seen here comfortably resting on a layer of all the garbage produced by his men. He has just listened to a speech by Luis Cervantes hypocritically justifying looting in the name of the Revolution. As if his aide's hypocrisy had left a bad taste in his mouth, his response is to rinse with beer, spit it out, and call Cervantes "long-winded." It is then Cervantes' turn to be disgusted. Cervantes, who is always ready to give long rousing speeches in which he speaks of the Revolution in abstract terms, becomes squeamish whenever he faces the less appealing consequences of the Revolution: the violence, the cruelty, and the filth. Demetrio on the other hand has the integrity to face up to reality and feels contempt for those like his aide who do not.

The stark juxtaposition of beautifully poetic landscapes and the brutally frank descriptions of the conditions of war endows Azuela's prose with freshness, tension, and realism. That realism, however, rests primarily on the predominance of dialogue in the novel. This is the story of *los de abajo* and Azuela uses their voices to tell it. The accurate representation of the speech patterns of different social classes is one of the major contributions of this novel to Mexican literature. The speech of the characters helps define their personalities but also marks them as to social class and level of education. There is, of course, a great contrast between the speech of educated middle-class characters like Luis Cervantes and Alberto Solís and the peasants, but even among the peasants there is great variety. The one notable exception to Azuela's linguistic realism is that obscenities are totally and unconvincingly absent from the speech of the novel's characters. Whether for reasons of his own prudishness or due to publishing standards in 1915, as in the following dialogue, Azuela employs ellipses wherever the dialogue would call for obscenities:

> "Güero Margarito! My darling Güero! Come defend me from
> these . . . ! Please my sweet Güerito! . . . Come and show them
> you're a real man and they're nothing but a bunch of sons
> of . . . !" (p. 70)

The absence of profanity in the dialogue is particularly remarkable given the author's total frankness in all other regards.

Another aspect of the novel's realism is related to Azuela's other profession as a physician. Diseases, the treatment of wounds, pathological conditions, and in general the facial features of characters are rendered with great clinical attention and care. Scrofulous lips are noted, as are the marks of venereal disease, and a man with a deformed goatlike foot.

As a physician trained in the nineteenth century, Azuela also reveals an interest in physiognomy. According to this nineteenth-century pseudo-science, a person's moral character could be predicted from his physical features. Manteca has "frowning murderer's eyes" and Pancracio has "the repulsively immutable, hard profile, with his projecting jaw" and "flat sloping forehead, and ears glued to his skull," and is "on the whole, beastlike in his appearance." Güero Margarito is described as "a little round man with a handlebar mustache and truly evil blue eyes that disappeared between his cheeks and his forehead when he laughed." When he holds his pistol "for eternal seconds" to a prisoner's chest, Margarito's "eyes shone in a strange way, and his pudgy face, his swollen cheeks, glowed with supreme sensual pleasure." Although Azuela is not rigorously applying physiognomic principles, the descriptions of his most criminal characters do depend on popularized concepts of that pseudoscience.

Related to Azuela's interest in clinical descriptions of his characters' features is his depiction of race in the novel. A major feature of the Revolution and of *The Underdogs* is the prominent role of combatants and leaders with Indian blood. Azuela contributes to the foregrounding of the Indian that takes place in the postrevolutionary culture of Mexico. Although Benito Juárez, a full-blooded Indian, is one of the most famous presidents of Mexico and Porfirio Díaz was a *mestizo,* official Mexican culture, far from drawing attention to Indianness, had done everything possible to relegate it to the background. Azuela's novel is one of the works that begins to change the official attitude toward Mexico's enormous indigenous population. The first time Demetrio is described in the novel, Azuela establishes an iconography that will later be adopted by the Mexican muralists: "Demetrio buckled on the cartridge belt and picked up the rifle. Tall, strong, red-faced, beardless, he wore a white cotton shirt and trousers, a wide-brimmed straw *sombrero* and *huaraches"* (p. 1). Although readers unfamiliar with Mexican culture may not be alert to the details, an absence of facial hair, thick lips (mentioned many times in the novel), and the use of traditional clothing are tokens of Indian blood. The following description, however, is unambiguous about Demetrio's race: "On his chestnut horse, Demetrio felt rejuvenated. His eyes recovered their particular metallic luster, and on his coppery, full-blooded Indian cheeks, the blood flowed again red and hot"(p. 29). The moment is one of euphoria as Demetrio, who has recovered from wounds, and his men set off again to fight the Revolution, and Azuela wants to underscore his Indianness.

A conceit that appears on the first page and runs throughout the novel is the use of animal imagery to describe the characters. The fact that it is used almost exclusively to describe the revolutionaries emphasizes their savagery and bestial instincts. Significantly the novel begins with an incident in which a noise is heard and Demetrio and his wife wonder if it is a human being or an animal.

"It's not an animal. . . . Just hear Palomo bark. . . . It's got to
be a person."
The woman's eyes searched the darkness of the sierra.
"Maybe Federales," answered the man who squatted, eating in
a corner, a clay pot in his right hand and three rolled *tortillas*
in the other. (p. 1)

In this case those at first mistaken for animals indeed turn out to be Federales. The characters described as animals in the novel make up an impres-
sive menagerie including an ant, a scorpion, a bird of prey, a bull, monkeys,
and most often, as in the following two examples, dogs: "women with olive
skin, flashing eyes, and ivory teeth, with revolvers at their waists, cartridge
belts across their chests, and huge palm *sombreros* on their heads, come and
go between the groups like stray dogs" (p. 45) and "Demetrio, who didn't
understand, raised his eyes to her; they faced each other like two strange dogs
sniffing each other warily. Unable to hold the girl's fiercely provocative gaze,
Demetrio lowered his eyes" (p. 46).

This literary device of confusing animals and humans culminates toward
the end of the novel in a passage of great descriptive beauty and biting com-
mentary about human nature. It is a passage that could be taken as a representation of the whole novel in microcosm:

> In the arena, Codorniz and Meco were setting loose two cocks
> with long, extremely sharp spurs. One was dark red, with beau-
> tiful obsidian highlights; the other was gold, with feathers like
> copper scales blazing with fire.
>   The fight was very brief, and in its ferocity it was almost hu-
> man. As if moved by a spring, the roosters leaped on each other.
> Raised feathers on their curving necks, eyes like corals, combs
> erect, their legs tense, for an instant they didn't even touch the
> ground, their plumage, beaks and claws all confused into one;
> the dark-red one broke loose and was thrown, legs up, beyond
> the line. His cinnabar eyes went out, the leathery lids closing
> slowly, and his fluffed feathers trembled convulsively in a pool
> of blood. (pp. 81–82)

The description deftly blends *modernista* sensuousness with Azuela's vibrant,
staccato prose. The graphic violence, as in the novel as whole, is mixed with
beauty. Exotic materials (obsidian, gold, copper, fire, coral, and cinnabar)
are enlisted in the description of the fighting cocks, but the scene ends
with feathers trembling "convulsively in a pool of blood." Here too, as in the
Revolution, beauty and power are wasted. Azuela inverts the commonplace

comparison of humans to animals he employs throughout the novel and finally sets the record straight. These unnatural, trained animals have been
taught to fight like humans: "The fight was very brief, and in its ferocity it
was almost human." This haunting phrase is Doctor Azuela's condemnation
of the worst in human nature.

Azuela's View of the Revolution

Since the publication of *The Underdogs* readers have struggled to understand
and have argued about Azuela's view of the Revolution. The question has
been asked often: does the novel itself put forth a defense of the revolutionary process or is its ultimate message counterrevolutionary? The prominence
of the novel in the culture of postrevolutionary Mexico has meant that both
positions have been heatedly defended. Azuela certainly has furnished sufficient support for either interpretation in his novel.

Writing about Dostoevky's *The Brothers Karamazov,* the Russian theorist
Mikhail Bakhtin explained that most critics had made the mistake of choos-
ing one or another character as the spokesperson for the author. Bakhtin argued instead that it was the chorus of different voices and viewpoints of the
characters that spoke for Dostoevsky.[20] I believe the same is true of Azuela's
The Underdogs.

At different points in the novel, characters speak of their motivation in
joining Madero's uprising against Díaz and then against Madero's assassin,
Huerta. The novel begins by showing us the burning of Demetrio's home by
Federal troops. We later learn, from the account he gives Luis Cervantes, that
the local *cacique* Don Mónico instigated the attack of the Federales for personal reasons. We learn that Anastasio Montañés joins the uprising because
he has murdered someone, Venancio because he accidentally poisoned his
girlfriend with an aphrodisiac, and Güero Margarito seems to find his life as
a Villista officer more to his liking than working as a waiter.

Besides the motivations of *los de abajo,* the novel also presents those of the
two middle-class characters who have joined the Revolution, Luis Cervantes
and Alberto Solís. Luis Cervantes, a former medical student and right-wing
journalist first joins Huerta and then switches sides, driven by his oppor-
tunism. Cervantes, who becomes Demetrio's aide, is cynical, hypocritical,
and cowardly. The end of the novel finds him in El Paso, living off the loot
he captured and practicing medicine. To use Azuela's phrase, he is one of

---

[20] Mikhail Bakhtin, *Problems of Dostoevky's Poetics* (Minneapolis: University of Minnesota
Press, 1984).

those who saw the forest but not the trees and benefited personally from the Revolution. Alberto Solís becomes a revolutionary for idealistic reasons, but by the time he appears in the novel he is thoroughly disillusioned.

There are aspects of Azuela's own revolutionary experience present in both characters. Like Solís, Azuela was an early idealistic supporter of Madero who left his medical practice to join the rebels. The fact that Cervantes studied medicine and seeks refuge in El Paso when the Revolution degenerates into civil war between Villistas and Carrancistas would seem to echo Azuela's own experiences. Neither Solís nor Cervantes, however, speaks for the author. Countless statements by Cervantes contribute to a cynical reading of the Revolution. Two of Solís' speeches form the basis for many pessimistic interpretations of the novel. When Solís first meets Cervantes, he gives vent to his profound disappointment. What he has seen in the Revolution has made Solís lose faith in his compatriots whom he describes as an "unredeemed race." Solís' words are prompted by Cervantes asking him what events brought on his disenchantment:

> "Events? . . . Insignificant matters, mere nothings: gestures that most people don't notice; the sudden life of a line that contracts, of eyes that flash, of closing lips; the fleeting meaning of a phrase that is lost. But they're events, gestures and expressions whose cumulative logic and natural expression also make up the fearsome and grotesque grimace of a race . . . of an unredeemed race! . . ." He drank down another glass of wine, paused for a long time and then continued, "You might ask why I continue with the revolution. The revolution is a hurricane, and the man who gives himself to her is not a man anymore, he is the miserable dry leaf swept by the wind. . . ." (p. 38)

Although Azuela is very conscious of race throughout the novel, by "race" here Solís does not mean Indians versus whites. He is using "race" in its nineteenth-century sense as a synonym for national character. He despairs of the Mexican people.

Later after the battle of Zacatecas, immediately after he has described Demetrio's feat of heroism, and just before he dies from a stray bullet, Solís returns to his analysis of "the psychology of our race":

> "How beautiful the Revolution is even in its savagery!" declared Solís, moved. Then in a low and vaguely melancholic voice:
> "What a shame that what is coming won't be the same. We have to wait a bit. Until there are no more combatants, until the only shots heard are those of the mobs given over to the delights

of looting. Until shining diaphanously, like a drop of water, we can see the psychology of our race condensed in two words: steal, kill! . . . My friend, what a disappointment, if we who offered all our enthusiasm, our very lives to overthrow a miserable assassin, instead turn out to be the builders of an enormous pedestal so that a hundred or two hundred thousand monsters of the same species can raise themselves! . . . A nation without ideals, a nation of tyrants! . . . All that blood spilled, and all in vain!" (pp. 43–44)

Coming, as it does, immediately before Solís is anticlimactically killed by a stray bullet, these words have the force of a last will and testament and have impressed many readers as prophetic.

So where does Mariano Azuela stand on the subject of the Mexican Revolution? The bravery and doggedness of Demetrio Macías and his men are as evident as their bestiality and desire for pillage. The key to understanding Azuela's stance may very well be in the 1945 lecture cited earlier. In France, Barbusse and his communists welcomed and published *The Underdogs* because they must have seen it as a work that advanced the cause of the international struggle of workers. Demetrio himself may fail, but as the novel ends he remains symbolically at his post waiting for those who will come after him to continue the fight. The French monarchists read the same novel and saw a depiction of the ignorance of the revolutionaries, their brutality, venality, and the futility of the bloodshed, concluding that Azuela was a champion of their reactionary cause. Both readings of the novel are valid, and yet both are misreadings because they select part rather than the whole of Azuela's vision.

The ambiguity that makes such divergent readings possible is carefully crafted into the novel. Mariano Azuela was careful to maintain his position as an independent writer who set down the beauty and the savagery of the Mexican Revolution as he himself witnessed it. Azuela's willingness to see and represent the contradictions of the Revolution is probably the main reason *The Underdogs* has continued to challenge and enthrall readers for almost a century.

Recommended Readings

About the Mexican Revolution

Brenner, Anita. *The Wind that Swept Mexico: The History of the Mexican Revolution of 1910–1942.* 184 photographs assembled by George R. Leighton. University of Texas Press, 2003. First published 1943.

Jowett, P. and A. de Quesada. *The Mexican Revolution 1910–20.* Illustrated by Stephen Walsh. Osprey Publishing, Ltd., 2006. [about the uniforms, weapons and military tactics, with many photographs and illustrations.]

Krauze, Enrique. *Mexico: Biography of Power: A History of Modern Mexico 1810–1996.* Chapters 10–14. Harper Collins, 1998.

Meyer, Michael C., William L. Sherman, and Susan M. Deeds, eds. *The Course of Mexican History.* Part VIII, The Revolution: The Military Phase, 1910–1920. Oxford University Press, 2003.

Knight, Alan. *The Mexican Revolution.* Volumes I and II. Cambridge University Press, 1986.

About Azuela's novel

Fuentes, Carlos. "The Barefoot Iliad." In Mariano Azuela, *The Underdogs.* Translated by Frederick H. Fornoff. Pittsburgh: University of Pittsburgh Press, 1992.

Menton, Seymour. "Epic Textures of *Los de abajo.*" In Mariano Azuela, *The Underdogs.* Translated by Frederick H. Fornoff. Pittsburgh: University of Pittsburgh Press, 1992.

Robe, Stanley L. *Azuela and the Mexican Underdogs.* Berkeley: University of California Press, 1979.

Ruffinelli, Jorge. "From Unknown Work to Literary Classic." In Mariano Azuela, *The Underdogs.* Translated by Frederick H. Fornoff. Pittsburgh: University of Pittsburgh Press, 1992.

Glossary

Adelita, La: The most famous ballad of the Mexican revolution, almost its anthem, tells the story of a soldier who is in love with a girl called Adelita.

aguardiente: Brandy.

arribeños: People from the highlands.

Arriba muchachos: Up and at 'em, boys!

arroyo: Brook or the dry bed of a stream.

atole: Warm drink made with corn.

cacique: Political boss, usually a powerful landowner.

cántaro: A large earthenware jug, usually for storing water.

Carranza, Venustiano: Governor of the state of Coahuila who rebelled against Huerta when he overthrew President Madero; president of Mexico, 1915–1920.

Carrancistas: Followers of Carranza.

carranclanes: Pejorative epithet used for the followers of Carranza by their enemies.

Carrera Torres: Alberto Carrera Torres was a revolutionary general.

Celaya: City in the state of Guanajuato where Villa's troops were defeated by Obregón. This defeat guaranteed Carranza's triumph in the civil war that broke out between the revolutionaries after they defeated Huerta's Federales.

champurrao/champurrado: A drink made with corn meal and chocolate.

charro: Mexican cowboy

chomite: Wraparound skirt made of homespun material; of Amerindian origin.

chorizo: A sausage.

Ciudadela: The Citadel, where the uprising against Madero began in 1913.

codorniz: Quail.

cofradía: A religious organization, or sodality.

comadre: *Comadrazgo* is literally the relationship that exists between the godmother and the parents of the child. *Comadre* is also the word used by women who are friends or neighbors to refer to each other.

compadre: *Compadrazgo* is literally the relationship that exists between the godfather and the parents of a child. *Compadre* is often used to mean much the same as "friend," "buddy," "pal."

compañero: Companion, comrade.

curro: Akin to "city slicker."

curruca: Linnet, a bird.

Díaz, Félix: Nephew of Porfirio Díaz who led the rebellion that overthrew Madero.

División del Norte: The Division of the North, Pancho Villa's victorious army.

Don: Title of respect.

Federales: The federal troops under General Victoriano Huerta who fought against the revolutionaries.

gorrudos: The revolutionaries were called *gorrudos* (big hats) because of their large *sombreros.*

güero: Blond.

huaraches: sandals

Huerta: Victoriano Huerta, Madero's commander in chief who joined the rebel forces, overthrew Madero and had him killed.

jacal: An adobe hut with a thatched palm roof.

jacalito: A small *jacal.*

jefe: Chief, boss.

Juanes: Common soldiers in the federal army, from the common first name Juan.

leva: A form of forcible conscription, or draft, employed by Huerta's government.

Madero: Francisco I. Madero, wealthy landowner who started the revolution against Porfirio Díaz and became president of Mexico (1911–1913). He was assassinated when General Huerta seized power.

mano: Short for *hermano,* as in "brother," "buddy," or "pal"; akin to *compadre.*

manteca: Lard.

Mauser: A repeating rifle of German manufacture in common use at the time of the Mexican Revolution.

"Meet your father": This idiomatic expression is rich in pejorative meanings. It suggests that the speaker is your superior, your boss, your master. It also implies that he may be your father, that he has enjoyed your mother and that you are a bastard. It is a hallmark of Mexican *machismo* as defined by Octavio Paz in *The Labyrinth of Solitude.*

mescal: Strong alcoholic beverage similar to *tequila.*

metate: A concave stone used for grinding corn; a corn mill.

mocho/mochito: A religious or political conservative; a term used by insurgents to refer to federal troops.

muchachos: Boys.

Natera: Pánfilo Natera, a revolutionary general active since 1910, who joined the Carrancistas against Huerta in 1913 and took Zacatecas.

Obregón: Álvaro Obregón, a revolutionary general who sided with Carranza against Huerta; president of Mexico, 1920–1924.

Orozco: Pascual Orozco first fought for Madero against Díaz, then rebelled against Madero and was defeated by Victoriano Huerta. At the time of the action of this novel he is leading a band of counterrevolutionaries against Villa's troops.

Orozquistas: Followers of General Orozco.

pacíficos: Name given to those who did not fight in the Revolution.

pelón: Literally, "cropped head," an insulting way to refer to the federal troops who had regulation haircuts.

peón: A field hand.

pintada: Literally, "the painted one."

rancheros: Small farmers, not ranchers.

rebozo: A shawl typically worn by Mexican women.

rurales: Rural police force.

señá: Short for *señora,* as in Señá Remigia.

serranos: People from the sierras, the mountains.

Urbina: General Tomás Urbina, first a Constitutionalist then one of Villa's lieutenants.

Villa: General Francisco Villa, also known as Pancho Villa, born Doroteo Arango. He rebelled against Díaz in support of Madero and then against Huerta when he overthrew Madero. He broke with Carranza and was defeated by Obregón.

Related Texts

Anita Brenner's Review of
The Underdogs

This is Anita Brenner's review of The Under Dogs *translated by E. Munguía, Jr., the first English translation of* Los de abajo *which was published in 1929. Anita Brenner is most known for her panoramic account of the Mexican Revolution,* The Wind that Swept Mexico.

What follows is the complete text of the review.

New York Evening Post, August 31, 1929.
Blood and Struggle of Mexico Incarnate in *Underdogs*
Azuela Etches Scenes Brutally Realistic

The Under Dogs. (Los de Abajo.) By Mariano Azuela. Brentano's.
$3.50 [Translated by E. Munguía, Jr.]

Reviewed by Anita Brenner

For thousands of years Mexico has been a country of artists, of people whose actions are a matter of passion, or a matter of taste; the Spanish-Indian weld has given this national bent new features, but as much today as when Cortez landed on the shores of Vera Cruz, Mexico's contribution to human achievement is artistic. However, that part of the world which concerns itself with such matters has been little aware of the fact and only now is it vaguely beginning to see the unique strength and unique beauty of that contribution.

    Modern Mexico—the new spirit which focuses in art but which pervades all constructive activity—is barely ten years old. The country is in social chaos, and presents an economic, moral and political panorama which shocks many visitors into despair or into a peculiar vicious resentment. Even the friendliest are apologetic. Within this upheaval, and in years whose full tragedy and horror few imaginations have comprehensively grasped, this remarkable people inevitably turns to an artistic crystallization of its pain, and of its desires. Physical violence and cultural power are so intimately linked again that it seems native Mexico has emerged with its ancient philosophy that beauty and life spring from necessary death, as crops grow.

"The Under Dogs" is thus not an isolated masterpiece by an isolated genius. In spirit and content it is at one with contemporary Mexican painting, architecture, sculpture, music. It is almost exactly a parallel in literature of José Clemente Orozco's monumental series of black-and-white scenes of the revolution—dramatic, rapid, passionately realistic. It is a pity that several of those sketches were not used to illustrate "The Under Dogs," for the drawings made specifically for the purpose, though legitimate Orozcos, are hasty echoes of the grand series.

Mariano Azuela, like Orozco, and like most of their great creative Mexican contemporaries, worked and thought in the midst of the turmoil. "Los de Abajo" was born of Azuela's years with a band transformed in the course of Villa's career from twenty sweating and singing outcasts into a flamboyant army banqueting on frijoles and champagne in looted mansions. The last scene was written in a mountain cave overlooking the catastrophic end of this band, as a sketch, to become a last chapter later, when the author was an exile on the other side of the Río Grande.

Full of pain, grief, great compassion; and quivering with life, the story races in rich native idiom from canyon to canyon, more a drama in construction and length than a novel. Each picturesque brutal scene flashes hundreds of similar scenes in the minds of Mexican readers, for of all these extraordinary pictures, there is not one that is extraordinary to any resident during the revolution, nor is any one in the vivid range of common experience omitted. Too rapid a foreign reader, however, will mistake fatigue for futility, and his flogged nerves may not permit him to sense below the carnage an inarticulate text that these men who were killed to no immediate practical purpose and who died in charred crops without realizing that they were part of a great spiritual change were not less heroic because they were not underwritten by idealistic post-revolutionary social dogma.

Other books by Azuela build, like the period in which they are laid, to that conclusion. "Los Caciques," a tragedy in a village preyed upon by profiteers dealing in rotten maize and land values; "Mala Yerba," a pitiful account of complaisant peasants outraged by a family of Spanish immigrants, have each the definite social implication which made the author, a tranquil provincial physician, become an armed revolutionary. Throughout his entire work runs a profound loathing for parasitism, and a special hate of absentee landlordism which makes him directly comparable to some Russian novelists. But Azuela possesses an equally profound national pride which is peculiarly Mexican and is the key of creative revolutionary Mexico. Azuela, Orozco and their contemporaries all accept, embrace and portray the things of which the average literate Mexican heretofore has been ashamed, the things not pretty and yet so dominant that they make their country utterly different from the rest of the Western world. The artistic realism which this pride predetermines and the enormous comprehensive compassion with which it is coupled, produce results which persons whose initial views are dissimilar might easily suppose to be pessimistic or bitterly critical.

Unhappily, the sentimental English version of the Spanish title helps to give that erroneous impression. "The Under Dogs" was written as a simple descriptive account of the mass in revolution, a mass then by no means the under dog, but rather the deepest and hottest fire of the volcano to which Azuela's mad poet compares the upheaval. Perhaps unavoidably, too, the English version [by Munguía] has lost the supple and compact, original rhythm, is at times unduly stiff. To extract clear English from the earthy, etched speech of Azuela required marvels of ingenuity which the translator performed. But it was not necessary to inject quaintness and even crudeness into an originally manly, poised style by rendering literally and awkwardly such phrases as "the ultimate faint rays of the moon," . . . "vultures of prey" . . . Demetrio laid his hand on his hair which covered his head" . . . "His words faithfully interpreted the general opinion" . . . and many others current in Spanish but unusual and confusing in English. However, it was a task for a devotee; and even though "The Under Dogs" is a somewhat adulterated "Los de Abajo," it retains the fierce, splendid integrity which makes it one of the great modern books in the Spanish tongue.

Waldo Frank's Review of Enrique Munguía's Translation of *Los de abajo,* and Anita Brenner's *Idols behind Altars.*

What follows is Waldo Frank's double review of Enrique Munguía's translation of Los de abajo, *and Anita Brenner's* Idols behind Altars.

The New Republic LX October 23, 1929, pp. 275–276.
The Mexican Invasion

The Underdogs (Los de Abajo), by Dr. Mariano Azuela, translated by Enrique Munguía. New York: Brentano's. $2.50

Idols behind Altars, by Anita Brenner, New York: Payson and Clarke. 359 pages. $5.

The country to our south has greater treasures for us than its oil and its gold. It is a land immeasurably rich in human spirit. There is some reason for José Vasconcelos' visionary notion that his nation's chaos should help us create *"la raza cósmica."* For in Mexico, there seems to be all pasts—of fact and of legend. Atlantis, Egypt, China, Africa, Spain and Europe seem to have come together here to create a way of life that is not similar to any past or to any present way in the world. In Mexico there are Indians whose daily crafts precisely carry on the profound arts of cultures buried when Cortés landed; in Mexico, a Communist steeped in Moscow and Paris paints a fresco in the *Palacio Nacional.* Mexico the ancient already possesses a dimension which may be the future. No wonder its people, busied since independence with self-discovery and self-articulation, have proved so listless—perhaps tragically careless—in the exploitation of their oil and ore, and have abandoned these practical tasks to the British, the Americans and the French.

This greater treasure, so distinct from the spirit of Europe that it may indeed create a new world, and so vital that it cannot fail to create one, is now becoming expansive. The mines and the wells lie passive, until the foreigner steals in and claims their booty. But this other kind of wealth does not wait for the stranger. It is getting itself embodied in plastic, in myriad crafts, in word, in music: and it is invading the United States.

Here are two examples in book form of the Mexican invasion. Early examples, for the invasion has scarcely begun. They herald a campaign of esthetic, emotional, intellectual infiltration which should last for centuries, and which may have effect on our American spirit as deep as that which American armies, later American engineers and business men, have had on Mexico. Since our Manifest Destiny first stole an empire from Mexico and added it to the United States, the penetration of our commerce and industry has fatefully proceeded. Mexico lives today within the orbit of our economics; no political force can thrive in Mexico that does not come to terms, tacit or avowed, with American money. This means, of course, that Mexico is very close to us; and will come closer, until the line which separates San Antonio and Los Angeles on the one side from Monterey and Chihuahua on the other grows not less real, but more entirely symbolic. As our money forces go down, cutting their lanes of communication, something from Mexico is beginning to come up. Imperial roads work both ways. Ere now, although built for armies and for commercial caravans, they have carried a Word. Saint Paul traveled the legionary and mercantile routes of Rome; so had the Greeks before him, so did the Patrists a little later. As our oil-inspectors, our banker-diplomats, our salesmen pass along the well traveled road to Mexico, whom will they meet bound north?

Dr. Azuela's novel follows kindred work by the great painter Orozco, who has illustrated this American edition. It is a tale of the Revolution. But the translated title "Underdogs" is a mistake. "Los de Abajo" has a connotation of piety and respect, above all, of potential wonder: it is the term for the humble, in a Catholic language—the humble, from whom salvation is to be expected. The word "Underdogs" lacks this overtone which is the spirit of the story. But the translation on the whole is excellent. It was no easy task to English this luminous, crass, subtle, spring-time Mexican Spanish. Nor is it without significance that the work was done by a Mexican lawyer, Enrique Munguía, attached as advocate to his country's embassy in Washington.

Azuela's book has been called photographic realism: but Homer and Cervantes antedated Daguerre, wherefore I consider the description ill-chosen. His portrayal of the blind whirl of revolution has been called bitterly satiric: it seems to me rather to be merely faithful and humbly clairvoyant. If you look with an intelligent eye at men in business—or at men in civil war—you are likely to judge that they are fools. But if you are an artist, you will find that there is beauty in them. And if you are a great artist, you will find (even if you have never heard of Spinoza and utterly reject the Epistles of

Saint Paul) that they are divine. Doctor Azuela is intelligent, and a great artist. He is a silent man, and his hands and heart are busy all the day, healing the plagues of the lowly. He does not talk about what he saw in the Mexican revolution. Probably, even to himself he is not confiding. But his pages reveal his complete and therefore prophetic vision. He saw the folly of men, and the divinity. His book is significant, because both these qualities are in it; the beauty, the tenderness, the vital splendor, the immaculate life of this Mexico of his tale are important, precisely because these traits reside within and emanate from the cruelty, the sordidness, the filth and desperation of the Mexico he portrays.

Moreover, the book is well joined as a Greek ode. A story of indescribable confusion, it has the body of an inner order—an order not in the least intellectual or studied; an order that is organic. And this, too, is important. The terrible materials of this chaos which Azuela describes are integrally related: seen as a whole, they fall into place, its esthetic form proves that this chaos is on the way to being an organic world: the book depicts the ignorance and horror of the Mexican struggle; but within them, plainly, is wisdom and revelation. You might admit that no man could record so low a story and make it beautiful, who was not a great man. I prefer to insist that no man could have done this who did not belong to a potentially great people.

Miss Brenner's book will be read with full appreciation by those who have already tasted Mexico in such tales as Azuela's, in such music as that of Carlos Chavez, in the cartoons of Posada, in the paintings of Rivera, Angel, Orozco, Lozano, or—best of all—in the crafts of Michoacan and Guadalajara. For "Idols behind Altars" is a remarkable synthesis, in personal form, of all such elements. Americans will find the volume hard to classify. Is it criticism? or history, or an imaginative portrait? Like everything real which comes from Mexico, it is above all, art. Miss Brenner is a Mexican not alone by birth, but as well by choice. Her father, I believe, is an American. She is at home on both shores of the muddy Rio Grande. She has sat familiarly with Gamio, under the falsely named Pyramids of Teotihuacan; but she has sat no less competently in the class-room of Franz Boaz. She is sound in learning, gifted in the use of sharp pictorial language; and she loves the land which she has begun to portray. These are all elements in her nature likely to mislead the conventional American critic, who does not look for beauty in the head of an archeologist, nor for erudition in the eyes of a poet.

Miss Brenner has endeavored to paint a portrait of Mexico. Naturally, her work is not a complete portrayal. But it has lines and colors more revealing of the spirit of that land than any I have found elsewhere in print. To gather

her materials, she needed to be a student: for the secret of so much that moves silent across the Mexican fields in the modern Indian or *meztizo*, lies in the buried idols and the crumbled temples of Maya and Toltec. To integrate her materials, she needed to be a creator. For Mexico is itself unborn: Mexico has not yet converged from her chaos. To make her work live, she needed to be a mystic lover of the land. For Mexico is in hard and miserable confusion: its loveliness is tortured by the circumstance of its envied position in an imperialistic world, tortured so painfully that only a Mexican artist who is something of a prophet can avoid despair.

I feel that, with all these qualifications, Miss Brenner has been remarkably successful. In her pages, you will come to feel the Indian, to know his village; you will understand why peons living in squalor can produce wool work and pottery that equals the archaic Egyptian. You will meet the modern Mexican artist—that amazing cohort whom the great Vasconcelos gathered under Obregon and who, in a few years, put on the walls of official buildings, here in America, a plastic expression possibly unequalled in the Occident since the death of the Goths. Her work suffers stylistically through the fact that the author is too close to Mexico always to write a wholly idiomatic English. But since her book brings very close the mystery and splendor of Mexico, this blemish is easily forgiven.

Waldo Frank.

Insurgent Mexico
by John Reed
First published in 1914

Part Two
FRANCISCO VILLA

CHAPTER ONE: *Villa Accepts a Medal*

It was while Villa was in Chihuahua City, two weeks before the advance on Torreon, that the artillery corps of his army decided to present him with a gold medal for personal heroism on the field. In the audience hall of the Governor's palace in Chihuahua, a place of ceremonial, great luster chandeliers, heavy crimson portières, and gaudy American wallpaper, there is a throne for the governor. It is a gilded chair, with lion's claws for arms, placed upon a dais under a canopy of crimson velvet, surmounted by a heavy, gilded, wooden cap, which tapers up to a crown.

The officers of artillery, in smart blue uniforms faced with black velvet and gold, were solidly banked across one end of the audience hall, with flashing new swords and their gilt-braided hats stiffly held under their arms. From the door of that chamber, around the gallery, down the state staircase, across the grandiose inner court of the palace, and out through the imposing gates to the street, stood a double line of soldiers, with their rifles at present arms. Four regimental bands grouped in one wedged in the crowd. The people of the capital were massed in solid thousands on the Plaza de Armas before the palace.

"*Ya viene!*" "Here he comes!" "Viva Villa!" "Viva Madero!" "Villa, the Friend of the Poor!"

The roar began at the back of the crowd and swept like fire in heavy growing crescendo until it seemed to toss thousands of hats above their heads. The band in the courtyard struck up the Mexican national air, and Villa came walking down the street.

He was dressed in an old plain khaki uniform, with several buttons lacking. He hadn't recently shaved, wore no hat, and his hair had not been brushed. He walked a little pigeon-toed, humped over, with his hands in his trousers pockets. As he entered the aisle between the rigid lines of soldiers he seemed slightly embarrassed, and grinned and nodded to a *compadre* here and there in the ranks. At the foot of the grand staircase, Governor Chao and Secretary of State Terrazzas joined him in full-dress uniform. The band threw off all restraint, and, as Villa entered the audience chamber, at a signal from someone in the balcony of the palace, the great throng in the Plaza de Armas uncovered, and all the brilliant crowd of officers in the room saluted stiffly.

It was Napoleonic!

Villa hesitated for a minute, pulling his mustache and looking very uncomfortable, finally gravitated toward the throne, which he tested by shaking the arms, and then sat down, with the Governor on his right and the Secretary of State on his left.

Señor Bauche Alcalde stepped forward, raised his right hand to the exact position which Cicero took when denouncing Catiline, and pronounced a short discourse, indicting Villa for personal bravery on the field on six counts, which he mentioned in florid detail. He was followed by the Chief of Artillery, who said: "The army adores you. We will follow you wherever you lead. You can be what you desire in Mexico." Then three other officers spoke in the high-flung, extravagant periods necessary to Mexican oratory. They called him "The Friend of the Poor," "The Invincible General," "The Inspirer of Courage and Patriotism," "The Hope of the Indian Republic." And through it all Villa slouched on the throne, his mouth hanging open, his little shrewd eyes playing around the room. Once or twice he yawned, but for the most part he seemed to be speculating, with some intense interior amusement, like a small boy in church, what it was all about. He knew, of course, that it was the proper thing, and perhaps felt a slight vanity that all this conventional ceremonial was addressed to him. But it bored him just the same.

Finally, with an impressive gesture, Colonel Servin stepped forward with the small pasteboard box which held the medal. General Chao nudged Villa, who stood up. The officers applauded violently; the crowd outside cheered; the band in the court burst into a triumphant march.

Villa put out both hands eagerly, like a child for a new toy. He could hardly wait to open the box and see what was inside. An expectant hush fell upon everyone, even the crowd in the square. Villa looked at the medal, scratching his head, and, in a reverent silence, said clearly: "This is a hell of a little thing to give a man for all that heroism you are talking about!" And the bubble of Empire was pricked then and there with a great shout of laughter.

They waited for him to speak—to make a conventional address of acceptance. But as he looked around the room at those brilliant, educated men, who said that they would die for Villa, the peon, and meant it, and as he caught sight through the door of the ragged soldiers, who had forgotten their rigidity and were crowding eagerly into the corridor with eyes fixed eagerly on the *compañero* that they loved, he realized something of what the Revolution signified.

Puckering up his face, as he did always when he concentrated intensely, he leaned across the table in front of him and poured out, in a voice so low that people could hardly hear: "There is no word to speak. All I can say is my heart is all to you." Then he nudged Chao and sat down, spitting violently on the floor; and Chao pronounced the classic discourse.

CHAPTER TWO: *The Rise of a Bandit*

Villa was an outlaw for twenty-two years. When he was only a boy of sixteen, delivering milk in the streets of Chihuahua, he killed a government official and had to take to the mountains. The story is that the official had violated his sister, but it seems probable that Villa killed him on account of his insufferable insolence. That in itself would not have outlawed him long in Mexico, where human life is cheap; but once a refugee he committed the unpardonable crime of stealing cattle from the rich *hacendados*. And from that time to the outbreak of the Madero revolution the Mexican government had a price on his head.

Villa was the son of ignorant peons. He had never been to school. He hadn't the slightest conception of the complexity of civilization, and when he finally came back to it, a mature man of extraordinary native shrewdness, he encountered the twentieth century with the naïve simplicity of a savage.

It is almost impossible to procure accurate information about his career as a bandit. There are accounts of outrages he committed in old files of local newspapers and government reports, but those sources are prejudiced, and his name became so prominent as a bandit that every train robbery and hold-up and murder in northern Mexico was attributed to Villa. But an immense body of popular legend grew up among the peons around his name. There are many traditional songs and ballads celebrating his exploits—you can hear the shepherds singing them around their fires in the mountains at night, repeating verses handed down by their fathers or composing others extemporaneously. For instance, they tell the story of how Villa, fired by the story of the misery of the peons on the Hacienda of Los Alamos, gathered a small army and descended upon the Big House, which he looted, and distributed the spoils among the poor people. He drove off thousands of cattle from the Terrazzas [Terrazas] range and ran them across the border. He would suddenly descend upon a prosperous mine and seize the bullion. When he needed corn he captured a granary belonging to some rich man. He recruited almost openly in the villages far removed from the well-traveled roads and railways, organizing the outlaws of the mountains. Many of the present rebel soldiers used to belong to his band and several of the Constitutionalist generals, like Urbina. His range was confined mostly to southern Chihuahua and northern Durango, but it extended from Coahuila right across the Republic to the State of Sinaloa.

His reckless and romantic bravery is the subject of countless poems. They tell, for example, how one of his band named Reza was captured by the rurales and bribed to betray Villa. Villa heard of it and sent word into the city of Chihuahua that he was coming for Reza. In broad daylight he entered the city on horseback, took ice cream on the Plaza—the ballad is very explicit on this point—and rode up and down the streets until he found Reza strolling with his sweetheart in the Sunday crowd on the Paseo Bolivar, where he shot him and escaped. In time of famine he fed whole districts, and took care of entire villages evicted by the soldiers under Porfirio Diaz's outrageous land law. Everywhere he was known as The Friend of the Poor. He was the Mexican Robin Hood.

In all these years he learned to trust nobody. Often in his secret journeys across the country with one faithful companion he camped in some desolate spot and dismissed his guide; then, leaving a fire burning, he rode all night to get away from the faithful companion. That is how Villa learned the art of war, and in the field to-day, when the army comes into camp at night, Villa flings the bridle of his horse to an orderly, takes a serape over his shoulder, and sets out for the hills alone. He never seems to sleep. In the dead of night he will appear somewhere along the line of outposts to see if the sentries are on the job; and in the morning he returns from a totally different direction. No one, not even the most trusted officer of his staff, knows the least of his plans until he is ready for action.

When Madero took the field in 1910, Villa was still an outlaw. Perhaps, as his enemies say, he saw a chance to whitewash himself; perhaps, as seems probable, he was inspired by the Revolution of the peons. Anyway, about three months after they rose in arms, Villa suddenly appeared in El Paso and put himself, his band, his knowledge of the country and all his fortune at the command of Madero. The vast wealth that people said he must have accumulated during his twenty years of robbery turned out to be 363 silver *pesos,* badly worn. Villa became a Captain in the Maderista army, and as such went to Mexico City with Madero and was made honorary general of the new *rurales*. He was attached to Huerta's army when it was sent north to put down the Orozco Revolution. Villa commanded the garrison of Parral, and defeated Orozco with an inferior force in the only decisive battle of the war.

Huerta put Villa in command of the advance, and let him and the veterans of Madero's army do the dangerous and dirty work while the old line Federal regiments lay back under the protection of their artillery. In Jimenez Huerta suddenly summoned Villa before a court-martial and charged him with insubordination—claiming to have wired an order to Villa in Parral, which order Villa said he never received. The court-martial lasted fifteen minutes, and Huerta's most powerful future antagonist was sentenced to be shot.

Alfonso Madero, who was on Huerta's staff, stayed the execution, but President Madero, forced to back up the orders of his commander in the field, imprisoned Villa in the Penitentiary of the capital. During all this time Villa never wavered in his loyalty to Madero—an unheard-of thing in Mexican history. For a long time he had passionately wanted an education. Now he wasted no time in regrets or political intrigue. He set himself with all his force to learn to read and write. Villa hadn't the slightest foundation to work upon. He spoke the crude Spanish of the very poor—what is called *pelado*. He knew nothing of the rudiments or philosophy of language; and he started out to learn those first, because he always must know the *why* of things. In nine months he could write a very fair hand and read the newspapers. It is interesting now to see him read, or, rather, hear him, for he has to drone the words aloud like a small child. Finally, the Madero government connived at his escape from prison, either to save Huerta's face because Villa's friends had demanded an investigation, or because Madero was convinced of his innocence and didn't dare openly to release him.

From that time to the outbreak of the last revolution, Villa lived in El Paso, Texas, and it was from there that he set out, in April, 1913, to conquer Mexico with four companions, three led horses, two pounds of sugar and coffee, and a pound of salt.

There is a little story connected with that. He hadn't money enough to buy horses, nor had any of his companions. But he sent two of them to a local livery stable to rent riding horses every day for a week. They always paid carefully at the end of the ride, so when they asked for eight horses the livery stable man had no hesitation about trusting them with them. Six months later, when Villa came triumphantly into Juarez at the head of an army of four thousand men, the first public act he committed was to send a man with double the price of the horses to the owner of the livery stable.

He recruited in the mountains near San Andres, and so great was his popularity that within one month he had raised an army of three thousand men;

in two months he had driven the Federal garrisons all over the State of Chihuahua back into Chihuahua City; in six months he had taken Torreon; and in seven and a half Juarez had fallen to him, Mercado's Federal army had evacuated Chihuahua, and Northern Mexico was almost free.

CHAPTER THREE: *A Peon in Politics*

Villa proclaimed himself military governor of the State of Chihuahua, and began the extraordinary experiment—extraordinary because he knew nothing about it—of creating a government for 300,000 people out of his head.

It has often been said that Villa succeeded because he had educated advisers. As a matter of fact, he was almost alone. What advisers he had spent most of their time answering his eager questions and doing what he told them. I used sometimes to go to the Governor's palace early in the morning and wait for him in the Governor's chamber. About eight o'clock Sylvestre Terrazzas, the Secretary of State, Sebastian Vargas, the State Treasurer, and Manuel Chao, then Interventor, would arrive, very bustling and busy, with huge piles of reports, suggestions and decrees which they had drawn up. Villa himself came in about eight-thirty, threw himself into a chair, and made them read out loud to him. Every minute he would interject a remark, correction or suggestion. Occasionally he waved his finger back and forward and said: *"No sirve."* When they were all through he began rapidly and without a halt to outline the policy of the State of Chihuahua, legislative, financial, judicial, and even educational. When he came to a place that bothered him, he said: "How do they do that?" And then, after it was carefully explained to him: "Why?" Most of the acts and usages of government seemed to him extraordinarily unnecessary and snarled up. For example, his advisers proposed to finance the Revolution by issuing State bonds bearing 30 or 40 per cent interest. He said, "I can understand why the State should pay something to people for the rent of their money, but how is it just to pay the whole sum back to them three or four times over?" He couldn't see why rich men should be granted huge tracts of land and poor men should not. The whole complex structure of civilization was new to him. You had to be a philosopher to explain anything to Villa; and his advisers were only practical men.

There was the financial question. It came to Villa in this way. He noticed, all of a sudden, that there was no money in circulation. The farmers who produced meat and vegetables refused to come into the city markets any more because no one had any money to buy from them. The truth was that those possessing silver or Mexican bank-notes buried them in the ground. Chihuahua not being a manufacturing center, and the few factories there having closed down, there was nothing which could be exchanged for food. So, like a blight, the paralysis of the production of food began all at once and actual starvation stared at the town populations. I remember hearing vaguely of several highly elaborate plans for the relief of this condition put forth by Villa's advisers. He himself said: "Why, if all they need is money, let's print some." So they inked up the printing press in the basement of the Governor's palace and ran off two million pesos on strong paper, stamped with the signatures of government officials, and with Villa's name printed across the middle in large letters. The counterfeit money, which afterward flooded El Paso, was distinguished from the original by the fact that the names of the officials were signed instead of stamped.

This first issue of currency was guaranteed by absolutely nothing but the name of Francisco Villa. It was issued chiefly to revive the petty internal commerce of the State so that the poor people could get food. And yet almost immediately it was bought by the banks of El Paso at 18 to 19 cents on the dollar because Villa guaranteed it.

Of course he knew nothing of the accepted ways of getting his money into circulation. He began to pay the army with it. On Christmas Day he called the poor people of Chihuahua together and gave them $15 a piece outright. Then he issued a short decree, ordering the acceptance of his money at par throughout the State. The succeeding Saturday the marketplaces of Chihuahua and the other nearby towns swarmed with farmers and with buyers. Villa issued another proclamation, fixing the price of beef at seven cents a pound, milk at five cents a quart, and bread at four cents a loaf. There was no famine in Chihuahua. But the big merchants, who had timidly reopened their stores for the first time since his entry into Chihuahua, placarded their goods with two sets of price marks—one for Mexican silver money and bank-bills, and the other for 'Villa money.' He stopped that by another decree, ordering sixty days' imprisonment for anybody who discriminated against his currency.

But still the silver and bank-bills refused to come out of the ground, and these Villa needed to buy arms and supplies for his army. So he simply proclaimed to the people that after the tenth of February Mexican silver and bank-bills would be regarded as counterfeit, and that before that time they could be exchanged for his own money at par in the State Treasury. But the large sums of the rich still eluded him. Most of the financiers declared that it was all a bluff, and held on. But lo! on the morning of February tenth, a decree was pasted up on the walls all over Chihuahua City, announcing that from that time on all Mexican silver and bank-notes were counterfeit and could not be exchanged for Villa money in the Treasury, and anyone attempting to pass them was liable to sixty days in the penitentiary. A great howl went up, not only from the capitalists, but from the shrewd misers of distant villages.

About two weeks after the issue of this decree, I was taking lunch with Villa in the house which he had confiscated from Manuel Gomeros and used as his official residence. A delegation of three peons in sandals arrived from a village in the Tarahumare to protest against the Counterfeit Decree.

"But, *mi General,*" said the spokesman, "we did not hear of the decree until to-day. We have been using bank-bills and silver in our village. We had not seen your money, and we did not know. . . ."

"You have a good deal of money?" interrupted Villa suddenly.

"Yes, *mi General.*"

"Three or four or five thousand, perhaps?"

"More than that, *mi General.*"

"Señores," Villa squinted at them ferociously, "samples of my money reached your village within twenty-four hours after it was issued. You decided that my government would not last. You dug holes under your fireplaces and put the silver and bank-notes there. You knew of my first proclamation a day after it was posted up in the streets of Chihuahua, and you ignored it. The Counterfeit Decree you also knew as soon as it was issued. You thought there was always time to change if it became necessary. And then you got frightened, and you three, who have more money than anyone else in the village, got on your mules and rode down here. Señores, your money is counterfeit. You are poor men!"

"*Valgame dios!*" cried the oldest of the three, sweating profusely.

"But we are ruined, *mi General!*—I swear to you—We did not know—We would have accepted—There is no food in the village—"

The General in Chief meditated for a moment.

"I will give you one more chance," he said, "not for you, but for the poor people of your village who can buy nothing. Next Wednesday at noon bring all your money, every cent of it, to the Treasury, and I will see what can be done."

To the perspiring financiers who waited hat in hand out in the hall, the news spread by word of mouth; and Wednesday at high noon one could not pass the Treasury door for the eager mob gathered there.

Villa's great passion was schools. He believed that land for the people and schools would settle every question of civilization. Schools were an obsession with him. Often I have heard him say: "When I passed such and such a street this morning I saw a lot of kids. Let's put a school there." Chihuahua has a population of under 40,000 people. At different times Villa established over fifty schools there. The great dream of his life has been to send his son

to school in the United States, but at the opening of the term in February
he had to abandon it because he didn't have money enough to pay for a half
year's tuition.

No sooner had he taken over the government of Chihuahua than he put
his army to work running the electric light plant, the street railways, the telephone, the water works and the Terrazzas flour mill. He delegated soldiers
to administer the great haciendas which he had confiscated. He manned the
slaughterhouse with soldiers and sold Terrazza's beef to the people for the
government. A thousand of them he put in the streets of the city as civil police, prohibiting on pain of death stealing, or the sale of liquor to the army.
A soldier who got drunk was shot. He even tried to run the brewery with
soldiers, but failed because he couldn't find an expert maltster. "The only
thing to do with soldiers in time of peace," said Villa, "is to put them to
work. An idle soldier is always thinking of war."

In the matter of the political enemies of the Revolution he was just as simple, just as effective. Two hours after he entered the Governor's palace the
foreign consuls came in a body to ask his protection for 200 Federal soldiers
who had been left as a police force at the request of the foreigners. Before
answering them, Villa said suddenly: "Which is the Spanish consul?" Scobell, the British vice-consul, said: "I represent the Spaniards." "All right!"
snapped Villa. "Tell them to begin to pack. Any Spaniard caught within the
boundaries of this State after five days will be escorted to the nearest wall by
a firing squad."

The consuls gave a gasp of horror. Scobell began a violent protest, but
Villa cut him short.

"This is not a sudden determination on my part," he said; "I have been
thinking about this since 1910. The Spaniards must go."

Letcher, the American consul, said: "General, I don't question your mo-
tives, but I think you are making a grave political mistake in expelling the
Spaniards. The government at Washington will hesitate a long time before
becoming friendly to a party which makes use of such barbarous measures."

"Señor Consul," answered Villa, "we Mexicans have had three hundred
years of the Spaniards. They have not changed in character since the *Con-
quistadores*. They disrupted the Indian empire and enslaved the people. We
did not ask them to mingle their blood with ours. Twice we drove them out
of Mexico and allowed them to return with the same rights as Mexicans, and
they used these rights to steal away our land, to make the people slaves, and
to take up arms against the cause of liberty. They supported Porfirio Diaz.
They were perniciously active in politics. It was the Spaniards who framed
the plot that put Huerta in the palace. When Madero was murdered the

Spaniards in every State in the Republic held banquets of rejoicing. They thrust on us the greatest superstition the world has ever known—the Catholic Church. They ought to be killed for that alone. I consider we are being very generous with them."

Scobell insisted vehemently that five days was too short a time, that he couldn't possibly reach all the Spaniards in the State by that time; so Villa extended the time to ten days.

The rich Mexicans who had oppressed the people and opposed the Revolution, he expelled promptly from the State and confiscated their vast holdings. By a simple stroke of the pen the 17,000,000 acres and innumerable business enterprises of the Terrazzas family became the property of the Constitutionalist government, as well as the great lands of the Creel family and the magnificent palaces which were their town houses. Remembering, however, how the Terrazzas exiles had once financed the Orozco Revolution, he imprisoned Don Luis Terrazzas, Jr., as a hostage in his own house in Chihuahua. Some particularly obnoxious political enemies were promptly executed in the penitentiary. The Revolution possesses a black book in which are set down the names, offenses, and property of those who have oppressed and robbed the people. The Germans, who had been particularly active politically, the Englishmen and Americans, he does not yet dare to molest. Their pages in the black book will be opened when the Constitutionalist government is established in Mexico City; and there, too, he will settle the account of the Mexican people with the Catholic Church.

Villa knew that the reserve of the Banco Minero, amounting to about $500,000 gold, was hidden somewhere in Chihuahua. Don Luis Terrazzas, Jr., was a director of that bank. When he refused to divulge the hiding-place of the money, Villa and a squad of soldiers took him out of his house one night, rode him on a mule out into the desert, and strung him up to a tree by the neck. He was cut down just in time to save his life, and led Villa to an old forge in the Terrazzas iron works, under which was discovered the reserve of the Banco Minero. Terrazzas went back to his prison badly shaken, and Villa sent word to his father in El Paso that he would release the son upon payment of $500,000 ransom.

CHAPTER FOUR: *The Human Side*

Villa has two wives, one a patient, simple woman who was with him during all his years of outlawry, who lives in El Paso, and the other a cat-like, slender young girl, who is the mistress of his house in Chihuahua. He is perfectly open about it, though lately the educated, conventional Mexicans who have been gathering about him in ever-increasing numbers have tried to hush up the fact. Among the peons it is not only not unusual but customary to have more than one mate.

One hears a great many stories of Villa's violating women. I asked him if that were true. He pulled his mustache and stared at me for a minute with an inscrutable expression. "I never take the trouble to deny such stories," he said. "They say I am a bandit, too. Well, you know my history. But tell me; have you ever met a husband, father or brother of any woman that I have violated?" He paused: "Or even a witness?"

It is fascinating to watch him discover new ideas. Remember that he is absolutely ignorant of the troubles and confusions and readjustments of modern civilization. "Socialism," he said once, when I wanted to know what he thought of it: "Socialism—is it a thing? I only see it in books, and I do not read much." Once I asked him if women would vote in the new Republic. He was sprawled out on his bed, with his coat unbuttoned. "Why, I don't think so," he said, startled, suddenly sitting up. "What do you mean—vote? Do you mean elect a government and make laws?" I said I did and that women already were doing it in the United States. "Well," he said, scratching his head: "if they do it up there I don't see that they shouldn't do it down here." The idea seemed to amuse him enormously. He rolled it over and over in his mind, looking at me and away again. "It may be as you say," he said; "but I have never thought about it. Women seem to me to be things to protect, to love. They have no sternness of mind. They can't consider anything for its right or wrong. They are full of pity and softness. Why," he said, "a woman would not give an order to execute a traitor."

"I am not so sure of that, *mi General,*" I said. "Women can be crueler and harder than men."

He stared at me, pulling his mustache. And then he began to grin. He looked slowly to where his wife was setting the table for lunch. *"Oiga,"* he said, "come here. Listen. Last night I caught three traitors crossing the river to blow up the railroad. What shall I do with them? Shall I shoot them or not?"

Embarrassed, she seized his hand and kissed it. "Oh, I don't know anything about that," she said. "You know best."

"No," said Villa. "I leave it entirely to you. Those men were going to try to cut our communications between Juarez and Chihuahua. They were traitors—Federals. What shall I do? Shall I shoot them or not?"

"Oh, well, shoot them," said Mrs. Villa.

Villa chuckled delightedly. "There is something in what you say," he re-marked, and for days afterward went around asking the cook and the cham-bermaids whom they would like to have for President of Mexico.

He never missed a bull-fight, and every afternoon at four o'clock he was to be found at the cock-pit, where he fought his own birds with the happy enthusiasm of a small boy. In the evening he played faro in some gambling hall. Sometimes in the late morning he would send a fast courier after Luis Leon, the bull-fighter, and telephone personally to the slaughter-house, ask-ing if they had any fierce bulls in the pen. They almost always did have, and we would all get on horseback and gallop through the streets about a mile to the big adobe corrals. Twenty cowboys cut the bull out of the herd, threw and tied him and cut off his sharp horns, and then Villa and Luis Leon and anybody else who wanted would take the professional red capes and go down into the ring; Luis Leon with professional caution, Villa as stubborn and clumsy as the bull, slow on his feet, but swift as an animal with his body and arms. Villa would walk right up to the pawing, infuriated animal, and, with his double cape, slap him insolently across the face, and, for a half hour, would follow the greatest sport I ever saw. Sometimes the sawed-off horns of the bull would catch Villa in the seat of the trousers and propel him vio-lently across the ring; then he would turn and grab the bull by the head and wrestle with him with the sweat streaming down his face until five or six *com-pañeros* seized the bull's tail and hauled him plowing and bellowing back.

Villa never drinks nor smokes, but he will outdance the most ardent *novio* in Mexico. When the order was given for the army to advance upon Torreon, Villa stopped off at Camargo to be best man at the wedding of one of his old *compadres*. He danced steadily without stopping, they said, all Monday night, all Tuesday, and all Tuesday night, arriving at the front on Wednes-day morning with blood-shot eyes and an air of extreme lassitude.

CHAPTER FIVE: *The Funeral of Abram Gonzales*

The fact that Villa hates useless pomp and ceremony makes it more impres-sive when he does appear on a public occasion. He has the knack of ab-solutely expressing the strong feeling of the great mass of the people. In February, exactly one year after Abram Gonzales was murdered by the Fed-erals at Bahimba Cañon, Villa ordered a great funeral ceremony to be held in the City of Chihuahua. Two trains, carrying the officers of the army, the consuls and representatives of the foreign colony, left Chihuahua early in the morning to take up the body of the dead Governor from its resting-place under a rude wooden cross in the desert. Villa ordered Major Fierro, his

Superintendent of Railroads, to get the trains ready—but Fierro got drunk and forgot; and when Villa and his brilliant staff arrived at the railway station the next morning the regular passenger train to Juarez was just leaving and there was no other equipment on hand. Villa himself leaped on to the already moving engine and compelled the engineer to back the train up to the station. Then he walked through the train, ordering the passengers out, and switched it in the direction of Bachimba. They had no sooner started than he summoned Fierro before him and discharged him from the superintendency of the railroads, appointing Calzado in his place, and ordered the latter to return at once to Chihuahua and be thoroughly informed about the railroads by the time he returned. At Bachimba Villa stood silently by the grave with the tears rolling down his cheeks. For Gonzales had been his close friend. Ten thousand people stood in the heat and dust at Chihuahua railway station when the funeral train arrived, and poured weeping through the narrow streets behind the army, at the head of which walked Villa beside the hearse. His automobile was waiting, but he angrily refused to ride, stumbling stubbornly along in the dirt of the streets with his eyes on the ground.

That night there was a *velada* in the Theater of the Heroes, an immense auditorium packed with emotional peons and their women. The ring of boxes was brilliant with officers in their full dress, and wedged behind them up the five high balconies were the ragged poor. Now, the *velada* is an entirely Mexican institution. First there comes a speech, then a "recitation" on the piano, then a speech, followed by a patriotic song rendered by a chorus of awkward little Indian girls from the public school with squeaky voices, another speech, and a soprano solo from "Trovatore" by the wife of some government official, still another speech, and so on for at least five hours. Whenever there is a prominent funeral, or a national holiday, or a President's anniversary, or, in fact, an occasion of the least importance, a *velada* must be held. It is the conventional and respectable way of celebrating anything. Villa sat in the left hand stage box and controlled the proceedings by tapping a little bell. The stage itself was brilliantly hideous with black bunting, huge masses of artificial flowers, abominable crayon portraits of Madero, Piño Suarez and the dead Governor, and red, white and green electric lights. At the foot of all this was a very small, plain, black wooden box which held the body of Abram Gonzales.

The *velada* proceeded in an orderly and exhausting manner for about two hours. Local orators, trembling with stage fright, mouthed the customary Castilian extravagant phrases, and little girls stepped on their own feet and murdered Tosti's "Good-bye." Villa, with his eyes riveted on that wooden box, never moved nor spoke. At the proper time he mechanically tapped the little bell, but after a while he couldn't stand it any longer. A large fleshy Mexican was in the middle of Handel's "Largo" on the grand piano, when Villa stood erect. He put his foot on the railing of the box and leaped to the stage, knelt, and took up the coffin in his arms. Handel's "Largo" petered out. Silent astonishment paralyzed the audience. Holding the black box tenderly in his arms as a mother with her baby, not looking at anyone, Villa started down the steps of the stage and up the aisle. Instinctively, the house rose; and as he passed out through the swinging doors they followed on silently behind him. He strode down between the lines of waiting soldiers, his sword banging on the floor, across the dark square to the Governor's palace; and, with his own hands, put the coffin on the flower-banked table waiting for it in the audience hall. It had been arranged that four generals in turn should stand the death watch, each for two hours. Candles shed a dim light over the table and the surrounding floor, but the rest of the room was in darkness. A dense mass of silent, breathing people packed the doorway. Villa unbuckled his sword and threw it clattering into a corner. Then he took his rifle from the table and stood first watch.

CHAPTER SIX: *Villa and Carranza*

It seems incredible to those who don't know him, that this remarkable figure, who has risen from obscurity to the most prominent position in Mexico in three years, should not covet the Presidency of the Republic. But that is in entire accordance with the simplicity of his character. When asked about it he answered as always with perfect directness, just in the way that you put it to him. He didn't quibble over whether he could or could not be President of Mexico. He said: "I am a fighter, not a statesman. I am not educated enough to be President. I only learned to read and write two years ago. How could I, who never went to school, hope to be able to talk with the foreign ambassadors and the cultivated gentlemen of the Congress? It would be bad for Mexico if an uneducated man were to be President. There is one thing that I will not do,—and that is to take a position for which I am not fitted. There is only one order of my Jefe (Carranza) which I would refuse to obey,—if he would command me to be a President or a Governor." On behalf of my paper I had to ask him this question five or six times. Finally he became exasperated. "I have told you many times," he said, "that there is no possibility of my becoming President of Mexico. Are the newspapers trying to make trouble between me and my Jefe? This is the last time that I will answer that question. The next correspondent that asks me I will have him spanked and sent to the border." For days afterward he went around grumbling humorously about the *chatito* (pugnose) who kept asking him whether he wanted to be President of Mexico. The idea seemed to amuse him. Whenever I went to see him after that he used to say, at the end of our talk: "Well, aren't you going to ask me to-day whether I want to be President?"

He never referred to Carranza except as "my Jefe," and he obeyed implicitly the slightest order from "the First Chief of the Revolution." His loyalty to Carranza was perfectly obstinate. He seemed to think that in Carranza were embodied the entire ideals of the Revolution. This, in spite of the fact that many of his advisers tried to make him see that Carranza was essentially an aristocrat and a reformer, and that the people were fighting for more than reform.

Carranza's political program, as set forth in the plan of Guadelupe, carefully avoids any promise of settlement of the land question, except a vague endorsement of Madero's plan of San Luis Potosi, and it is evident that he does not intend to advocate any radical restoration of the land to the people until he becomes provisional president—and then to proceed very cautiously. In the meantime he seems to have left it to Villa's judgment, as well as all other details of the conduct of the Revolution in the north. But Villa, being a peon, and feeling with them, rather than consciously reasoning it out, that the land question is the real cause of the Revolution, acted with characteristic promptness and directness. No sooner had he settled the details of government of Chihuahua State, and appointed Chao his provisional governor, than he issued a proclamation, giving sixty-two and one-half acres out of the confiscated lands to every male citizen of the State, and declaring these lands inalienable for any cause for a period of ten years. In the State of Durango the same thing has happened and as other states are free of Federal garrisons, he will pursue the same policy.

CHAPTER SEVEN: *The Rules of War*

On the field, too, Villa had to invent an entirely original method of warfare, because he never had a chance to learn anything of accepted military strategy. In that he is without the possibility of any doubt the greatest leader Mexico has ever had. His method of fighting is astonishingly like Napoleon's. Secrecy, quickness of movement, the adaptation of his plans to the character of the country and of his soldiers,—the value of intimate relations with the rank and file, and of building up a tradition among the enemy that his army is invincible, and that he himself bears a charmed life,—these are his characteristics. He knew nothing of accepted European standards of strategy or of discipline. One of the troubles of the Mexican federal army is that its officers are thoroughly saturated with conventional military theory. The Mexican soldier is still mentally at the end of the eighteenth century. He is, above all, a loose, individual, guerrilla fighter. Red-tape simply paralyzes the machine. When Villa's army goes into battle he is not hampered by salutes, or rigid respect for officers, or trigonometrical calculations of the trajectories of projectiles, or theories of the percentage of hits in a thousand rounds of rifle fire, or the function of cavalry, infantry and artillery in any particular position, or rigid obedience to the secret knowledge of its superiors. It reminds one of the ragged Republican army that Napoleon led into Italy. It is probable that Villa doesn't know much about those things himself. But he does know that guerrilla fighters cannot be driven blindly in platoons around the field in perfect step, that men fighting individually and of their own free will are braver than long volleying rows in the trenches, lashed to it by officers with the flat of their swords. And where the fighting is fiercest—when a ragged mob of fierce brown men with hand bombs and rifles rush the bullet-swept streets of an ambushed town—Villa is among them, like any common soldier.

Up to his day, Mexican armies had always carried with them hundreds of the women and children of the soldiers; Villa was the first man to think of swift forced marches of bodies of cavalry, leaving their women behind. Up to his time no Mexican army had ever abandoned its base; it had always stuck closely to the railroad and the supply trains. But Villa struck terror into the enemy by abandoning his trains and throwing his entire effective army upon the field, as he did at Gomez Palacio. He invented in Mexico that most demoralizing form of battle—the night attack. When, after the fall of Torreon last September, he withdrew his entire army in the face of Orozco's advance from Mexico City and for five days unsuccessfully attacked Chihuahua, it was a terrible shock to the Federal General when he waked up one morning and found that Villa had sneaked around the city under cover of darkness, captured a freight train at Terrazzas [Terrazas] and descended with his entire army upon the comparatively undefended city of Juarez. It wasn't fair! Villa found that he hadn't enough trains to carry all his soldiers, even when he had ambushed and captured a Federal troop train, sent south by General Castro, the Federal commander in Juarez. So he telegraphed that gentleman as follows, signing the name of the Colonel in command of the troop train: "Engine broken down at Moctezuma. Send another engine and five cars." The unsuspecting Castro immediately dispatched a new train.

Villa then telegraphed him: "Wires cut between here and Chihuahua. Large force of rebels approaching from south. What shall I do?" Castro replied: "Return at once." And Villa obeyed, telegraphing cheering messages at every station along the way. The Federal commander got wind of his coming about an hour before he arrived, and left, without informing his garrison, so that, outside of a small massacre, Villa took Juarez almost without a shot. And with the border so near he managed to smuggle across enough ammunition to equip his almost armless forces and a week later sallied out and routed the pursuing Federal forces with great slaughter at Tierra Blanca.

General Hugh L. Scott, in command of the American troops at Fort Bliss, sent Villa a little pamphlet containing the Rules of War adopted by the Hague Conference. He spent hours poring over it. It interested and amused him hugely. He said: "What is this Hague Conference? Was there a representative of Mexico there? Was there a representative of the Constitutionalists there? It seems to me a funny thing to make rules about war. It's not a game. What is the difference between civilized war and any other kind of war? If you and I are having a fight in a *cantina* we are not going to pull a little book out of our pockets and read over the rules. It says here that you must not use lead bullets; but I don't see why not. They do the work."

For a long time afterward he went around popping questions at his officers like this: "If an invading army takes a city of the enemy, what must you do with the women and children?"

As far as I could see, the Rules of War didn't make any difference in Villa's original method of fighting. The *colorados* he executed wherever he captured them; because, he said, they were peons like the Revolutionists and that no peon would volunteer against the cause of liberty unless they were bad. The Federal officers also he killed, because, he explained, they were educated men and ought to know better. But the Federal common soldiers he set at liberty because most of them were conscripts, and thought that they were fighting for the Patria. There is no case on record where he wantonly killed a man. Anyone who did so he promptly executed—except Fierro.

Fierro, the man who killed Benton, was known as "The Butcher" throughout the army. He was a great handsome animal, and the best and cruellest rider and fighter, perhaps, in all the revolutionary forces. In his furious lust for blood Fierro used to shoot down a hundred prisoners with his own revolver, only stopping long enough to reload. He killed for the pure joy of it. During two weeks that I was in Chihuahua, Fierro killed fifteen inoffensive citizens in cold blood. But there was always a curious relationship between him and Villa. He was Villa's best friend; and Villa loved him like a son and always pardoned him.

But Villa, although he had never heard of the Rules of War, carried with his army the only field hospital of any effectiveness that any Mexican army has ever carried. It consisted of forty box-cars enameled inside, fitted with operating tables and all the latest appliances of surgery, and manned by more than sixty doctors and nurses. Every day during the battle shuttle trains full of the desperately wounded ran from the front to the base hospitals at Parral, Jimenez and Chihuahua. He took care of the Federal wounded just as carefully as of his own men. Ahead of his own supply train went another train, carrying two thousand sacks of flour, and also coffee, corn, sugar, and cigarettes to feed the entire starving population of the country around Durango City and Torreon.

The common soldiers adore him for his bravery and his coarse, blunt humor. Often I have seen him slouched on his cot in the little red caboose in which he always traveled, cracking jokes familiarly with twenty ragged privates sprawled on the floor, chairs and tables. When the army was entraining or detraining, Villa personally would be on hand in a dirty old suit, without a collar, kicking mules in the stomach and pushing horses in and out of the stock-cars. Getting thirsty all of a sudden, he would grab some soldier's canteen and drain it, in spite of the indignant protests of its owner; and then tell him to go over to the river and say that Pancho Villa said that he should fill it there.

CHAPTER EIGHT: *The Dream of Pancho Villa*

It might not be uninteresting to know the passionate dream—the vision which animates this ignorant fighter, "not educated enough to be President of Mexico." He told it to me once in these words: "When the new Republic is established there will never be any more army in Mexico. Armies are the greatest support of tyranny. There can be no dictator without an army.

"We will put the army to work. In all parts of the Republic we will establish military colonies composed of the veterans of the Revolution. The State will give them grants of agricultural lands and establish big industrial enterprises to give them work. Three days a week they will work and work hard, because honest work is more important than fighting, and only honest work makes good citizens. And the other three days they will receive military instruction and go out and teach all the people how to fight. Then, when the Patria is invaded, we will just have to telephone from the palace at

Mexico City, and in half a day all the Mexican people will rise from their fields and factories, fully armed, equipped and organized to defend their children and their homes.

"My ambition is to live my life in one of those military colonies among my *compañeros* whom I love, who have suffered so long and so deeply with me. I think I would like the government to establish a leather factory there where we could make good saddles and bridles, because I know how to do that; and the rest of the time I would like to work on my little farm, raising cattle and corn. It would be fine, I think, to help make Mexico a happy place."

Part Four
A PEOPLE IN ARMS

CHAPTER THREE: *First Blood*

The water train pulled out first. I rode on the cow-catcher of the engine, which was already occupied by the permanent home of two women and five children. They had built a little fire of mesquite twigs on the narrow iron platform, and were baking *tortillas* there; over their heads, against the windy roar of the boiler, fluttered a little line of wash. . . .

It was a brilliant day, hot sunshine alternating with big white clouds. In two thick columns, one on each side of the train, the army was already moving south. As far as the eye could reach, a mighty double cloud of dust floated over them; and little straggling groups of mounted men jogged along, with every now and then a big Mexican flag. Between slowly moved the trains; the pillars of black smoke from their engines, at regular intervals, growing smaller, until over the northern horizon only a dirty mist appeared.

I went down into the caboose to get a drink of water, and there I found the conductor of the train lying in his bunk reading the Bible. He was so interested and amused that he didn't notice me for a minute. When he did he cried delightedly: "*Oiga,* I have found a great story about a chap called Samson who was *muy hombre*—a good deal of a man—and his woman. She was a Spaniard, I guess, from the mean trick she played on him. He started out being a good Revolutionist, a Maderista, and she made him a *pelon!*"

Pelon means literally "cropped head," and is the slang term for a Federal soldier, because the Federal army is largely recruited from the prisons.

Our advance guard, with a telegraph field operator, had gone on to Conejos the night before, and they met the train in great excitement. The first blood of the campaign had been spilt; a few *colorados* scouting northward from Bermejillo had been surprised and killed just behind the shoulder of the big mountain which lies to the east. The telegrapher also had news. He had again tapped the Federal wire, and sent to the Federal commander in Torreon, signing the dead Captain's name and asking for orders, since a large force of rebels seemed to be approaching from the north. General Velasco replied that the Captain should hold Conejos and throw out outposts to the north, to try and discover how large the force was. At the same time the telegrapher had heard a message from Argumedo, in command at Mapimi, saying that the entire north of Mexico was coming down on Torreon, together with the Gringo army!

Conejos was just like Yermo, except that there was no water tank. A thousand men, with white-bearded old General Rosalio Hernandez riding ahead, went out almost at once, and the repair train followed them a few miles to a place where the Federals had burned two railroad bridges a few months before. Out beyond the last little bivouac of the immense army spread around us, the desert slept silently in the heat waves. There was no wind. The men gathered with their women on the flat-cars, guitars came out, and all night hundreds of singing voices came from the trains.

The next morning I went to see Villa in his car. This was a red caboose with chintz curtains on the windows, the famous little caboose which Villa has used in all his journeys since the fall of Juarez. It was divided by partitions into two rooms—the kitchen and the General's bedroom. This tiny room, ten by twenty feet, was the heart of the Constitutionalist army. There were held all the councils of war, and there was scarcely room enough for the fifteen Generals who met there. In these councils the vital immediate questions of the campaign were discussed, the Generals decided what was to be done,—and then Villa gave his order to suit himself. It was painted a dirty gray. On the walls were tacked photographs of showy ladies in theatrical poses, a large picture of Carranza, one of Fierro, and a picture of Villa himself. Two double-width wooden bunks folded up against the wall, in one of which Villa and General Angeles slept, and in the other José Rodriguez and Doctor Raschbaum, Villa's personal physician. That was all. . . .

"*Que desea, amigo?* What do you want?" said Villa, sitting on the end of the bunk in blue underclothes. The troopers who lounged around the place lazily made way for me.

"I want a horse, *mi General.*"

"*Ca-r-r-r-ai-i [Caray],* our friend here wants a horse!" grinned Villa sarcastically amid a burst of laughter from the others. "Why, you correspondents will be wanting an automobile next! *Oiga,* señor reporter, do you know that about a thousand men in my army have no horses? Here's the train. What do you want a horse for?"

"So I can ride with the advance."

"No," he smiled. "There are too many *balassos [balazos]*—too many bullets flying in the advance. . . ."

He was hurrying into his clothes as he talked, and gulping coffee from the side of a dirty tin coffee-pot. Somebody handed him his gold-handled sword.

"No!" he said contemptuously. "This is to be a fight, not a parade. Give me my rifle!"

He stood at the door of his caboose for a moment, thoughtfully looking at the long lines of mounted men, picturesque in their crossed cartridge-belts and varied equipment. Then he gave a few quick orders and mounted his big stallion.

"*Vamonos!*" cried Villa. The bugles brayed and a subdued silver clicking ringing sounded as the companies wheeled and trotted southward in the dust. . . .

And so the army disappeared. During the day we thought we heard cannonading from the southwest, where Urbina was reported to be coming down from the mountains to attack Mapimi. And late in the afternoon news came of the capture of Bermejillo, and a courier from Benavides said that he had taken Tlahualilo.

We were in a fever of impatience to be off. About sundown Señor Calzado remarked that the repair train would leave in an hour, so I grabbed a blanket and walked a mile up the line of trains to it.

CHAPTER FOUR: *On the Cannon-Car*

The first car of the repair train was a steel-encased flat car, upon which was mounted the famous Constitutionalist cannon "El Niño," with an open caisson full of shells behind it. Behind that was an armored car full of soldiers, then a car of steel rails, and four loaded with railroad ties. The engine came next, the engineer and fireman hung with cartridge-belts, their rifles handy. Then followed two or three box-cars full of soldiers and their women. It was a dangerous business. A large force of Federals were known to be in Mapimi, and the country swarmed with their outposts. Our army was already far ahead, except for five hundred men who guarded the trains at Conejos. If the enemy could capture or wreck the repair train the army would be cut off without water, food or ammunition. In the darkness we moved out. I sat upon the breech of "El Niño," chatting with Captain Diaz, the commander of the gun, as he oiled the breech lock of his beloved cannon and curled his vertical mustachios. In the armored recess behind the gun, where the Captain slept, I heard a curious, subdued rustling noise.

"What's that?'

"Eh?" cried he nervously. "Oh, nothing, nothing!"

Just then there emerged a young Indian girl with a bottle in her hand. She couldn't have been more than seventeen, very lovely. The Captain shot a glance at me, and suddenly whirled around.

"What are you doing here?" he cried furiously to her. "Why are you coming out here?"

"I thought you said you wanted a drink," she began.

I perceived that I was one too many, and excused myself. They hardly noticed me. But as I was climbing over the back of the car I couldn't help stopping and listening. They had gone back to the recess, and she was weeping.

"Didn't I tell you," stormed the Captain, "not to show yourself when there are strangers here? I will not have every man in Mexico looking at you. . . ."

I stood on the roof of the rocking steel car as we nosed slowly along. Lying on their bellies on the extreme front platform, two men with lanterns examined each foot of the track for wires that might mean mines planted under us. Beneath my feet the soldiers and their women were having dinner around fires built on the floor. Smoke and laughter poured out of the loopholes. . . . There were other fires aft, brown-faced, ragged people squatting at them, on the car-tops. Overhead the sky blazed stars, without a cloud. It was cold. After an hour of riding we came to a piece of broken track. The train stopped with a jar, the engine whistled, and a score of torches and lanterns jerked past. Men came running. The flares clustered bobbing together as the foremen examined the damage. A fire sprang up in the brush, and then another. Soldiers of the train guard straggled by, dragging their rifles, and formed impenetrable walls around the fires. Iron tools clanged, and the "Wai-hoy!" of men shoving rails off the flat-car. A Chinese dragon of workmen passed with a rail on their shoulders, then others with ties. Four hundred men swarmed upon the broken spot, working with extraordinary energy and good humor, until the shouts of gangs setting rails and ties, and the rattle of sledges on spikes, make a continuous roar. It was an old destruction, probably a year old, made when these same Constitutionalists were retreating north in the face of Mercado's Federal army, and we had it all fixed in an hour. Then on again. Sometimes it was a bridge burned out, sometimes a hundred yards of track twisted into grape vines by a chain and a backing engine. We advanced slowly. At one big bridge that it would take two hours to prepare, I built by myself a little fire in order to get warm. Calzado came past, and hailed me. "We've got a hand-car up ahead," he said, "and we're going along down and see the dead men. Want to come?"

"What dead men?"

"Why, this morning an outpost of eighty *rurales* was sent scouting north from Bermejillo. We heard about it over the wire and informed Benavides on the left. He sent a troop to take them in the rear, and drove them north in a running fight for fifteen miles until they smashed up against our main body and not one got out alive. They're scattered along the whole way just where they fell."

In a moment we were speeding south on the hand-car. At our right hand and our left rode two silent, shadowy figures on horseback—cavalry guards, with rifles ready under their arms. Soon the flares and fires of the train were left behind, and we were enveloped and smothered in the vast silence of the desert.

"Yes," said Calzado, "the *rurales* are brave. They are *muy hombres. Rurales* are the best fighters Diaz and Huerta ever had. They never desert to the Revolution. They always remain loyal to the established government. Because they are police."

It was bitter cold. None of us talked much.

"We go ahead of the train at night," said the soldier at my left, "so that if there are any dynamite bombs underneath——"

"We could discover them and dig them out and put water in them, *carramba! [caramba!]*" said another sarcastically. The rest laughed. I began to think of that, and it made me shiver. The dead silence of the desert seemed an expectant hush. One couldn't see ten feet from the track.

"*Oiga!*" shouted one of the horsemen. "It was just here that one lay." The brakes ground and we tumbled off and down the steep embankment, our lanterns jerking ahead. Something lay huddled around the foot of a telegraph pole—something infinitely small and shabby, like a pile of old clothes. The *rurale [rural]* was upon his back, twisted sideways from his hips. He had been stripped of everything of value by the thrifty rebels—shoes, hat, underclothing. They had left him his ragged jacket with the tarnished silver braid, because there were seven bullet holes in it; and his trousers, soaked with blood. He had evidently been much bigger alive—the dead shrink so. A wild red beard made the pallor of his face grotesque, until you noticed that under it and the dirt, and the long lines of sweat of his terrible fight and hard riding, his mouth was gently and serenely open as if he slept. His brains had been blown out.

"*Carrai! [Caray!]*" said one guard. "There was a shot for the dirty goat! Right through the head!"

The others laughed. "Why, you don't think they shot him there in the fight, do you, *pendeco? [pendejo]*" cried his companion. "No, they *always* go around and make sure afterward——"

"Hurry up! I've found the other," shouted a voice off in the darkness.

We could reconstruct this man's last struggle. He had dropped off his horse, wounded—for there was blood on the ground—into a little dry arroyo. We could even see where his horse had stood while he pumped shells into his Mauser with feverish hands, and blazed away, first to the rear, where the pursuers came running with Indian yells, and then at the hundreds and hundreds of bloodthirsty horsemen pouring down from the north, with the Demon Pancho Villa at their head. He must have fought a long time, perhaps until they ringed him round with living flame—for we found hundreds of empty cartridges. And then, when the last shot was spent, he made a dash eastward, hit at every step; hid for a moment under the little railroad bridge, and ran out upon the open desert, where he fell. There were twenty bullet holes in him. They had stripped him of all save his underclothes. He lay sprawled in an attitude of desperate action, muscles tense, one fist clenched and spread across the dust as if he were dealing a blow; the fiercest exultant grin on his face. Strong, savage, until one looked closer and saw the subtle touch of weakness that death stamps on life—the delicate expression of idiocy over it all. They had shot him through the head three times—how exasperated they must have been!

Crawling south through the cold night once more. . . . A few miles and then a bridge dynamited, or a strip of track wrecked. The stop, the dancing torches, the great bonfires leaping up from the desert, and the four hundred wild men pouring furiously out and falling upon their work. . . . Villa had given orders to hurry. . . .

About two o'clock in the morning I came upon two *soldaderas* squatting around a fire, and asked them if they could give me *tortillas* and coffee. One was an old, gray-haired Indian woman with a perpetual grin, the other a slight girl not more than twenty years old, who was nursing a four-months baby at her breast. They were perched at the extreme tip of a flat-car, their fire built upon a pile of sand, as the train jolted and swayed along. Around them, backed against them, feet sticking out between them, was a great, inconglomerate mass of sleeping, snoring humans. The rest of the train was by this time dark; this was the only patch of light and warmth in the night. As I munched my *tortilla* and the old woman lifted a burning coal in her fingers to light her corn-husk cigarette, wondering where her Pablo's brigade was this night; and the girl nursed her child, crooning to it, her blue-enameled earrings twinkling,—we talked.

"Ah! it is a life for us *viejas*," said the girl. "*Adio [Ay, Dios]*, but we follow our men out in the campaign, and then do not know from hour to hour whether they live or die. I remember well when Filadelfo called to me one morning in the little morning before it was light—we lived in Pachuca—and said: 'Come! we are going out to fight because the good Pancho Madero has been murdered this day!' We had only been loving each other eight months, too, and the first baby was not born. . . . We had all believed that peace was in Mexico for good. Filadelfo saddled the burro, and we rode out through the streets just as light was coming, and into the fields where the farmers were not yet at work. And I said: 'Why must I come?' And he answered: 'Shall I starve, then? Who shall make my *tortillas* for me but my woman?' It took us three months to get north, and I was sick and the baby was born in a desert just like this place, and died there because we could not get water. That was when Villa was going north after he had taken Torreon."

The old woman broke in: "Yes, and all that is true. When we go so far and suffer so much for our men, we are cruelly treated by the stupid animals of Generals. I am from San Luis Potosi, and my man was in the artillery of the Federacion when Mercado came north. All the way to Chihuahua we traveled, the old fool of a Mercado grumbling about transporting the *viejas*. And then he ordered his army to go north and attack Villa in Juarez, and he forbade the women to go. Is that the way you are going to do, *desgraciado?* I said to myself. And when he evacuated Chihuahua and ran away with my man to Ojinaga, I just stayed right in Chihuahua and got a man in the Maderista army when it came in. A nice handsome young fellow, too,—much better than Juan. I'm not a woman to stand being put upon."

"How much are the *tortillas* and coffee?" I asked.

They looked at each other, startled. Evidently they had thought me one of the penniless soldiers crowded on the train.

"What you would like," said the young woman faintly. I gave them a peso.

The old woman exploded in a torrent of prayer. "God, his sainted Mother, the Blessed Niño and Our Lady of Guadelupe have sent this stranger to us tonight! Here we had not a centavo to buy coffee and flour with. . . ."

I suddenly noticed that the light of our fire had paled, and looked up in amazement to find it was dawn. Just then a man came running along the train from up front, shouting something unintelligible, while laughter and shouts burst out in his wake. The sleepers raised their curious heads and wanted to know what was the matter. In a moment our inanimate car was alive. The man passed, still yelling something about "*padre*," his face exultant with some tremendous joke.

"What is it?" I asked.

"Oh!" cried the old woman. "His woman on the car ahead has just had a baby!"

Just in front of us lay Bermejillo, its pink and blue and white plastered adobe houses as delicate and ethereal as a village of porcelain. To the east, across a still, dustless desert, a little file of sharp-cut horsemen, with a red-white-and-green flag over them, were riding into town. . . .

Part Five
CARRANZA—AN IMPRESSION

When the Treaty of Peace was signed in Juarez which ended the Revolution of 1910, Francisco Madero proceeded south toward Mexico City. Everywhere he spoke to enthusiastic and triumphant throngs of peons, who acclaimed him The Liberator.

In Chihuahua he addressed the people from the balcony of the Governor's palace. As he told of the hardships endured and the sacrifices made by the little band of men who had overthrown the dictatorship of Diaz forever, he was overcome with emotion. Reaching inside the room he pulled out a tall, bearded man of commanding presence, and, throwing his arm about his shoulder, he said, in a voice choked with tears:

"This is a good man! Love and honor him always."

It was Venustiano Carranza, a man of upright life and high ideals; an aristocrat, descended from the dominant Spanish race; a great land-owner, as his family had always been great land-owners; and one of those Mexican nobles who, like a few French nobles such as Lafayette in the French Revolution, threw themselves heart and soul into the struggle for liberty. When the Madero Revolution broke out Carranza took the field in truly medieval fashion. He armed the peons who worked upon his great estates, and led them to war like any feudal overlord; and, when the Revolution was done, Madero made him Governor of Coahuila.

There he was when Madero was murdered at the Capital, and Huerta, seizing the Presidency, sent a circular letter to the Governors of the different States, ordering them to acknowledge the new dictatorship. Carranza refused even to answer the letter, declaring that he would have no dealings with a murderer and a usurper. He issued a proclamation calling the Mexican people to arms, proclaiming himself First Chief of the Revolution, and inviting the friends of liberty to rally around him. Then he marched out from his capital and took the field, where he assisted in the early fighting around Torreon.

After a short time Carranza marched his force from Coahuila, where things were happening, straight across the Republic into the State of Sonora, where nothing was happening. Villa had begun heavy fighting in Chihuahua State, Urbina and Herrera in Durango, Blanco and others in Coahuila, and Gonzales near Tampico. In times of upheaval like these it is inevitable that there shall be some preliminary squabbling over the ultimate spoils of war. Among the military leaders, however, there was no such dissension; Villa having just been unanimously elected General Chief of the Constitutionalist Army by a remarkable gathering of all the independent guerrilla leaders before Torreon,—an unheard-of event in Mexican history. But over in Sonora, Maytorena and Pesquiera were already squabbling over who should be Governor of the State, and threatening revolutions against each other. Carranza's reported purpose in crossing to the West with his army was to settle this dispute. But that doesn't seem possible.

Other explanations are that he desired to secure a seaport for the Constitutionalists on the West; that he wanted to settle the Yaqui land question; and that in the quiet of a comparatively peaceful State he could better organize the provisional government of the new Republic. He remained there six months, apparently doing nothing whatever, keeping a force of more than 6,000 good fighters practically inoperative, attending banquets and bull-fights, establishing and celebrating innumerable new national holidays, and issuing proclamations. His army, twice or three times as big as the disheartened garrisons of Guaymas and Mazatlan, kept up a lazy siege of those places. Mazatlan fell only a short time ago, I think; as did Guaymas. Only a few weeks ago Provisional-Governor Maytorena was threatening counter-revolutions against General Alvardo, Chief of Arms of Sonora, because he would not guarantee the Governor's safety, and evidently proposing to upset the Revolution because Maytorena was uncomfortable in the palace at Hermosillo. During all that time not a word was said about any aspect of the land question, as far as I could learn. The Yaqui Indians, the expropriation of whose lands is the blackest spot in the whole black history of the Diaz régime, got nothing but a vague promise. Upon that the whole tribe joined the Revolution. But a few months later most of them went back to their homes and began again their hopeless campaign against the white man.

Carranza hibernated until early in the spring of this year, when, the purpose of his Sonora sojourn evidently having been accomplished, he turned his face toward the territory where the real Revolution was being fought.

Within that six months the aspect of things had entirely changed. Except for the northern part of Nueva Leon, and most of Coahuila, northern Mexico was Constitutionalist territory almost from sea to sea, and Villa, with a well-armed, well-disciplined force of 10,000 men, was entering on the Torreon campaign. All this was accomplished almost single-handed by Villa; Carranza seems to have contributed nothing but congratulations. He had, indeed, formed a provisional government. An immense throng of opportunist politicians surrounded the First Chief, loud in their protestations of devotion to the Cause, liberal with proclamations, and extremely jealous of each other and of Villa. Little by little Carranza's personality seemed to be engulfed in the personality of his Cabinet, although his name remained as prominent as ever.

It was a curious situation. Correspondents who were with him during these months have told me how secluded the First Chief finally became. They almost never saw him. Very rarely did they speak with him. Various secretaries, officials, Cabinet members, stood between them and him— polite, diplomatic, devious gentlemen, who transmitted their questions to Carranza on paper and brought them back his answers written out, so that there would be no mistake.

But, whatever he did, Carranza left Villa strictly alone, to undergo defeats if he must, or make mistakes: so much so that Villa himself was forced to deal with foreign powers as if he were the head of the government.

There is no doubt that the politicians at Hermosillo sought in every way to make Carranza jealous of Villa's growing power in the north. In February the First Chief began a leisurely journey northward, accompanied by 3,000 troops, with the ostensible object of sending reinforcements to Villa and of making his provisional capital in Juarez when Villa left for Torreon. Two correspondents, however, who had been in Sonora, told me that the officers of this immense bodyguard believed that they were to be sent against Villa himself.

In Hermosillo Carranza had been remote from the world's news centers. No one knew but what he might be accomplishing great things. But when the First Chief of the Revolution began to move toward the American border, the attention of the world was concentrated upon him; and the attention of the world revealed so little to concentrate upon, that rumors rapidly spread of the non-existence of Carranza; for example, one paper said that he was insane, and another alleged that he had disappeared altogether.

I was in Chihuahua at the time. My paper wired me these rumors and ordered me to go and find Carranza. It was at the immensely exciting time of the Benton murder. All the protestations and half-veiled threats of the British and American governments converged upon Villa. But by the time I had received the message Carranza and his Cabinet had arrived at the Border and broken the six months' silence in a startling way. The First Chief's declaration to the State Department was practically this:

"You have made a mistake in addressing representations in the Benton case to General Villa. They should be addressed to me as First Chief of the Revolution and head of the Provisional Constitutionalist Government. Moreover, the United States has no business to address, even to me, any representations concerning Benton, who was a British subject. I have received no envoy from the government of Great Britain. Until I do I will make no answer to the representations of any other government. Meanwhile, a thorough investigation will be made of the circumstances of Benton's death, and those responsible for it will be judged strictly according to law."

At the same time Villa received a pretty plain intimation that he was to keep out of international affairs, and Villa gratefully shut up.

That was the situation when I went to Nogales. Nogales, Arizona, and Nogales, Sonora, Mexico, really form one big straggling town. The international boundary runs along the middle of the street, and at a small customs-house lounge a few ragged Mexican sentries, smoking interminable cigarettes, and evidently interfering with nobody, except to collect export taxes from everything that passes to the American side. The inhabitants of the American town go across the line to get good things to eat, to gamble, to dance, and to feel free; the Mexicans cross to the American side when somebody is after them.

I arrived at midnight and went at once to a hotel in the Mexican town where the Cabinet and most of the political hangers-on of Carranza were staying; sleeping four in a room, on cots in the corridors, on the floor, and even on the stairs. I was expected. A temperamental Constitutionalist consul up the line, to whom I had explained my errand, evidently considered it of great importance; for he had telegraphed to Nogales that the entire fate of the Mexican Revolution depended upon Mr. Reed's seeing the First Chief of the Revolution immediately upon his arrival. However, everybody had gone to sleep, and the proprietor, routed out of his back office, said that he hadn't the slightest idea what the names of any of the gentlemen were or where they slept. Yes, he said, he had heard that Carranza was in town. We went around kicking doors and Mexicans until we stumbled upon an unshaven but courteous gentleman who said that he was the Collector of Customs for the whole of Mexico under the new government. He waked up in turn the Secretary of the Navy, who routed out the Secretary of the Treasury; the Secretary of the Treasury finally flushed the Secretary of Hacienda, who finally brought us to the room of the Secretary of Foreign Relations, Señor Isidro Fabela. Señor Fabela said that the First Chief had retired and couldn't see me; but that he himself would give me immediately a statement of just what Carranza thought about the Benton incident.

Now none of the newspapers had ever heard of Señor Fabela before. They were all clamoring to their correspondents, wanting to know who he was. He seemed to be such an important member of the provisional government, and yet his antecedents were not known at all. At different times he apparently filled most of the positions in the First Chief's Cabinet. Rather medium height and distinguished-looking, suave, courteous, and evidently very well educated, his face was decidedly Jewish. We talked for a long time, sitting on the edge of his bed. He told me what the First Chief's aims and ideals were; but in them I could discern nothing of the First Chief's personality whatever.

"Oh, yes," he said, "of course I could see the First Chief in the morning. Of course he would receive me."

But when we came right down to cases, Señor Fabela told me that the First Chief would answer no questions outright. They had all to be put in writing, he said, and submitted to Fabela first. He would then take them to Carranza and bring back his answer. Accordingly, the next morning I wrote out on paper about twenty-five questions and gave them to Fabela. He read them carefully.

"Ah!" he said; "there are many questions here that I know the First Chief will not answer. I advise you to strike them out."

"Well, if he doesn't answer them," I said, "all right. But I would like to give him a chance to see them. He could only refuse to answer them."

"No," said Fabela, politely. "You had better strike them out now. I know exactly what he will answer and what he will not. You see, some of your questions might prejudice him against answering all the rest, and you would not want that to occur, would you?"

"Señor Fabela," I said, "are you sure that you know just what Don Venus-tiano won't answer?"

"I know that he won't answer these," he replied, indicating four or five which dealt rather specifically with the platform of the Constitutionalist government; such as land distribution, direct elections, and the right of suffrage among the peons.

"I will bring back your answers in twenty-four hours," he said. "Now I will take you to see the Chief; but you must promise me this: that you will not ask him any questions,—that you will simply go into the room, shake hands with him, and say 'How do you do,' and leave again immediately."

I promised, and, together with another reporter, followed him across the square to the beautiful little yellow municipal palace. We stood a while in the patio. The place was thronged with self-important Mexicans button-holing other self-important Mexicans who rushed from door to door with portfolios and bundles of papers. Occasionally, when the door of the Department of the Secretaryship opened, a roar of typewriters smote our ears. Officers in uniform stood about the portico waiting for orders. General Obregon, Commander of the Army of Sonora, was outlining in a loud voice the plans for his march south upon Guadalajara. He started for Hermosillo three days afterward, and marched his army four hundred miles through a friendly country in three months. Although Obregon had shown no startling capacity for leadership, Carranza had made him General-in-Chief of the Army of the North-West, with a rank equal to Villa's. Talking to him was a stout, red-haired Mexican woman in a black satin princess dress embroidered with jet, with a sword at her side. She was Colonel Ramona Flores, Chief-of-Staff to the Constitutionalist General Carrasco, who operates in Tepic. Her husband had been killed while an officer in the first Revolution, leaving her a gold-mine, with the proceeds of which she had raised a regiment and taken the field. Against the wall lay two sacks of gold ingots which she had brought north to purchase arms and uniforms for her troops. Polite American concession-seekers shifted from one foot to the other, hat in hand. The ever-present arms and ammunition drummers poured into the ears of whoever would listen, praises of their guns and bullets.

Four armed sentries stood at the palace doors, and others lounged around the patio. There were no more in sight, except two who flanked a little door half-way down the corridor. These men seemed more intelligent than the others. Anybody who passed was scrutinized carefully, and those who paused at the door were questioned according to some thorough formula. Every two hours this guard was changed; the relief was in charge of a general, and a long colloquy took place before the change was effected.

"What room is that?" I asked Señor Fabela.

"That is the office of the First Chief of the Revolution," he answered.

I waited for perhaps an hour, and during that time I noticed that nobody entered the room except Señor Fabela and those he took with him. Finally he came over to me and said:

"All right. The First Chief will see you now."

We followed him. The soldiers on guard threw up their rifles.

"Who are these señores?" asked one.

"It's all right. They are friends," answered Fabela, and opened the door.

It was so dark within that at first we could see nothing. Over the two windows blinds were drawn. On one side was a bed, still unmade, and on the other a small table covered with papers, upon which stood a tray containing the remains of breakfast. A tin bucket full of ice with two or three bottles of wine stood in a corner. As our eyes became accustomed to the light, we saw the gigantic, khaki-clad figure of Don Venustiano Carranza sitting in a big chair. There was something strange in the way he sat there, with his hands on the arms of the chair, as if he had been placed in it and told not to move. He did not seem to be thinking, nor to have been working,—you couldn't imagine him at that table. You got the impression of a vast, inert body—a statue.

He rose to meet us, a towering figure, seven feet tall it seemed. I noticed with a kind of shock that in that dark room he wore smoked glasses; and, although ruddy and full-cheeked, I felt that he was not well,—the thing you feel about tuberculous patients. That tiny, dark room, where the First Chief of the Revolution slept and ate and worked, and from which he hardly ever emerged, seemed too small—like a cell.

Fabela had entered with us. He introduced us one by one to Carranza, who smiled a vacant, expressionless smile, bowed slightly, and shook our hands. We all sat down. Indicating the other reporter, who could not speak Spanish, Fabela said:

"These gentlemen have come to greet you on behalf of the great newspapers which they represent. This gentleman says that he desires to present his respectful wishes for your success."

Carranza bowed again slightly, and rose as Fabela stood up, as if to indicate that the interview was over.

"Allow me to assure the gentlemen," he said, "of my grateful acceptance of their good wishes."

Again we all shook hands; but as I took his hand I said in Spanish:

"Señor Don Venustiano, my paper is your friend and the friend of the Constitutionalists."

He stood there as before, a huge mask of a man. But as I spoke he stopped smiling. His expression remained as vacant as before, but suddenly he began to speak:

"To the United States I say the Benton case is none of your business. Benton was a British subject. I will answer to the delegates of Great Britain when they come to me with representations of their government. Why should they not come to me? England now has an Ambassador in Mexico City, who accepts invitations to dinner from Huerta, takes of his hat to him, and shakes hands with him!

"When Madero was murdered the foreign powers flocked to the spot like vultures to the dead, and fawned upon the murderer because they had a few subjects in the Republic who were petty tradesmen doing a dirty little business."

The First Chief ended as abruptly as he had begun, with the same immobility of expression, but he clenched and unclenched his hands and gnawed his mustaches. Fabela hurriedly made a move toward the door.

"The gentlemen are very grateful to you for having received them," he said, nervously. But Don Venustiano paid no attention to him. Suddenly he began again, his voice pitched a little higher and louder:

"These cowardly nations thought they could secure advantages by standing in with the government of the usurper. But the rapid advancement of the Constitutionalists showed them their error, and now they find themselves in a predicament."

Fabela was plainly nervous.

"When does the Torreon campaign begin?" he asked, attempting to change the subject.

"The killing of Benton was due to a vicious attack on Villa by an enemy of the Revolutionists," roared the First Chief, speaking louder and louder and more rapidly; "and England, the bully of the world, finds herself unable to deal with us unless she humiliates herself by sending a representative to the Constitutionalists; so she tried to use the United States as a cat's paw. More shame to the United States," he cried, shaking his fists, "that she allowed herself to join with these infamous Powers!"

The unhappy Fabela made another attempt to dam the dangerous torrent. But Carranza took a step forward, and, raising his arm, shouted:

"I tell you that, if the United States intervenes in Mexico upon this petty excuse, intervention will not accomplish what it thinks, but will provoke a war which, besides its own consequences, will deepen a profound hatred between the United States and the whole of Latin America, a hatred which will endanger the entire political future of the United States!"

He ceased talking on a rising note, as if something inside had cut off his speech. I tried to think that here was the voice of aroused Mexico thundering at her enemies; but it seemed like nothing so much as a slightly senile old man, tired and irritated.

Then we were outside in the sunlight, with Señor Fabela agitatedly telling me not to publish what I had heard,—or, at least, to let him see the dispatch.

I stayed at Nogales a day or two longer. The next day after my interview, the typewritten paper upon which my questions had been printed was returned to me; the answers written in five different handwritings. Newspaper men were in high favor at Nogales; they were treated always with the utmost courtesy by the members of the Provisional Cabinet; but they never seemed to reach the First Chief. I tried often to get from these Cabinet members the least expression of what their plans were for the settlement of the troubles which caused the Revolution; but they seemed to have none, except a Constitutional Government. During all the times I talked with them I never detected one gleam of sympathy for, or understanding of, the peons. Now and again I surprised quarrels about who was going to fill the high posts of the new Mexican Government. Villa's name was hardly ever mentioned; when it was it was in this manner:

"We have every confidence in Villa's loyalty and obedience."

"As a fighting man Villa has done very well—very well, indeed. But he should not attempt to mingle in the affairs of Government; because, of course, you know, Villa is only an ignorant peon."

"He has said many foolish things and made many mistakes which we will have to remedy."

And scarcely a day passed but what Carranza would give out a statement from headquarters:

"There is no misunderstanding between General Villa and myself. He obeys my orders without question, as any common soldier. It is unthinkable that he would do anything else."

I spent a good deal of time loafing around the Municipal Palace; but I never saw Carranza again but once. It was toward sunset, and most of the Generals, drummers, and politicians had gone to dinner. I lounged on the edge of the fountain in the middle of the patio, talking with some soldiers. Suddenly the door of that little office opened, and Carranza himself stood framed in it, arms hanging loosely by his sides, his fine old head thrown back, as he stared blindly over our heads across the wall to the flaming clouds in the west. We stood up and bowed, but he didn't notice us. Walking with slow steps, he came out and went along the portico toward the door of the palace. The two guards presented arms. As he passed they shouldered their rifles and fell in behind him. At the doorway he stopped and stood there a long time, looking out on the street. The four sentries jumped to attention. The two men behind him grounded their arms and stopped. The First Chief of the Revolution clasped his hands behind his back, his fingers working violently. Then he turned, and pacing between the two guards, went back to the little dark room.

Idols behind Altars
by Anita Brenner
First published in 1929
© by Payson & Clarke LTD

CHAPTER TEN: *Travail*

I.

The revolution in the south was Zapata, the story of a cause. The revolution in the north was Villa, and this was the legend of a man. Villa, the hero of women, poets, and the unredeemed poor, crystallized his philosophy in significant slang. *"Qué chico se me hace el mar para hacer un buche de agua . . .* I'll use the ocean to gargle!"

Dorotea [Doroteo] Arango, later Francisco Villa, was the son of a peasant stable-cleaner on a ranch in Chihuahua. Almost shorn of legend, he appears in boyhood a shock-headed, grubby-faced, morose youth, chopping wood in the forests, peddling buttons and trifles on a cinnamon coloured burro for maize to deceive the family hunger.

At the age of fourteen, say the ballads, with considerable scandal he removed the tyrannic foot from his neck. Villa had a beautiful sister. The son of the hacendado was lustful and greedy, in feudal tradition. One night he was seen in the shadow of the family hut. The boy bullied a confession out of his sister. Then he vowed furiously vengeance. First he went to the seducer and demanded that he marry the girl. The hacendado laughed at him. He went again, and this time he was the subject of a petulant order. "They just about broke my bones in the beating they gave me", said he always at this point of his story.

He began to save pennies most patiently, and after many weeks he bought a very old, very rusty gun. In the bush of a trail through which his consecrate enemy sporadically rode, Villa watched nightly for six months. At last luck turned Don Juan his way. Villa, stepping out in his path, properly muttering bitterness and triumph, shot the young man (who had long forgotten the presumptuous peon and his raped sister) quite dead. Then he took himself and his not very trusty gun to the hills.

He was captured by government rangers and put in jail. An order came to convey him to another jail. This he knew for his death warrant, according to the infamous Diaz "fugitive law". An innocent removal from one jail to another jail, on horseback across open country, was almost infallibly the first step of its application. Next came a stop at a creek, where the prisoner was asked if he were thirsty, and was allowed to stoop down for a drink. The finale was an official note recording the death of an escaping criminal.

"My jailmates told me goodbye sadly," Villa would preface this chapter of his reminiscences. "At a beautiful little river, the captain said to me, 'Muchacho, aren't you thirsty?'

"'Are you going to kill me already?' I asked him. He looked me up and down, and down and up, and then said, 'Drink, boy, no one will hurt you.' Afterwards he admitted that he really had orders to apply fugitive justice to me, but that I looked like such a fine youth, and promised so well, that he relented. Since then I've never doubted my luck."

He broke out of jail and again took to the hills, where, with his *compadre* or "pal" Urbina, he followed the only profession now open to him, that of banditry. Beginning with an occasional pack burro here, and a stray steer there, they managed within a comparatively short time to build up a thriving business. The gang stole cattle from rich ranches, dried the meat and sold it at a distance from its point of disappearance. The system was perfectly organized and Villa was a bold and capable chief. Supply therefore never failed the demand for their popular delicacy.

However probably the rangers grew troublesome, because Villa crossed the border and, he said, as one of Roosevelt's Rough Riders learned American army tactics and represented the stars and stripes in Cuba. With the first stir of the revolution of 1910 he was back in Mexico ambitiously. It was at this time he took the name of Villa, after a famous bandit of his native province. He succeeded Villa the First like a conscientious Elisha, staged sensational raids on haciendas with a flourish, gave to the poor money, food, and advice; showered manna and serenaded the yawning Lady Revolution chivalrously.

Personal attraction, skill as a leader, many promises, and some excellent oratory on his behalf, gathered to him as good a gang as any outlaw heart might desire. Villa, bandit, became then Villa crusading guerrilla. He preached revolt, paralleling Madero's fantastic soap-boxing in central Mexico, Carrillo Puerto's idealistic beginnings in Yucatan, the A.B.C. lessons in socialism of Plutarco Elias Calles the country schoolmaster. He was ardently Maderista, but he went very little into theory. He promised the only justice he conceived, which was a reversal of the good things from top to bottom, with prizes for the brave.

When Madero became president Villa was told by a political leader, who called himself a "red," that Madero was not a revolutionist, but merely a reformer, and pointed to his uncomfortable writhing in the face of the

American Ambassador as proof of the saviour's unworthiness. Villa thereupon turned against him, but when Huerta, Madero's Minister of War, betrayed him with the compliance of the American representative, Villa remorsefully turned against Huerta too. Popular sympathy turned with him.

To Villa came then poor devils of peasants, out for loot and social vengeance; adolescent dreamers, disturbed by too obvious misery too often; philosophers and poets, the intellectual martyrs of a suffering mass, hoping to bring Utopia, or at least frijoles, to that mass; cut-throats and jailbirds, finding safety in numbers, and other advantages; girls who had not yet learned resignation to justice, and women who did not give a hang about either justice or the proletariat. They all chased their dreams on horseback and they did it Villa fashion.

"We learned," one of the men on his personal staff relates, "*berrenda* tactics. The berrenda is a very swift deer that is everywhere and nowhere, here today and yonder also today. We learned real values, such as horseflesh and distance, with our bodies. We learned to ride like hell, to eat when there was food and to sing when there was none. When we had to move, and move fast and silently, we shifted from horse's back to horse's back night into day at a gallop. He knew the roads, we thought, by smell. It was glorious, and heartbreaking. Men, good men, killed and more killed, and ten in the place of each come also to get killed. But how we loved him!"

Huerta's government pursued Villa listlessly. When Huerta fell Villa became an accepted fighting candidate, a champion of Mexican destinies. He swept the entire north in his train. The peasants who stayed at home, spied for him, fed him, and dreamed about what he was going to do for them. Once several of them were captured by Villa's opposition and tortured to tell his whereabouts.

"Where is Villa?"

"*Pues,* señor, who knows?"

"If you don't tell where he is you'll be shot."

"Yes, señor." And so on through the lot, each interview ending with the promised execution.

The guerrilla band was now become the famous "Invincible Division of the North". Villa and Carranza, both northern men, first allies against Huerta, split, each disclaiming they wanted the presidency, but each determined to be autonomous. Began the struggle that rocked Mexico, the great furnace that twisted and melted and smudged the accumulated building of four centuries. The land lay sacrificed, darkly patient, Villa, with the United States supposedly behind him; (because, it was whispered, he had been thought potentially malleable) with a well equipped and almost disciplined army, was hailed the Napoleon of Mexico. His name blossomed internationally, and hope and hurrahs made that image: horse, pistol, mustaches, amours—the Mexican Bad Man. It was then Villa expressed a desire to gulp the ocean.

John Reed described the guerrilla at this time: "He is the most natural human being I ever saw. Natural in the sense of being nearest to a wild animal. He says almost nothing and seems so quiet as to be almost diffident. His mouth hangs open and if he isn't smiling he's looking gentle. All except his eyes, which are never still and full of energy and brutality. They are intelligent as hell and as merciless. The movements of his feet and legs are awkward—he always rode a horse—but those of his hands and arms are extraordinarily simple and direct. They're like a wolf's."

Austere physical discipline and pure hero-worship made many men fit seconds to their chief. Stories are multiple of their exploits, not a few like the tale of how Villa and his personal escort alone, won a renowned battle. They had gone out to reconnoiter, and stumbled into the pickets of a large detachment of Carranzistas. "There comes Pancho Villa with the whole Division of the North!" shouted one of the enemy scouts, terrified.

"Yes, you son of an unlucky mother, the whole Division of the North," Villa yelled back, "and if you don't surrender, we'll disembowel the lot of you!" They surrendered; and were forced to wait, disarmed, several mortifying hours until a few squads of the Division of the North came to march them into corral.

Villa breathed power. His lieutenants whitened if his dinner went wrong, for ill-temper made their chief's suspicions dynamic, and he was very suspicious. His one friend, he said, was his gun. Disloyalty maddened him. He would risk his life and the success of a big offensive to punish it, as he did in the case of his old friend "Butcher Urbina." "And though you hide under a pebble," Villa had said to him, "'if you ever betray me, I'll dig you out and bury you again." Urbina despatched, Villa galloped home to his dinner; a frugal one as usual.

Two luxuries the Bad Man allowed himself. The first, which he did not consider a luxury at all, was women. The second was flattery. He was always deeply touched by loyalty; and he so craved friendship that he wooed even its monstrous caricatures. The merest court fool could "fondle his beard", as one says in Spanish. He had a poet laureate whose sole and important duty was to add to the many verses already sung about and to Don Pancho. When Villa listened it might be death to disturb him. The story is told of an orderly, driven frantic by an equally frantic officer in doubt about a clearly unnecessary execution, who entered in the middle of a stanza. Villa shot him over the neck of the guitar.

So long as the revolution in the north was guerrilla warfare, of the Mexican type, whose strength lies in elusiveness and sudden ubiquity, Villa could indeed be the Invincible Division of the North. Personal trusts and distrusts for army hierarchy, impulses for campaign plans, emotions for political consciousness, and long-sensitive instinct about when to swoop and when to run, were equipment for handling a genial gang, than which none could be fitter. His later big army, requiring some kind of military operative form, marching against troops under Obregon's literate strategy, defeated Villa.

The military genius on his staff was Felipe Angeles, a brilliant, cultured, tactful man, one of several who hoped Villa would be the physical lever of national rehabilitation. Better a primitive, they thought, comparing him with Carranza, than a schemer. Had Villa kept the wisdom, or the humbleness, that earlier made him listen to Angeles, Carranza's bright young generals might not have disproved the invincibility of the Division of the North. "But I committed the folly," Villa afterwards admitted, "of believing myself a military genius." The biggest frog-in-the-puddle urge that after all generated his power, made him shortsighted, hotheaded, and measured his downfall. Yet because of that urge, he jumped human hurdles lithely and picturesquely. It was very appealing.

II.

I was graduated from *Maderista* and the nursery to *Villista* when his heroes came to Aguascalientes retreating before the Carranza army under Obregon, and established their headquarters for what proved to be Villa's biggest and last campaign. They came confident still, singing ballads of their triumphs, vowing in verse to make of Carranza's beard a cockade for their beloved Don Pancho. Convincing, this account of an early triumph:

> Allright, you old drunkard Huerta
> your bad heart will skip a beat
> when you learn, in Zacetacas
> your Barrón has met defeat.
>
> You may be thinking, said Villa
> there is a hard fight ahead
> but I've got my little roosters
> of those that to spurs are bred.

All the streets of Zacatecas
that day were paved with dead;
and the hills around the city
looked like a monstrous sheep-herd.

The Federals were so frightened
most of them ran away
dressed like Indians and like women
while their comrades round them lay.

The Division of the North traveled in the manner classic to Mexican revolutionaries. Troop trains scrambled and trudged in ceaselessly, bristling
with soldiers, gorged to the windows with women and spoils that spilled out
on the roof and the ground. Slung under the cars in blankets, men rode in
asleep. One with the weariest, brownest face in the world, on the girder
which held the wheel within six inches of his head, had lashed an important
alarm clock.

They camped in front of our house, a soldier to a tree. His woman un-
rolled the blankets and spread a petate on the roots, drove nails into the
trunk for hats and dug out a niche for an image. If you adventurously walked
the avenue you had to be careful or you'd step on somebody's baby and dive
into somebody's stew. Sometimes, when the women quarreled—one re-
members about a revolutionary army, first the women—they rolled over and
over in the dust, their hands buried in each other's hair, biting, scratching,
dirty skirts flying and beads scattering, till the men, tired of this amusement
(which didn't end, like a cock-fight) roughly pushed them apart.

There was always the noise of bugles and the shuffled march of sandaled
feet; always the smell of scorching frijoles and prickling chile, always the rattle of gossip, always the patter of women's hands making tortillas and never
a moment there was not the wail of a new child and the haunt of an old song.
The churches were full. Young girls would come to the picket fence and beg
for flowers to take to Our Lady. Once a soldier, who looked very small for a
soldier, came too, asking for roses to offer Guadalupe; answering to the ban-
ter that only women take flowers to Our Lady, that he was a woman, and
removing his hat from a newly cropped head to prove it.

A great tourist hotel across a field from our garden was turned into a
hospital. One day we had the medical staff and some officers to lunch. The
doctors, odorous of their make-shift calling, ate hardboiled eggs out of the
shells with their knives, and told tales—a soldier who, dying, shouted Viva

Carranza! in the teeth of the Villistas around him . . . tales of limbs gangrened and hacked off in the quick, without anesthetics (there were none) with a flip of a *machete*. . . . We were sent away from the table after this story. So we went to a window and watched the regiment take a bath in the irrigation canal that ran down the length of the avenue. There wasn't enough room for all the army in the water, so it promenaded by turns nude along the thoroughfare, between washes.

Threading details of those days they are strange. Mobile youngsters with baskets, hanging to the shawls of their mothers, spiraling before the doors of the warehouse for the moment the dispensary of maize. Which were Villista people and which servants, or the wives of peons off trailing in one of the other armies, one could not tell. Their rebozos were all the same colour, dusty; they all turned their faces up to the big posters nearly every day new on a nearby wall, nearly all of them (for I went there and spelled them aloud to the crowd, which was very appreciative) promising liberties and other advantages in the name of the face on the poster, General Blank.

A colonel about to be married came to ask my mother for pretty ices, which were ordered made. At midnight on the night of his wedding a rhythmic crash with the butt of a gun on our front door set the nurses to singing hymns. It was his orderly bearing a tray of festal food, "with the colonel's compliments." The soldier women wistfully would knock on the high door of the cattle-corral and ask for milk. There was never enough for all of them, and on the ranch the soldiers were quartering the cattle. I'd see a circle of men around a plunging, bellowing calf, with ropes tied to its hoofs and a soldier hanging on each, in a tug-of-war to split a haunch first. Live meat ripped open glints rose and blue in the sun . . .

My father went once to "Butcher Urbina" to protest such waste. The general received him, he says, in a little room, sitting on bags of maize and coins. At first Urbina wanted to shoot him for an impudent foreigner, remarking that also, somebody in the army could wear to great comfort his to-be-discarded shoes. But neither Urbina nor my father were very ill-tempered that day, and the general graciously gave a sealed order to be presented to the lieutenants on the ranch. It read: "Don't kill Mr. Brenner's milch cows, but kill all the rest of them."

A former groom, tired of being Carranzista, came home with wornout sandals and many scraps of white damask from rifled churches, to make new baby-clothes for the Infant Christ, he said. He had tales of how the women danced to the *Cucaracha,* that mad chant, with their mouths open and their skirts pulled up on their legs, after a battle yelping:

The little cockroach, the little cockroach
Will not travel any more,
Because it wants some, because it has no
Marihuana smoke to blow!

They would carry gilded chairs and parrots plundered from mansions, on their horses, and tire of the chairs and use them for firewood, as if they had been pianos or big altar-pieces.

This man found a wallet of Villa money, worthless the moment the town changed generals, and spent it therefore breathlessly all in one day, with my delighted help. We bought several bushels of doughnuts and three crates of green figs, and five pairs of enormous shoes and several dozen bandannas. Then he tired of singing the *Cucaracha* and learned the *Adelita,* and went off with the piece of an army; came back talking about Chihuahua, where they were hanging so many people that the trees were black clusters of buzzards. The corpses made such curious gestures and faces after they'd hung a while, he said, that it was very interesting to observe them. The city came on Sundays, sight-seeing, and drank lemonade and ate peanuts on the site, to refresh itself.

One day Villa himself, a pair of mustaches on a round amiable face, two very taut short legs, a cloud of dust and a plunging horse, galloped suddenly past the front door, and this meant a battle almost in the backyard. He was reviewing some specially imported savages, fighters from the north. He disappeared at the end of the double-file of great bronze Indians, naked except for red loincloths, arrows fastened to their belts, beads dropping on bare chests and feathers twisted into heavy black hair that hung, tangled, over their eyes on a line with their necks; bulged forearms thrust through man-high bows, and profiles of unbearable sharpness—a carved immobile frieze.

Aeroplanes droned industriously on the other side of the irrigation ditch that day. That night, rumble of carts, spies to be shot or rich men who would not contribute to revolutions, to be threatened and possibly hanged. Bugles, endless shuffle of feet; and music from bivouac dancing, till dawn. Morning of shining sun and new-hatched ducks in the garden pool, and salmon pink carnations just burst into bloom. Behind the Hill of the Cross, where we usually went on picnics, a shaking, a lazy grumbling, growing monotonously louder. . . With noon, the house walls quivered sympathetically and women began running in, dipping their shawls in the pool (disturbing the pale green ducks) to freshen the mouths of their wounded . . . Cows mooing, servants whimpering. . .

Then a line of stretchers, first slackly spaced, then linked like a moving factory-belt, past the door, to the hospital. Blood drops dimpling the dust, and feet making mud of it. Buckets of filth showered heavily from the hospital windows, making little hills of dark stained cotton below them. Voices following the filth, calling to Jesus to let them die. From the hospital, meeting the belt of stretchers, a shifting line of coffins, a black ribbon hung on the day.

Villa had lost. That night he shuffled and bugled his army away. Then the jigging sound of the Cucaracha, smells of burning, and shadows—hardly more sensed than shadows—of bodies gibbeted on trees . . . New faces ringing the trees in the avenues, more women cooking and quarreling, more naked swollen-bellied children wedging their faces into the garden to watch the baby ducks beginning to paddle. Again girls asking for flowers to take to the Virgin. New colour of official money. Pink tickets this time.

Carranza became president. Villa was again in the hills. He and the few hundred men he retained managed to keep Mexico discomforted. He flared out against the United States, flamed erratically from mountain to valley, crippled railroads, burned ranches, frustrating even the gestures of reconstruction. Chihuahua he captured by smuggling into it soldiers who were peasants disguised as peasants, in their civilian white, with crates of vegetables and chickens to feed the hungry city. Once in, they turned off the lights and opened a bombardment on the garrison. What a *vacilada!*

Villa held Chihuahua for the sole purpose, he said, of "showing the gringoes that Carranza is a poor devil and Villa a real man." His last gesture was the Columbus raid. This invasion of United States territory brought to his relish upon him the same general who once had cordially, or diplomatically, embraced him. Villa with his seasoned rebels and his intimacy with the hills, against Pershing with several thousand lumbering, cannon-hampered, rule-encumbered recruits, played Mexican mountain cat to American domestic rat. The battles were farce. Villa would squat in high caves and review the Pershing army regularly. He got himself killed and resuscitated in the American press, daily. He had a gorgeous time. Popular sympathy was his again, and many new poems garlanded him. This is one song of the moment:

> Mother mine of Guadalupe
> Bless this soldier of your nation,
> Tomorrow I march to the war,
> The war against intervention.

> Oh beautiful Guadalupe
> Sacred and beloved Virgin
> You must not let the gringoes
> Consume the blood of your children.

Maybe they think that the Indians
Have by now all disappeared,
But there are plenty of us
To whom liberty is still dear.

Maybe they have guns and cannons,
Maybe they are a lot stronger,
We have only rocks and mountains
But we know how to last longer.

Go look somewhere else for riches
Must you with greed be so blind
That you can't see you have left us
Nothing except the rind?

Came the overthrow of Carranza, Villa's personal target, by Obregon. Overtures from the new president found the guerrilla wisely ready to settle. But he settled at his pleasure. At one swoop he lighted with his men on Mexico's biggest coal-mines. Right hand on the telegraph instrument and left on a dynamite bomb, Villa, renegade again and bandit, exacted from the president the privileges he was granted; or at least that is the tale. He was given an enormous hacienda, money and machinery enough for all of his "boys," and the consideration due a retiring gentleman. Simultaneously the sub, semi, and pseudo Villas also went back to the land, and with him changed their titles from General to Don. It was a neatly dramatic forging of machetes to tractors.

When Villa was peacefully assassinated in the fall of 1924, his epitaph was a universal sigh of regret and relief. He left behind him, stories to find in the bottles of old people whose guerrilla day is past, and stories that flow from the fountain pens of the poets who rather hoped but never quite believed Villa would save whatever it was they wanted saved; songs, many songs, and a scattering of wives who harvest the only material crops of that fame which is now legend.

ANTI-ELECTION RIOTS
Demonstrations dissolved by Diaz police. Mexico City, 1892.

DRAWING BY POSADA
Solemn entrance of Francisco I. Madero into the capital, 1911.

THE HANGED MAN
Scene of the Revolution

THE PILGRIMS

DANCE OF THE TOP-HAT
Drawing by José Clemente Orozco